Her Soul

Family Secrets series
Book Eight

By

Rebekah McClew

Dedication:

This book is for the family I found in fiction. You were never just characters to me. You were companions through long nights, difficult days, and the quiet spaces in between. Finishing your story felt like saying goodbye to something real. I'm not sure I'll ever fully let you go. And to the readers who loved them as I did, thank you for giving them a life beyond these pages.

I didn't write this book easily. There were days I avoided it, nights I doubted it, and moments I thought the ending would never come. But this story deserved to be finished and so did the people inside it. This is for them. And for anyone who kept going, even when it was hard.

Chapter One

Death Please

After two hundred years it was finally time, I had been called up in front of the council awaiting my verdict. The day had arrived that my suffering would end, and I would be put to death for my crimes. Serving the last hundred years under the councils' direction until I had grown bored of all the games they played, after all. What was the point? After a while nothing had any meaning, there was rarely justification for what they required of us. At one time I had truly believed they protected the human and vampire world. Except once you were in the center of it, you found out the truth, the darker sinister secrets, some might have had good intentions when it all started except after a while it was nothing more than a move for power. Stuck in their service we deluded ourselves that we were still protecting others, doing the right thing, even turning it into a game to challenge or keep ourselves from admitting just how bad it was. Once you've done something often enough the excitement was gone, rarely was there a way to get that rush anymore. I had no real reason to live, all those I had grown up with or loved died many years ago. I hadn't cared if I were to see another day begin or not. I had been stolen out of my parent's home and raised by a fellow vampire who taught me everything he knew and then he took the easy way out. He left me and a few others to live with the council while he went off to die.

My hands were tightly bound behind my back as I stood in the center of the room. There were other vampires along each side curious just how I would be put to death, and if I would change my mind at the last second. It felt as if the council was counting this as part of the execution, taking an incredibly long time to reach their verdict as the entire council sat there barely saying a word. Speaking telepathically to each other deliberating over my fate. Rarely did the council ever speak out loud to share their reasoning on matters unless they were to simply ask a question, again, was rare. Then Gerard, the lead vampire stood as the room hushed quietly out of respect. He walked over slowly and deliberately towards me as the other four council members continued to sit in their seats showing no expression either way. Stopping right before me. I had kept my attention on him waiting any moment for his judgment to come swiftly.

"Life is an interesting thing; anything that exists has the potential of being started as well as permanently stopped. You have served us well; you have fought for us while you have even stood against us. You have helped keep us going as the world around us changed and evolved. There is one mistake you have made we cannot overlook. You knowingly made the mistake of letting mortals know of your existence. Although the mess has been cleaned up, we cannot risk another situation like this happening again where they find out the very location of the council. Langston, what does redemption mean to you?" Never once moving or allowing anything to distract him, he stared me directly in the eyes while he spoke.

I was almost expecting him to end it all right then, I had committed the crime I was accused of. What kind of redemption could he be speaking of? Not that mortals thought much of it other than thinking an insane man went into the most violent storm to set off explosives. I cleaned up the mess myself which is why I hadn't stuck around the first time, and there were a few loose ends I took care of, so there truly was nothing left for me.

"Redemption means nothing to me. I accept my fate." I had known others who were let off for worse offenses; it all depended on the person's reputation with the council; however, I was assured my offense would be unforgivable, I had made sure of that.

"Perhaps Langston is not quite grasping what we are implying," Lydia stood up from her chair making her way down to me, "we vampires have existed for a very long time, and we demand order. You live under the protection of the council as well as benefit from us as a group, and because of this we fare much better than those who attempt to blend in with mortals on their own. They get exposed or dissected by humans. We have protection as a collective. We have lived for so long because of our rules and our needs as vampires are different from that of humans. We permanently bond with those who changed us; we each have the chance of having a soul mate unique to us that marriage is unnecessary. Our loyalties are to each other; we live and die for this bond. You are being rewarded your freedom if you wish for redemption, otherwise, you will die today." Her voice wavered slightly.

I certainly hadn't expected what they were offering me. I was ready for death, for my final relief. I certainly wasn't ready for such a bold statement from them.

"What freedom are you talking about? I have no fear of my death?" I had not wanted it delayed any longer than necessary.

Walking over closer to me now standing behind me. I could feel her breath on my neck as she placed a hand on either of my shoulders now whispering extremely low to make sure that only I could hear her.

"I hate to see such a great specimen wasted. I have a job for you and if you do it well, then you will be as free as we are. No more contract or servitude to the council, you would still enjoy all the benefits as well as have others working below you that you would command. You would be free from ever appearing before the council again." Moving away from me she had looked so assured I would go along with their plan.

"I already have others who work below me; I live among the humans and uproot any time the council demands of it. Handling one more assignment is no reward for me. Death shall be my reward." As I said this, I could see Lydia frown.

She knew how stubborn I could be. Many years ago, we had been rather intimate until she had found she won the attention of Gerard. The power and control had been what lured her away.

"Unlike you, we do not possess the ability to walk among the humans during the daylight as you have. We are rather stuck in our situation until nightfall when we rule. If you wish to abandon those who need your protection during the day, we can accept that, however, we need this last assignment accomplished by you. We will swiftly end your life at the end of its completion. If you refuse you will stay in the burning coffin until you are nothing more than ash, I cannot promise you where we will choose to spread your ashes."

She no doubt stated this as if it was an insult to me. Saying nothing and only grinning at her. I knew it wasn't the response she wanted.

"After all, if an eternity has already soured your viewpoint, how much more so do you think it will be after you have spent several years in there?" Gerard was no longer making this easy, not that he would have necessarily stuck to his commitment.

I had seen him before promising eternal life to a human only to drain their life away entirely.

"Rest assured if you finish this you will have earned your death rightfully, and I would find it a pleasure to carry it out." Alexandra was rather eager to carry the sentence out.

The only expression she had shown on her face, the one most would cringe when seeing. The evil smirk on Alexandra's face was enough to make most die from fear in their place, however, if she was promising this, I knew she would not back down from it. She thrived from watching others die. It was very unusual to see her in agreement with Gerard and Lydia.

"What is it you wish for me to do?" Even though it was becoming much rarer for a vampire to walk during the day.

The ones who had special gifts were no longer passing on the traits so future vampires were stuck under shade or at night-fall. The old ancient ones could never walk amongst the light, no one knew where the ability had come from even though there were many theories, none were ever proven.

"This will take some time; you must be patient, however, trust me that I am sure you will find your reward worth it. There is a child who has been borne however she has been put in the care of another family to protect her. You are to find her, keep her safe until she comes into her power. Her power might already be active, if it is then she is being taught not to use it, otherwise we would have located her. Once you have her, you will bring her back to us to receive your final payment. If you're not able to get her here, then you are to collect the power from her and kill her. We have no real need of the little girl." Lydia leaned back in her chair as she spoke to me; I knew there had to be something more to this.

"What sort of creature is protecting this child? This seems simple enough that any vampire could handle it. What's so special about this child that any of you would need its gift?" I wasn't sure if I would get an honest answer if it was a coveted power.

I doubted they wanted other vampires to know about it, or they would not have bothered with me. Why would I want to waste my time protecting a child, especially if I was to care for her until she came into her power? That's not a swift payment unless they think she'll inherit whatever it was soon.

"That will be explained to you as soon as you find where she is. Her father has hidden her well; we do not know where she is except you knew her father personally. You should be able to find her based on your knowledge of him. Follow Aaron and he will show you what needs to be done once she has her powers. He will be able to fill you in on the rest." As Gerard made his last statements, he walked away from me with Lydia and Alexandra.

Usually, there were eighteen council members however to render a death verdict there only needed to be four present. As they left, I followed Aaron as he made his way down the long stretched-out hallway until we came to the private chambers of the council. Waiting for me on the table had been a rather large tattered-looking book along with glass vials. I assumed whatever magic they thought she had. It was in her bloodstream.

As Aaron explained she was a rather special child. Her father was a vampire while her mother managed to become pregnant and carry a child to term. What no one had been able to figure out had been her being pregnant in the first place. She was a vampire as well, and as far as anyone knew, only he had the ability for walking in the daylight. Listening to him explain this. I was curious about what this child must look like. Her mother had been born into a family of witches. She was the sixth generation to carry on their traditions; she was also the seventh daughter born to the family.

"As far as we know the little girl has three older sisters who have also been hidden. I wasn't sure why they were not sought after; except they were only focusing on this one. For some reason, they felt there was a stronger significance to her and not the others, not that I had kept after superstitions and such." Aaron continued to explain not looking at me as he put more items into the cloth satchel.

Not that the details meant much to me. It wasn't as if I was benefiting from this. All of this sounded much more troublesome than worrying about death; I could kill myself much faster even though there would be no honor in that. Sad after all these years, honor was the only driving motivator that I had. As Aaron handed me the burlap bag filled with the essential items they felt I would need.

'You're a guardian Aaron, why don't you sense her for the council and flit in and grab her and get out before whatever is guarding her figures it out." I was curious since a few guardians were stuck working for the council even though their mandatory time was almost up.

"We guardians have expressed to the council we were able to sense certain people or places because we had been there. We do not sense magic or random people or strangers we do not know. Also, our power is to preserve life, not end it. We may work for the council for now to pay a debt, however, killing will never be one of those things. If it comes to killing this young girl, you have no weapons included to do that, you can figure that out yourself." Not explaining anymore, he shifted himself to another room.

The council might have believed him, but I knew first-hand they could find anyone simply by concentrating on something that belong to, a scent, place or anything associated with the person. I could only guess it helped not having to track down people by stating this. Working for the council had been rough on the guardians. I admit I was impressed by their fearless stance when it came to murder and torture, preferring death over administering it to someone else. The council could only push them so far and I often wondered if they were afraid of them but then if they were, they would have had them exterminated by now. They must have found some benefit in having them here. I kept thinking it was too emotionally crush those who cared for them knowing they were stuck here.

I was now left in the room on my own. Thinking over my plan of attack. Depending on how difficult it was to locate this child, especially if she is being protected by magic then it could either be relatively quick or due to the experience of the one guarding her, it could take years. Compared to my age, a few years wasn't that long at all. Reading the slip of paper of the person. I was to investigate. I couldn't believe it; I knew everything there was to know about this man and he supposedly had a child?

There was no one to stop me as I left the council chambers making my way down the long hallway and outside. There were only a few who had stared at me most likely curious about what exactly the assignment would have been. Not giving them the satisfaction of finding out I had kept my expression rather plain, after all this was to be kept silent while only myself and the council knew what they were planning. Except for one thing they had yet to share with me, what they wanted it for. What exactly this power could do and why they needed it? I understood why they could not just kidnap the child if they found her; none had experience raising a child, at least none of the council members. Vampires were incapable of bearing them and when would we willingly spend time with one? Sure, there were a few that still wanted children, mainly those who the choice had been taken from. The rest of us were thankful for being what we were, it took care of that problem.

The second reasoning had been a simple fact it would draw unwanted attention to the vampire world as well as the council if for any reason humans started to investigate us, it was hard enough blending in as each century passed. They would prefer others not to know where they accumulated their power from.

With only a burlap sack slung over my shoulder, a wide brim hat to cover most of my face from those around me as well as my long black trench coat. I had made my way home for now. No purpose in searching for something I had no idea where it was yet. Let alone a clue as to where to start first. Living near the lake. I hadn't been that far away from the council; I always lived nearby for security reasons. During some centuries it had simply been to keep the villagers out with their pitch forks and torches while in other centuries it had been to divert attention from the council. Walking up the front steps of my estate home, the door had already been held open for me as I simply walked in without saying a word. Most of the staff had stood there rather surprised to see me alive still. Not bothering to say a word. I made my way directly to my study leaving the sack on the table. Making my way over to my liquor cabinet, pulling out the brandy and pouring myself a glass, gulping it down rather quickly I knew he was standing right behind me most likely waiting for an answer, he wanted to know what the rest of the staff was curious about.

What would happen now to me since I hadn't been killed on the spot?

"I have not been doomed to death however to receive my reward of it. I must finish one more assignment for them." Still leaning against the wall not even looking at Brunswick I knew that was not exactly the answer he was looking for.

"I am surprised that Lydia even agreed to let you die at all, seems she will lose her weekend visiting place if you die." There was no secret that she still paid visits to me after all this time.

"It was not left up to her even though it was clear she would have kept me around." Physically turning now, throwing my half drank glass into the fireplace causing the glass to shatter on the ground as the fire itself roared in anger from the liquid.

"Am I to assume there is more to this?" Closing the door behind him this time making sure no one was waiting in the hallway to listen in.

"There is some power the council wants and to collect it I must find a child and wait until it develops its power, they were not sure if it was born with it or when it would come. They seem rather sure it would happen at all. They wanted me to collect the power from it and then I am expected to kill it, that is if I couldn't take off with the child. I'm sure they knew I didn't want to be bothered with it. Then I was to return the power to the council to receive my reward of death. I've only a name to go on as well as who her father was. I am sure I can find where they last lived, however, there is no record showing the age of the child I must find. I will leave first thing in the morning for Drezin's manor; he may no longer be alive however it still stands. I might find a clue there." Walking over to my desk preparing for ideas as to finding this child I heard the slight whisper from Brunswick as he was leaving.

"I shall make sure any services you need when you leave in the morning are ready for you." I knew from the tone of his voice he sounded as surprised as I was to find out whose child it was.

Other than the manor. I had no other idea where to

search, this was the first I had even heard that he and his partner even had children. Opening the top drawer, I had a few odd pictures left in there. Leafing through them I pulled one out in particular examining it. We were out in the middle of a field during one of those rare times goofing off when we were younger. Before things had become much more complicated for us to even care. Lydia had worn her favorite red beret while Drezin stood there next to Thea, his natural soul mate. Neither had stayed when the presidium stepped back letting the lesser council underneath them take over the minor events. Both Drezin and Thea had slipped away disappearing from their former lives no longer interested in serving the council. Not that they were ever a threat, but Drezin had helped me quite a bit at times. However, they had preferred a simpler, quieter existence away from man and vampire. They had made it quite clear they did not agree with the council, however, even they knew it was safer to stay away and not challenge their power.

Taking my attention away from the picture I heard that familiar sound I was used to hearing. Not needing to be announced. I knew she was standing there. Without looking up from the picture I was not in the mood. I had already had enough from the council. Regardless of who it happened to be.

"What do you want?" I kept it simple and to the point, keeping my voice steady.

It had not been the weekend yet and I had hoped she would not be making an appearance before I left tomorrow. I should have known she would come.

"Who knew you would be sentimental over a silly picture? I wanted to make sure you would be able to carry out the task; after all, it does happen to be your childhood friend's daughter. Besides, there is no real reason for you to die. I can make sure your last reward is something much different." Her voice had gone rather soft towards the end of her statement.

I already knew what she was getting at.

"There is nothing you could offer me that I could not get myself. Prove to me there is a reason I should live," this had been the first time I looked up at her waiting for a response, one I had known would not come, "just as I had thought." Setting the picture back in the drawer I looked away from her as I moved away from my desk.

"The great Langston is giving up far too easily. If you die, there is so much your about to miss." She tried to make it sound as if there was something that could be interesting however eventually nothing was different.

"Did Gerard send you or did you come because of your own choice? I'm not much for company right now." Moving over to pick up another glass and a bottle of brandy, taking it into the other room with me. I hadn't even bothered to see if she was following even though I was positive she would.

"There is more to this than you know, and I need to make sure it's done right. When you find this child, you are to simply protect her from a distance. You are not to get involved except when it is time to take the power from her and finish the job." The tone in her voice had changed rather quickly.

Even I knew there had to be more to this than they were telling me, after all, why would they need to kill the child if there had not been? Could it produce more of its power if it survived? However, I had noticed a certain sound in her voice I had yet to hear before.

"Do I detect a bit of jealousy?" I knew it could not have been for the child, after all, she never once wanted a child.

She never once fought the idea of becoming a vampire. The idea of never worrying about being pregnant or raising a child thrilled her so why the tone? She was the one who had chosen us out from the others at the time to join her and my mentors' group. She may have been changed by the same vampire however she was a student of him centuries before we had come along.

"I am jealous of nothing except I know you too well, you distract quite easily." Lydia had made her way over to me as I sat down on the corner of my bed.

Looking up at her and her familiar expression. I had

grown to know quite well. There was much she was keeping from me.

"I could always disappear with this child, and you would never find either of us? Perhaps you should fill me in if you know me so well?" Reaching out for her and pulling Lydia closer to me.

I knew she would never resist.

"You know I would tell you everything if I could, except this time I cannot. Besides you can consider the part we are not telling you a gift personally from me." Just from her answer alone, I knew I would eventually find out, and somehow, I had the feeling I was not going to like it.

"Whatever happened with us?" As I slid my hands up her back underneath her shirt, she arched forward to kiss me on the forehead.

"You don't have what I want. Are we really going to get into this again? Besides. I am not here for my weekend visit; Gerard is no doubt waiting for me so I must get back." She stood up except I pulled her closer now kissing her fully on the lips.

I hadn't cared if Gerard was waiting or not. She can be late if she is going to come over here and not tell me the full reason why?

"I don't care if Gerard is waiting for you, let him wait, he will never be me." I had heard no arguments from her as she placed her hands on either side of my hips.

I knew what she had wanted, she wasn't the only one. Starting to pull her down onto the bed with me I heard the door open. I swear he always had the worst timing, or I guess in his case perfect timing.

"Do you honestly think I would let her come here to see you alone," nervously standing up quickly Lydia made her way past Gerard while he stood in the doorway, not even risking a glance at him as she passed, "I do not care what comes of you or how you live except it is imperative you collect this power for us and kill this child. She is not just a threat to us as the council; she is to you as well and the rest of the vampire world. If you don't do this, I'll make sure being alive truly becomes the worst nightmare you would ever dream of. The Presidium wants her dead." Not saying another word, he closed the door behind him as I continued to lie back on the bed.

Stretching out a little as I looked up at the ceiling above the bed. I never did have a use for the bed; it was simply to look aesthetically appealing for when humans had visited at times. Mortals seemed to be easily impressed and interested in the simple house tour I would give them. I would put their minds at rest by assuring them we were simple people as they were living normal everyday lives. That there was nothing to fear, if they had only known the truth there was much to fear and all of this had been for show. They would think we were simply eccentric mortals and nothing more. It's amazing when you think of it how much you can hide simply because of how something appears to look. I had only used this bed in my private room when Lydia would show up.

As the centuries passed, there was less need to prove ourselves to others. Before it had been all-show and now more preferred to keep to themselves not caring who their neighbor was or who else happened to be in the area as long as they left them alone. It had almost felt as though humans were adapting to our way of life. Not that I had wanted to trade the bed in for a coffin, we simply blocked out the light with thicker fabrics now. Not that I had to hide from the sunlight like the others. Not bothering to move as I heard the door open again, I could guess who it had been just from the sound of the footstep.

"Your things are ready whenever you wish to go, I thought after your visit tonight you might wish to leave early?" Never saying too much or attempting an in-depth conversation, Brunswick left the room.

No one had ever told me how to live my life or disagreed with the way I had lived it. I had done everything I wanted exactly the way I wanted it. I never bothered looking back or acknowledging if there were mistakes. Simply accepting whatever was done is over and will be done as I saw fit the next time the situation came up again. I could admit to myself I was rather arrogant and self-centered but then I never had a reason not to be. It probably helped that I had no problem taking responsibility for my own actions.

Brunswick was right; I would be far too restless to stick around until morning. One of my personal drawbacks I had yet to learn to conquer. My impatience had followed me from my human years; although there were few, I had changed by the time I was twelve, I was always rather selfish when I was younger but then it could have been attributed to my age. Only a few things if I had been reasoned with or benefited me that I would change a viewpoint or the way I handled something. The only time I had not been selfish had been when I almost ran into my original family, I had hidden to keep them safe, for far too many reasons, otherwise for the loyalty of my very few friends. Many of us who had been changed never wanted those we left behind to worry knowing eventually we would still be here when they were not, let alone the fact someone attacked us changing us physically this way.

I was always thankful not to be stuck looking the same age as I had when I changed. I could only guess the years of war-ravaged me enough to give me a bit of a tougher look. Certainly not the sort you would intentionally go after as a friend or an associate to be around. When I was younger most fell for the act simply because most trusted a child to be innocent and as I aged, I had enough time to study life around me to know how to get the upper hand. That's where my friends and I had differed from most vampires, we had aged after the change, not quickly, however we still aged. There was something special about the one who had changed us, and unfortunately, it was never anything anyone could explain to us why. Either way, I was thankful not to be stuck as a small child for the rest of my life as I had seen with some.

Not needing much and neither feeling in the wallowing mood from her having left right away, I forced myself up and out of my bedroom and back in my study. Brunswick had hidden the burlap bag in a secret compartment in the wall for when I would need it again later. I had no desire to carry it all over with me. I traveled with as little as possible. Only putting my hat and coat back on. I made my way back down to my favorite mode of transportation. I knew my staff had been watching however as always, I never paid much attention to them. Most had been handpicked by the council to keep an eye on me and Brunswick was the only one I had carefully chosen myself to work closely with. It had felt much better doing something rather than sitting and waiting to start. I would prefer to leave on foot however with the world changing as it had. I was stuck traveling much slower, except that had not meant I could not enjoy myself. I placed a small pack to the back end of my motorcycle and took off rather quickly. I liked leaving at night, there were far fewer people to contend with on the road.

My motorcycle had been a gift from Lydia. She knew my taste rather well, custom designed exactly the way I liked it, pure black other than the two small swirls of smoke running along either side of it, one swirl was red being Lydia's favorite color, and the other purple for my favorite color. The rest of the design resembled a spider web giving the bike a rather unique design; Lydia was always good at either decorating or accenting. Keeping my bike helmet on the back of the seat. I hadn't been too worried about wearing it. After all, how much more could I die; besides if it was permanent, it was what I had been after anyway.

Being careful not to draw too much attention to myself. I took off leaving the estate in a rush. I knew it would take a while before I would get to Drezin's home and hopefully, most of the traps had already been sprung by others trespassing, otherwise I was also going to have a bit of an adventure. I could also venture a guess they would still be there, or I would have heard from the council about someone being injured going in there, most likely they had left that to me.

As I had always lived in the direct city. My childhood friend on the other hand lived far out in the country keeping as private as possible, usually doing his best to stay off the minds of the council or the presidium. It had only taken a few hours, with a two hundred forty-eight cc Double Overhead Camshaft, inline twin engine, and a six-speed transmission and riding at one hundred miles per hour. I hadn't thought it would take me very long at all. Eventually, I planned on upgrading my bike however, for now, I couldn't complain too much, after all it was free. In the distance just a bit or at least long before any human eyesight would have seen it, there was a large man-made lake surrounding the property with large spruce trees and vines to fill in the open space. Drezin had certainly made sure no one had seen his home or property from the road. Carefully slowing up now following the dirt road. I kept my hearing alert as well as eyesight for any traps along the dirt path. It wasn't as if he invited strangers to visit or ever expected company. So far nothing out of the ordinary other than now looking deserted as well as overgrown.

I had been surprised to see the front iron gates broken open, not that I saw any bodies lying around. Leaving my bike safely in the center of the drive. I slowly made my way up to the front door. I had thought about simply letting myself in one of the many windows or the back door except I had known him rather well. He would have been prepared for this. The easiest solution and most avoided would have been to use the front door.

Smiling to myself. I couldn't help it when I read the message on the door mat. It warned any possible visitors very clearly. It read, "this isn't a welcome mat, I'm not a liar." Then the note on the wall of the house stated, "no one is welcome here. I will not answer the door to you and give no sympathy if you are stupid enough to go any further. Go away! I love my life in hell, and we are most likely naked."

Careful not to step directly in front of the door, I grabbed the rock on the ground first tossing it onto the non-welcoming mat in front of me. As I had done this it disappeared falling downward into a shaft below. Getting closer and now staring down there were sharp looking steel blades facing upward ready to impale any unwelcomed intruders. Brunswick wondered why I placed a bag full of water in a plastic bag in my pocket. Now taking it out and opening the top seal and tossing the water on the doorknob it not only sizzled, but it also exploded outward and as I guessed. Would have sent metal pieces of the knob into the intruder's body. It never surprised me the length Drezin was willing to go to keep others out. Pulling out a rubber glove now from my pocket. I reached in where the knob used to be to push down the wire inside now to open his homemade door. Still not entering yet. I had waited just a minute. Ripping out the bush next to the door and throwing it in, fire ignited from the sides setting it on fire as it allowed it to plummet through the now new opening in the floor from inside the house. Taking careful steps as I entered, lowering myself as the flames shot across me, I had to avoid the exposed hole still in the floor.

I was sure he wouldn't have to many traps set but then if he knew he was going to die. He might have set up as many as he could, simply to get even with those who did not belong in his home. When I had heard he passed, it was sent to me in written form by Lydia explaining no one knew the circumstances. Personally, I had always assumed it was the council, I had searched trying to find any proof I could, whoever had killed him did a great job at covering their tracks. That alone was very unlike the council and there was usually something left behind, they were not that clean when they killed someone, in a way they took pride in what they did and always felt fully justified, even if they were wrong.

Instead of sticking to the first-floor office off to the side. I was heading for his private office only a few had known of. First, I had to collect the key from upstairs. Not touching the banister, I had been sure the shiny substance was something I hadn't wanted to risk touching. Testing the steps first they had not moved or broken underneath me. Safely making my way up the stairs to the first door I had come to, I slowly touched the side panel expecting to be shocked or blown away. Nothing had happened as I pulled the panel from the wall. Behind it there was a small box shape facing me as I reached in for the key. Pulling it out and replacing the panel. I made my way back down the stairs. On the end of each post had been a pineapple shape décor. I always thought it had looked awful, except Drezin had not picked it for its looks however more for its functional use.

Twisting the top of the pineapple so that the top half was now flat it revealed where a key would fit. Placing the key inside. The stairs now began to slide backward, at least enough for a person to walk to the side left of them opposite of where the key had gone in. Taking the key out I walked in rather quickly, the timer set for the stairs to slide back was certainly not set for someone taking their time. As I moved in each light I had passed turned on. There were no traps in here but then Drezin most likely assumed if someone had known about this private office, it was someone he trusted. Now for the difficult task which was to find out any information I could about his daughter. He had trusted me with so much and yet I had never known he had children, something he kept silent. Not that I could blame him. Perhaps he was concerned about the council's control and what they might do, but then I also wondered if it had to do with his daughters' magic they would inherit somehow? I was still uncertain if I would kill the child or not. After all. I owed Drezin my loyalty far before any loyalty to the council or assignment.

There were so many files on almost every project that he had worked on, even a file he had been working on around the time he had been reported dead. I had already been through these papers so many times before, I was sure if he had a record of any children, I would have found it from before. He never kept any photos or drawings here either of himself or his wife. If there was something he wanted to keep secret, there was one place I could think of and that spot I had yet to get into. I skipped searching it earlier because the counsel was close along with a few of their personal assassins. I hadn't wanted to bring their attention to the room. They seemed satisfied when I left without anything.

His most secret room was below the hidden room beneath the stairs. The only reason I had known it existed had been the simple fact he brought me down in it once with him. Except when I had gone in, he turned over many papers and frames before I was allowed into the room with him, perhaps he did have their picture. At least if I could see a picture, I could get some idea of how old the girls were. As far as I knew the youngest could be four or five years old by now, her father had passed five years ago while her mother simply disappeared leaving no trace as to her situation.

There were very few pictures on the wall even in here although most knew who his wife had been. Studying the picture this time I still wondered where she had gone or what happened to her. She was very much like a sister to me as he was a brother. As I looked there seemed to be a red smear in the far corner of the picture. Taking down the frame and placing it on the desk. I broke the glass with my fist pulling the picture out. It had been folded over quite well. The small red smudge was not one at all, it was the edge of a fingertip. The person attached had been Genevieve her sister. At least now I had a second place to check.

Thanks to all the technology it was much easier finding people then it had been in the past. Centuries ago, I would have had to ask about the description or had something to go off. Now all I needed was a name, picture, and access to a computer. Even we demons were stuck falsifying our information just to blend in. It had looked as though we had generations of family and possessions to be passed down even though it was ourselves that kept them.

My next stop had been to see Genevieve; I wasn't sure how she would be now or if she would even be in the last place she was listed at. I wound up leaving my bike at Drezin's home safely hidden under thick brush. I felt it would be safer here than the airport. That and I refused to pay to park my bike when I was kind enough to pay for a ticket I didn't need. Having a cab drop me off, then I boarded the plane using a fake passport; I kept thinking at least I would end up at my destination faster this way; I would have to find temporary transportation while I was there. Sitting back in my chair attempting to relax as the plane was taking off, I could already feel my chair getting repeatedly kicked by the toddler from behind me.

"I'm so sorry; usually he's sleeping on these flights, with the delay he wound up sleeping beforehand." She seemed to be a single mother trying to control her son.

Not that I could blame him, I was just as bored only difference had been as an adult I knew how to control myself. I admired him for being able to get away with kicking my chair. Most of the time I hadn't really cared for children but then I hadn't cared for most adults either.

"Not to worry I'm not bothered by it at all; it's a rather soothing feeling almost as if I have my own chair massager." Smiling back at the women I could see a bit of relief in her expression.

I had to admit if she did not have the child with her, I would have possibly flirted with her. Sitting back in position as the child continued to kick my chair. It really hadn't bothered me but then rarely anything did, no matter what it had been I could tune it out. Leaning over to me the man in the seat beside me whispered something.

"It does bother me, if I had my choice I would have her thrown off the plane. If you can't handle your child, you should not have any. Besides airlines should know better than to allow children on in the first place, it's why more resorts are turning into couple's only retreats." Simply listening to him was interesting; I hadn't cared for his take on the situation although he had his right to his own opinion.

I simply pretended not to be interested closing my eyes and leaning back.

"Control your child or I will, you may not believe in punishing your child but while we are cooped up in this tiny hell hole, I will beat both of you if I must." Had been the rather loud shout from the man now.

From the nervous vibrations the women was giving off. I knew he had scared her as she pulled her son onto her lap.

"Come with me and we can have her moved to another area." I whispered in his ear, as I stood without hesitation the man followed me back to the end of the plane.

I rarely had difficulty getting others to follow my lead. Most seemed to be won over by my rather low tone, soothing sort of voice and the vibration I gave off. Opening the bathroom door, I had shoved him in closing the door quickly behind.

"You probably don't remember me, do you?" I asked the man, but he hadn't seemed a bit scared, any other mortal would have.

"I know who you are, anyone in the vampire world does, your one of the slaves to the council. These people on the plane are nothing important, especially that woman and child, why would you protect them? I only came back with you assuming we were going to wreak havoc." The all too familiar anger was building in his voice.

Something I was used to with vampires who hated concealing themselves from mortals feeling our race should rule the world instead of protecting and hiding from it. Many have forgotten they were mortal at one time.

"I am a slave of nothing, there isn't anything that could possibly hold any kind of power or fear over me, I only work for the council, and I work alone. I promise you I do not share your views." This was a man who at one time even the council had considered recruiting for their projects except he was too crazy for his own agenda; it would not have worked for them.

Being an assassin for the council you had to be psychotic however still in control at all times, something this man never learned. He was a vampire who happened to be too cocky for his own good. I made the mistake of not dealing with him when I should have otherwise he wouldn't be on this plane with me now.

He had been peddling little jobs even to the point he was successful enough to hide how he was doing them or that he was doing them himself in plain daylight, the fact he could walk in the light impressed the others until his own temper caused his own downfall. In such a small town if you were a vampire, you cleared out rather quickly since it was difficult to blend in with hunts going on every night. By those who were afraid of what they were not familiar with or just uneducated about. One of the last times I had seen him. I was already busy working on another assignment which he almost ruined for me by bringing attention to the area we were in. He had successfully proven he could not control his own emotions or temper.

For whatever reason he had lost his temper and decided not to care if anyone saw who or what he was. He had one simple assignment and blew it. He was meant to kill a person, not have anyone see him and dispose of the body where no one would find it. It didn't happen that way at all. I had already finished up my job and would have been gone long before the rest of the mess ensued however since I didn't have an alternate means of transportation, I had to pretend to be a visitor and take the bus out of town. When I had first stepped out onto the street, I had seen Jerome, another assassin for the council watching this man's every move while staying out of sight, I only knew where he was since I knew what to look for.

The bar across the street had been rather rustic and impressive looking, obviously it had been there for quite some time, and at least it wasn't anymore. The entire place was engulfed with flames as a lifeless body blocked the door from closing. The man's neck had been slit yet not one drop of blood on his clothes or the ground below him. Several motorcycles outside had been set ablaze as he lit his cigar from the fire. A very brave officer attempted to stop him as he was swiftly killed on the street in broad daylight being drained of his blood, dropping him to the ground as he turned and bolted out of the area leaving countless onlookers to realize what he was and what exactly he had left behind. It created instant panic and fear.

"You can't do anything to me; the council would kill you for exposing our kind here." Showing a smug expression on his face, apparently, he didn't know me well enough.

"I would have to say you owe me one, after all. I let you live after your last mistake. Besides, what they don't know won't hurt them." Moving quickly before he had a chance to react, snapping his neck to prevent anyone hearing him scream for help.

I liked the first-class bathrooms; they were not as crowded as the regular ones were. I knew it would signal the cabin pressure alarm however it should still be safe in the plane. I had waited a while before making my next move, after all I wanted to make sure I was close enough to my destination and no one had knocked on the bathroom door yet, it helped having the 'busy' label showing. For a mortal what I was about to do would have been near impossible, for myself no difficulty at all. Now that it was time, breaking the window and shoving the man through the hole. I watched as his body plummeted down to the ground. As I had assumed it would, the alarm had gone off. Making sure to scratch the outside of the plane, I wanted it to look as though we were hit by something on the outside breaking the window. Coming out of the bathroom rather quickly. I went and sat down as the stewardesses were warning everyone to put their oxygen mask on. We were almost to our destination as we were making an emergency landing, which was fine by me, I had wanted to end up on this end rather than over at the airport. This would save me some time in my traveling.

"Where's the rude man who was sitting next to you? I saw him get up with you." I was sure she was more worried he would do something to her rather than about his safety.

"Not sure?" As I winked at the kid, he gave me a huge smile.

Turning around I felt rather relaxed now that I had the use of both arm rests as we were descending to land in an open field. The pilots handled the situation rather nicely. I had no baggage to claim so as soon as no one was looking. I planned on sneaking off. They must have called in or radioed, looking out of the window there had been swirling lights down below as we landed. Getting off the plane on the slide we all lined up at the end in one piece and safely away from the plane, not that there was anything wrong with it other than the window. The emergency crew had already started taking a head count to see if

there were any fatalities or injuries due to the emergency landing. I could hear as the one flight attendant was explaining that
I had gone into the bathroom with the man, and he had never
come out, as she went to point me out, she was shocked. Looking
around she could no longer find me; I was already gone.

I was rather impressed by the view here, a place I hadn't
been to in several years. I liked where I lived, however, nothing
could ever compare to this countryside. I might have been able to
create my own personal garden however I never would where I
live now. At home. I was always reminded that I was living in the
city from the sounds and smells, here it was so vastly different
with the mountains in the distance, rolling hills and wildflowers
blanketing the ground. Not too often I get to enjoy a scene like
this and thankfully I wasn't in any hurry.

Chapter Two

The Child

After walking for several hours, I watched my surroundings, mainly for one reason. I knew I was being followed, not by humans, however, it was more vampires trying to be unseen by me. Not wanting to bring them along to my destination. I had been rather deliberate taking my time even stopping to sit by the stream for a while. I could attempt pretending to be mortal, I usually blended better than most vampires; however, my reputation within our own community made that impossible. If they had planned on ambushing me, they would have done it by now. I could see the small town in the distance; I wasn't sure how long they intended on following me or what they wanted, they might have assumed I was human since I was spending so much time out in the sun, I decided to stop by the local bar instead of going any further for now. At least this way I would find out what sort of town this had been. Opening the door there was not one person that had been looking away from me, almost as if they heard me coming. This had to be one of those rare towns completely occupied by vampires and I was the new one visiting. Perhaps that was why the others hid in the shadows; they were not light walkers like me? At least this will be an easy way to access the others and waste a few minutes.

"A mug or preferably a glass of Velvet Hemlock if you have it, if not I'll take a brandy" As I sat myself at one of the open barstools acting as though I was completely uninterested in the others around me.

Velvet Hemlock was a drink few vampires consumed, not that mortals would survive if they drank it. At least this way I would find out if my assumptions had been correct. Not bothering to correct me, the bartender quickly filled a glass full of it. As he set it down in front of me, I handed over the cash. It was one of my favorite drinks and I could only find it at vampire bars.

It was a drink with taste, dark berries like blackberry and plum. Honey eyed red grapes, a hint of cherry, slight cinnamon and cloves, elderflower. A soft velvety texture, with a hint of rose or violet ending with a hint of something poisonous like hemlock for bitterness and a splash of herbal mint, deep crimson red, a delightful life and death mingled. As I gulped it down, I was still aware of all the eyes that were watching my every move.

I lifted the delicate glass that didn't look like it belonged in a traditional bar, perhaps a Victorian home, Velvet Hemlock. The name alone sounds like something I should worship, almost holy or forbidden. taking the first sip, slight cinnamon, cloves, elderflower and black cherries, creamy thick across the tongue, then a hint of rose petals, soft, and a bit surprising. As the warmth of the liquid spread through my chest, a sharp edge of herbal bitterness stabbed through, almost like a truth I could barely handle. Pausing for a moment with a smile on my lips. swirling the liquid in the glass slightly to take in the aroma again, I felt intoxicated by the scent of rich fruit and dark petals and let the creamy hemlock settle in my veins. It burned; it soothed. It reminded me I was alive, in my own way. So much from a simple glass of pleasurable liquid, as if to offer oneself to beauty that has risk.

The taste lingered, but more than that, the name velvet hemlock. The moment the words left mine or anyone's lips, or printed on a menu, it demanded something from us, not just attention but awe. It wasn't a drink; it was a ritual, a personal poison. To say the name was to bow to it. The syllables softened like velvet, then struck sharp like poison.

I liked how it caught in my throat, made him pause. Even before the first drop touched his tongue, the name made me believe in its power, power over pleasure, over danger, over what it meant to live forever. It was worship, the way someone might kneel at altars or trace a relic with trembling fingers. The name was hymn and poison both, and I found myself signing along, deliberately, arrogantly, but with an undercurrent of reverence he couldn't fully suppress.

Because underneath the vanity, underneath the craving for praise, there was something softer. A flicker or longing to be worthy of something beautiful even if that something could kill. And velvet hemlock, just the name, promised both.

"I take it this town is either not used to outsiders or manners?" With my finished mug I had motioned I was finished with it.

"We usually do not get visitors during the daylight hours, what are you?" At least it made sense for him to ask.

"I am a light walker, vampire origin." Making it rather clear and as I had the eyes ceased staring at me feeling content with the information they heard.

"We also do not get many visitors here, are you passing through?" He seemed rather curious for my sudden visit.

I had to admit I had only been here once, that had to be at least eighty years ago, not that I had a reason for traveling here, let alone in this area.

"I happen to be looking for an old friend." Standing up from my seat not quite moving away from it, I wasn't sure if I wanted to share that information with any of them, who exactly I was looking for.

"Who might you be looking for? I might be able to assist. I've lived here for a very long time. I know everyone who has ever lived here." As he said this, I could feel all eyes on me again just as curious as he had been.

Looking at the door there had been two rather large men blocking the door.

"I take it she has already had some unwanted visitors. I'm here to offer protection." I hadn't needed to tell them who was searching for her before I came along; they were already acting as though they were ready to fight me.

"She has enough protection; you can leave now and if you don't, we will have a problem." With all the ones in the bar now standing I had not felt afraid for one second.

I had been up against worse. The only area that had not been blocked by the others now had been the front door since they moved in closer.

"She will need much more protection then what you can offer her, especially when the council comes for her." Tipping my hat slightly I made my way for the door as I noticed neither of the men standing near the door were interested in moving.

I could only guess they were waiting for me to announce I was leaving the small town. In my entire life I had yet to let anyone, or thing choose what I did with my life, and I was certainly not going to start now by being bullied out of a small town like this.

"What does the council want with her?" He seemed surprised to hear they were behind this.

"Should you really be surprised? After all, you said you know everyone that lives or had lived here, can't you think of one reason at all? I am their right-hand guard. However, my loyalty lies first and foremost with Drezin." Still not turning around the men in front of me finally backed away.

At least my reputation has preceded me or at least they had respect for the memory of Drezin, the majority of vampires at least knew him by name.

"Are you Langston?" I could hear the shock in his voice.

"The one and only." They all paid close attention now as I had said my last words as I continued walking out past the two men not waiting for any further replies.

At least they hadn't followed me right away onto the street but then it was still lit by the sun. I had hoped to finish a fight; sadly, not one presented themselves for one. Making my way out of the bar back into the light I continued my walk, not that any had offered where she was located, I walked towards the home I knew she had once lived in. Each house I passed I watched as the windows were drawn shut, not that it would have kept me out, no one had simply wanted to acknowledge me or be seen by me. I was aware many that hid from the council came here merely out of protection feeling it was safer in larger numbers. The old Victorian home I remembered, it still looked the same as the last time I had seen it, cream shutters, and trim. The rest of the house was stark white along with the traditional picket fence. Walking up to the house, it certainly looked in order until I came to the door. The handle had been twisted only barely hanging onto its place on the door. The door had been slightly ajar as I pushed it open the rest of the way; the home had been completely trashed inside. Either the place had already been searched through, or this was a ploy to make someone believe it had already been ransacked. I was fooled by neither. Although cluttered and looking destroyed it was far to organized to be a quick job.

Entering the house, I had not heard a sound, or even any slight scrapings from the wall or floorboards. Walking through looking around I had not seen much other than furniture torn to pieces on the floor along with broken dishes and plates scattered everywhere. Glass from one of the windows laid on the floor almost as if it had simply fallen out of its frame breaking in half. Flipping through several of the papers on the floor they had been scribblings of nothing interesting or important, definitely set there on purpose. Making my way to the upstairs I noticed a few tiny crayon marks on the banister. At least I knew a child had been here at some point. If I hadn't been looking for remnants of a child, I would have missed those. At the top of the steps each room had been in as much disrepair as the downstairs. She was certainly careful not to have any of the child's belongings thrown about on the floor. Flipping through the closet I had been looking for what most would not. Shoving what hanging clothing was left on their hangers. I searched the wallpaper along the wall until I found what I was looking for. The thinnest crack along the far side, I dug my fingers into the drywall grabbing a hold of the door that had been covered over, pulling it open. Knowing the family as well as I did, they always had some hidden place in their homes, I was the same way.

The wallpaper had not torn where I pulled back the door; at least it had been the natural area where it opened. The wallpaper had actually been wrapped around the door panel where it pushed back to unlock unlike a regular doorknob. With the floral pattern it blended in rather nicely. Stepping behind pulling the wall closed behind me. I made my way down the stairs in the very narrow passageway that I could only assume had led me past the first floor now down into the basement. Looking around there had not been very much down here. A few toys no doubt for occupying the child except I found one item that would help me more than anything else. It was a picture of Genevieve along with seven other children. I could only assume one of them had to be the child I was looking for. Genevieve tended to take pity on those children who were carelessly changed or left to die, a simple glance and you could tell not one of them had been related to the other.

Tucking the picture into my pocket. I walked around the room a bit more. In the corner of the room had been another door leading to the outside except I noticed one more interesting piece. I never would have noticed it if it had not been for the scent. Bending down touching the slight green spot on the ground. I knew immediately where to go next. The swamp, only this smell and stain would have been made from there and as I guessed had wiped off from their shoes. Making my way out of the basement I went straight for the swamp, no need in hiding my running speed since the entire town appeared to be vampire. I would have preferred heading somewhere that I had no personal connections or reasons to go, if I were to hide someone, apparently, she felt safer here then she should be. At least the swamp wasn't far from here, approximately eight miles. Closing in on the swamp I finally had to stop and listen for any sounds that would give away that someone would be out here.

"What are you doing here?" As I heard the voice, I knew it had been the only person that had ever been able to sneak up on me without my hearing.

Even back at my own home, I knew all along Gerard was making his way up the stairs at my estate. I loved or rather enjoyed a little too much seeing the look on his face letting him see that Lydia was still mine in some way. Only Genevieve had ever surprised me let alone been able to get away with sneaking up on me, and she meant business this time. Holding a rather sharp tactical knife in front of my throat as well as the same pressed against the back of my neck. She never used basic weapons; they were always ones she had either made herself or altered in some way to accomplish what she wanted.

"It's nice to see you also and I mean that figuratively, after all, I can't really see you behind me. Perhaps you can tell me why the council wants the little girl so badly?" I was never one to sidestep a question, I preferred to get to the point especially when I was not in the mood to play games, besides if she wished to kill me, I was fine by it, I was not trying to preserve my life by any means.

"I know you work for them and are here in their place, they are cowards unwilling to do their own dirty work." As she spoke the blades came closer to my throat.

"True, cowards they are however you are forgetting one simple element, I had stood by Drezin far longer than any of the council, I am simply here to offer my support, or to be honest I'm more curious what the council wants with a child?" I could hear her almost hissing at me with anger.

"You should have been here years ago if you wished to help." I could now feel the cold blade starting to enter my skin.

"I would have been if I only knew he had children he left behind. You've known me from our past and should know me better than that. I promise I have not changed one bit from the last time you knew me. I am still the despicable, womanizing, arrogant and most important narcissistic idiot you know and love." As I had said this, she lightened up with the blades giving in to a slight laugh.

At least she remembered me rather well.

"Regardless, if you have won me over or not, I still will not give you the girl. Besides you're not as narcissistic as you would like to think." She had sounded rather determined and I matched her tone of voice.

"Not to worry. I don't want her." Wiping away the grey sticky film that had come from my neck, the one thing I had really missed about being human, at least blood looked natural, almost pretty, probably why several vampires liked watching humans bleed to death being mesmerized by the color.

Watching as she put the knives back into their protective sheaths, I could also tell she had not changed at all. By far she had been the only one I had not been able to seduce. Not that I would ever tell her I admired her for her firm stance. Taking out the picture from my pocket I had already committed it to memory.

"You were a bit sloppy with your fake ransacking of the house; you might want this." Handing the picture over to her she hid her expression quite well.

I could hear children in the far distance and without waiting for her I started walking casually towards the sound. Genevieve hadn't bothered to stop me as she followed beside me, I could see seven children playing in the distance.

Not that I was an expert on children, all I could guess had been that they were all under the age of eighteen. Most of the children had looked so different from each other except for one child. As she looked directly at me, I had seen her father's eyes boring a hole into me. She had his same bright blue shining eyes and her mother's white hair. She had been so pale compared to the rest of the children, but then even her aunt came from a different father then her mother had. Her aunt had such a dark complexion as did the rest of the six children. Apparently, this was the child I was to protect until it had come time to kill her. She stood there waving at me as friendly as a child could, completely unaware of her future fate. I had still been undecided whether I would carry it out. If I had not, I knew there would be others to come along attempting to finish the job. As I walked over. The older children stopped playing being cautious not to let me out of their sight. They had taken after their mother not trusting anyone. The oldest girl had come over directly to the little one picking her up; she walked away quickly into the little house they had built to blend in with the swamp. Not wanting to press it I followed Genevieve into the other half of the house. At least for now I knew part of my job was secure, the little girl was indeed safe for now.

As soon as we closed the door behind us, I could hear the children outside resume playing again. One thing I couldn't figure out had been the difference with Drezin's daughter. There was something very different about her. Sitting down at Genevieve's table, she set out a glass for herself and a bottle of brandy. Reaching back into the cupboard she pulled a large, tinted glass bottle, turning she handed me just a bottle of vodka. She still remembered I had no need of a glass. Taking the top off the bottle, I took a swig before setting it back down on the table. I hoped she might start speaking but then she had been as distrusting as I was, not risking letting any information out that she hadn't needed to.

"I can't quite place it; I know there's something different about her, what is it or do I have to figure this one out myself?" Smiling at me rather devishly as she poured more brandy into her glass.

"Is it driving you crazy not knowing? Perhaps I should make you suffer and make you figure it out yourself?" She smirked at me.

I was beginning to feel the challenge coming on.

"You may not want me doing that? What is the kid's name? She does have one doesn't she, I admit I am curious what

Drezin, and Thea would name their child." I was ready to launch quite a few questions at her however I refrained hoping to find out the most important ones first.

"Her name is Kendra Langston Lewison, yes, I admit it is a bit different however fits her rather well. She is very much like her father in so many ways other than one, and you can stop giving me that strange look, yes, they had named her after you. Rather strange thing to do and still not tell you about her." Reaching back behind her she pulled open a drawer, reaching in she pulled out an envelope and now handing it to me I recognized the handwriting on the outside, it was from Drezin.

"What happened with the other two girls?" I might as well ask before she left the room.

"They are safe with other family members; both are vampires as well except this one. According to the council. It would be against the rules to allow her to live, which is why I have her and protect her for now. I have classes to teach since my children do not go to formal classes." Standing up I watched her leave the room.

Leaving me time to read the letter, I ripped it open not being cautious with it pulling the note out.

"I am fully aware that if you are reading this letter most likely you are here because of the council, not for actual visiting. I hope you take into consideration our pact and protect my daughter the same. Do not let the council get their hands on her; I know they would not wish to allow her to live. I would have sent her off with humans to live, she would have stood a better chance at hiding with them, however, I know how diligent you are, and you would have found her one way or another. She was much safer with family especially when she comes into her power. She is of course for the most part human. I am sure you have figured this out by now. I have no doubts I died because of the council, I admit I hated this and still wish not to acknowledge this to myself which may have been my reason for not telling you about her. The vampire fortune teller explained to me her permanent link to you. Even you must admit it's not right. No monster of any kind should ever be linked with a

human and how was I to know my own daughter would be human? When Najee and Nevaeh had access to the various portals, I had found it, not only a portal but a gateway to the gods. I know I sound insane, but it will make sense someday, I only wish I were there to experience it still. All the same I love her enough to give my life for her. My other two will be safe and capable of protecting themselves, however. Kendra needs you even though not as much as you will need her.

The letter simply ended with that. How was I to need anything from someone else? Especially from a human and what link was she to me? Setting the paper down I had been so absorbed I hadn't paid any attention to who might have walked in. I knew Genevieve was busy teaching the other children as Kendra came to stand in front of me wide-eyed and curious as to who I was. She seemed to be giving me a rather strange look, almost trying to figure out what I was thinking. Apparently, she must have lost her curiosity as she now saw something else she wanted. Walking into the kitchen she slid a chair over to the counter, looking up I could see the new object of attention. She climbed up the chair, then onto the countertop still not able to reach in to get the candy bar she wanted. Giving herself a slight jump, she had finally grabbed it except she missed the counter falling backward. Before she could come close to landing on either the chair or floor, I was up off my chair standing underneath catching her, trying to be careful not to grip her too hard. Never once had she let go of the candy bar as I set her down. She was much more interested in her prize then to be worried that she might have been injured. I wasn't sure just how vulnerable a human could be other than the simple fact she would have been hurt by what she was just doing. I watched her now partly out of curiosity as she tore the wrapper off eating her prize.

"How old are you?" I wasn't sure if she was old enough to tell me, I was having a hard time guessing her exact age.

Looking up at me she raised her hand up showing me her full palm and fingers. I had noticed the crescent moon on her hand, other than that I wasn't sure what she was trying to say.

"She's showing you on her hand how old she is, she's five years old. I'm not staying I just came in for juice and to see if Kendra was in here with you. Want a juice to?" The young girl had looked at Kendra as the little girl simply nodded now smiling.

Pulling out a juice for herself she also pulled one out for Kendra handing it to her with a straw already in it for her to drink. She picked her and took her outside with her.

I decided to follow behind them. I was curious what kind of an education they were receiving here. I guess I wouldn't be observing them quite yet; Genevieve was already finished for the day. The kids scattered for a while playing games until they had to come in for the evening. As I found the only one that required sleep was Kendra. All the children had taken off rather fast, even the one who grabbed Kendra as she held onto her.

"How often are you attacked here because of Kendra?" I was curious what sort of attacks to expect; I would always be prepared for anything just in case she had not told me.

"In town? Constantly. Living in the house, we were far too easy for anyone to find even with a few hidden rooms. We had the support of the others in town except when the council finally started snooping around making their intentions well known, than we were on our own. Since we have been staying in the swamp, you are the first to find us." She stated casually.

I was trying to decide whether I wanted to squeeze information from Lydia hoping to learn the real reason they wanted her power and what they planned to use it for.

Usually if the council wanted a power or anticipated it could be used by the council, it was promoted or heavily encouraged for that person to join the council in some form. At least she would be safe here for now except there were a few things I wanted to check on back at home, especially if I was going to make this an extended stay. Handing the note Drezin left for me to Genevieve, at least she would understand why I planned on making this a permanent stay for myself.

"I'm making a quick trip home and then I will be back, she should still be safe here with you except with so many children to care for, you will need some help. You're obviously doing just fine since you've been able to hide from the council this long. If anything, I can help make it easier for you. I won't be gone long, after all. I have a promise to keep, I just need to find out a few things about the council and sadly, my contacts are not here and it's far too easy to ease drop or catch wind of conversation if it's not done right." Not needing to say much more she simply nodded as I took one last glimpse of Kendra as I took off running.

I had planned on getting back as soon as possible. I could have made it with very few personal items, I've lived away from my estate before without anything, except I kept having that nagging feeling affecting my thoughts and I had to find out. I avoided the airlines this time since I was sure they would be looking for me. I would have to wait until enough time had passed before I were to fly again. Being careful of the direction I chose, and making sure no one was following me. When I was clearly out of range and certainly not giving any indication where or if I had found Kendra. I went into a store and picked up a phone calling home. I never carried or owned a cell phone since I hadn't wanted to be easily contacted at any moment or at worst, be easily tracked.

"Brunswick, I need you to dismiss the staff temporarily or at least until I give further notice, I am bringing something into the house, and I need to make sure no one else is there." I knew I could trust him; however, I had my phone tapped before.

I was far too aware of the signs, besides the council never fully trusted me so I was always under full surveillance. I mainly wanted to find out how involved the council was with this as well as who specifically was involved, after all I had a feeling not all of them were aware of this.

"Not a problem. Consider it done, will you be requiring any other assistance?" As he said this, I could hear a slight airy sound on the line.

Someone was either listening in on another phone in the house or was picking up air signal from where I was currently, which means someone might have found me at some point on my way back.

"No, I have it handled. I'll be there shortly." There was something I had to do before I stopped at the house.

After hanging up the phone I had gone into a different store picking up a large bag buying a few things. As I did, I stuffed the bag to make it appear full, then throwing a blanket over it. There was no way of telling if I had the child with me or not. I had been careful not to choose small or lumpy items; I wanted it as realistic as possible, filling it more with a rounded pillow, shoes at the bottom and a doll with hair extensions. That way with the smallest amount of hair sticking out it would blow in the wind naturally the way hair would. I realized this must have confused the saleswoman since I bought her new pair of extensions and took hers in exchange. After all, I wanted to make sure it had a mortal scent to it, otherwise it would be easy to tell all of this was a ploy. If I could throw the council's attention off for a while thinking the child was here with me, there might not be any attacks while I'm away, they would be more fully focused on me especially since I had the other workers leave.

Most of those had been hired or coerced by the council, no doubt will be in a hurry to report on me hoping to gain favor. As I neared home, I smelled two scents nearby. One I knew to be Lydia; the other one I wasn't too sure of. Coming up to the backdoor, Brunswick had the door already open for me to enter as usual.

"The house is empty as you asked, however I will warn you that since you called there are several watching the place now. Do you think it was wise to bring the child here?" I had even managed to fool Brunswick and with his comment it was perfect for anyone listening.

"I can't discuss it out here, follow me." Making my way to the office I closed the door behind us listening for anyone who might have followed us in or waited in here to ease drop.

Opening the closet, I tossed the mystery blanket and its contents into it.

"That is certainly no way to handle a child sir, if I may suggest a better accommodation?" He was rather concerned as he still believed the child had been wrapped up protecting it from being seen.

I certainly couldn't be angry with him; he knew me rather well and was right to assume I wouldn't know how to properly handle a child.

"I was only pretending to bring the child in with me, the item I threw in the closet was just a bag covered with a blanket filled with junk. Even I know you can't treat a child in that way, even though they can fit in any closet," I couldn't help getting a rise out of Brunswick, I may not know much about children, sadly I do know you simply cannot throw them into a closet, "how many council members or their lackeys would you say have been around here since I called?"

I could figure out a few simply by scent, however, I had been curious which staff member was keeping tabs on me now.

"At least twenty however they are minor with only two main council members keeping an eye on the place. I doubt they are interested in your sentencing; one is of course Lydia which I am sure you have guessed and the other Gerard." Now leaving me to myself, I had let Brunswick finish what he was working on.

I expected Lydia to make her appearance soon; I planned on getting information from her and hopefully we would not be interrupted at all.

I paced the floor for a while wondering how long it was going to take for her to make her entrance, even for her she had a hard time waiting if there was something she wanted. Brunswick had left for his own room keeping the door closed, I hoped by doing this they might assume the child was with him. Kicking off my shoes and sitting on my bed with a folder filled with notes, I scribbled down a few random ideas, however, making sure I had put them in a code form that only I would understand. If anyone had ever read through any of my notes, they would have assumed I was mad and not thinking clearly at all. The only other person who would have understood my made-up language would have been Drezin. As I flipped through the pages thinking over exactly what I was hoping to find out, I knew she was already on the balcony of my window as I heard her footsteps. The window opening slowly and deliberately, I could never understand why she thought she could sneak up on me. When all this time I had known her, she had never managed to do so. Her scent always gave her away before she had ever entered a room, a scent I had craved, as much as I was over her having fun, toying with Gerard, knowing it made him angry, she still visited me, it still felt good having her here.

As detached as I made myself appear to be from her, I still looked forward to her coming on our old weekends even though now from circumstances I was sure this would be a last visit.

"Where is the child? I assume you brought her back here. I saw you sneak in something, why did you bring her here?" She asked rather nervously.

I expected her to ask that.

"What? No hug for me? I might have only been gone for two days and yet you ask if I brought the girl here? Before I tell you, I want some answers." Moving away from the desk and dropping the book, I was writing in, on the bedside table.

Laying back on the bed getting comfortable I was ready for Lydia to resist telling me anything right away. She could be as secretive as she wanted to, however, if she hadn't answered my questions then I would prolong the agony until she possibly searched the house herself for the child. I wanted to know just how involved and why she was in all of this.

"You know I cannot give you anymore answers, now where is she. I am curious what she looks like? You were supposed to stay at a distance and not get involved, how could you have done this?" Walking closer to me yet staying a little further then she normally would have, I could only guess other members of the council were close by.

"Perhaps this is the best way of keeping her safe, after all, you know me, I can't help but get involved, especially when my loyalties are being tested." I wished I knew why my being involved angered her so much.

"There are just things you are not supposed to know that only the council is privileged to." She tried to sound stern except she was never good at faking it to me; she would never get angry with me unless she was pushed by someone else.

"You mean the fact that the council had killed Drezin and that it happens to be his child? How many council members are behind all of this?" Taking a step back I knew she wanted to leave and not answer anymore.

"You know I can't say anything, we are a collective and decide together how to better protect our own." She had weakly stated as she kept walking backward towards the window.

I was intent on keeping her here a bit longer. Getting up off the bed I walked towards her rather quickly grabbing her by the arm before she could make it out the window.

"Did any of the council come with you just now, other than Gerard?" Pressing her against the wall waiting for her answer, leaning in so close that I brushed my cheek against her face, I heard her let out a light sigh.

"Only Gerard, he is mainly here to find out if the child is here with you or not. I must report back to him." Not even looking at me. I knew there was something she was trying hard not to say.

"I wasn't aware that your being a council member made you below him. Surprised you would take a position where you had to answer to someone else? Not giving you much power, is he? Tell him yes, that she is here, then come back to me quickly. I have something to share with you." Letting her go I knew it would be tempting enough she would come back.

Watching her leave out the window, she went directly across the street to report the child was indeed with me, however she had not seen her for herself. As soon as she had told him the vehicle door shut leaving her on the sidewalk to watch it drive away. Making her way back up. I had always wondered why she refused to enter the front door or at least a regular door.

She had always insisted on entering either through the window in my office or the bay window to my bedroom. After she did this for the first few months, I had a trellis made with slightly wider awning and steps small enough for one foot at a time gradually heading to the ground. I wanted to make sure it hadn't looked as if I added stairs for her or she would never use it. Brunswick always kept some sort of shrub growing on it.

"Can I see her?" Almost saying it in an extremely low tone now, as though she might be afraid the child might do something to her.

It was difficult to shake the feeling she could actually be afraid of a child? What could a child do that would create so much fear unless I was not grasping the concept of magic? I had known a few magical beings in my time except they had rarely bothered us vampires. Even then as evil as the last one I had encountered; it certainly never struck a fear into me.

"Not yet, I need answers still, however, we will get to those soon." I swear I must be masochistic.

Wrapping my arms around her waist pulling her towards me. I leaned in to brush my lips softly over hers again, teasing her before I firmly kissed her lips. As I had. I smelled her scent. It was rather intoxicating; perhaps the addictive side of me for constantly inviting her or rather allowing her back in. Kissing her on the neck she had felt so good in my arms, she was different from most vampires where they had always been rather cold, I could feel the heat coming off from her body. I always thought it was the pesky shade part of her body wanting to come out. Most would die if they had been bitten by a vampire. However, her mother was a shade and her father a vampire, she inherited her abilities from both making her a light walker like me.

When we had broken up years ago, I should have made a clean break, perhaps it was also why I hadn't moved on to anyone else? I was always good at tormenting myself in a way no one else could. But then pain was very close to pleasure, and I had a rather disturbed way of looking at both. Even in death I had to be reminded I was still somewhat alive by the pain she could cause.

Leaning her up against the wall kissing her, she wrapped her arms around my neck. Her lips were so inviting I could hardly resist tasting them. Biting at her lower lip I could feel her trying to form words as I pressed my lips firmer against hers to stop her from saying anything.

"When do I get to see her?" She had still managed to get the words out.

"You're no fun; besides, I thought you might want to wait and see her with Gerard?" I knew he would still be waiting for her to report on seeing the girl.

"Why are you keeping her from me? You never keep anything from me?" She seemed genuinely surprised I hadn't just handed her over.

"My dear, I'm not the only one holding back, after all I have a feeling, the council is hiding something rather important from me or is it simply Gerard? I doubt I was the only one that could have found her?" Looking at her directly in the eyes I could always tell if she was lying to me.

"You're the only one they wouldn't have killed on sight; you have an agreement with her father. That's something the rest of us do not have. You knew her family better than any of us, besides, where did you find her? We heard you were far south when you called. It's not a surprise you're being watched." Smiling at her I had known I was being listened to, which is why I deviated my travel home.

"Why do I have a feeling not all the council is a part of this? It would explain why I would be sent, I don't work in groups, keep my mouth shut and hire out to any one of them, so I would never draw suspicions, so who out of you four really are interested in this? I want you to tell me what I haven't heard yet. You can make this easier, either way I always find out eventually what I want to know." Making my last statement as a matter of fact, after all, if I want to find out information, I had my ways of doing it and she knew it.

"Tell me what you've heard, and I'll let you know if you're accurate?" Smiling back, she was calling my bluff, I may have had my ways except it didn't hurt to take the easy way and I had learned much from her over the years.

After a while she learned even with me, she had to learn to keep her own mouth shut.

"Sorry not this time, besides, I have the child that is wanted so badly and if I don't find out what I want. I just might start making plans of my own." The look of surprise was quickly changed to a look of anger.

"You wouldn't dare, besides the council would be all over you before you had the chance to hide her." As she said this, she had pushed away from me walking over to the window.

"If they had that much power, they should have been able to find my exact location or where the child was, it wasn't that difficult. That's why if the woman I found is correct, not all the council knows about her." As greedy as I had known Gerard to be, I doubted the rest of the council would have known about this.

If they had. I would have been executed immediately that day instead of being sent off on another assignment. They could have easily found her if they truly gave it thought, I wasn't the only one with a strong connection to the family, besides Jerome could have found them just as easily, another top assassin for the council.

"I highly doubt the child would know anything about it." Lydia glared at me for a second.

"I'm not speaking about the child and your right, she has no clue about any of this, she doesn't even know about the power she's about to inherit, I'm speaking about the woman who happens to be my new source, after all, I can get it out of her so much easier then you and I get more from her." Smiling smugly at her I knew she would start acting jealous that I was spending time with another woman.

There were only three women who would be working around the council and as far as Lydia had known, any one of them would confide in me in a second.

"Drop the child off at the old fishery; we will appoint someone else to watch her, after that you may do as you wish."

Her tone was rather indignant.

"I already do whatever I want, there's no fun in that anymore." As I watched her leave at least without having to say a word, I could already guess the rest of the council had no idea about the child's power.

Gerard was the main one who wanted this and no doubt using Lydia to keep me in line to help. I hadn't even known of her existence except there had to be someone out there that did. Genevieve knew she would be inheriting her power by sixteen, however, she had not known the entire extent of it. Apparently, this was not something passed on by either parent, it was a blessing left to her from a rather magical creature who had not wanted to see the power die out with the very last remaining creatures of its kind. Personally, I felt it was more of a mutation if it could prevent the child's vampire side from taking over. If Gerard had the chance to become more powerful than the council, he would take that chance. He was just as addicted to power as Lydia had been, except I doubted she realized the unsettling truth. No matter how much she helped him. I doubt he would even bother keeping her around at that point. After all, why would he share such a power when he could have it all to himself? Letting out a sigh, I knew I could only protect her so much, and sadly she had let herself be around the most dangerous people. Deciding not to dwell on all of that again, I decided if they wanted the child, I was going to give them what they wanted.

It had been early morning when they came by to see if I truly had the child with me. As I had waited for nightfall, I knew whoever had truly been interested in collecting the child would be there at the old fishery. This way, even if a member of the council had not been there, I could guess which one it had been due to the messenger waiting to collect the child. Each member tended to use those who were loyal to them and no one else. Even I had two whom I had trusted to carry out what I needed done. Except this time, it really hadn't mattered as I simply had chosen someone at random. I wanted them to know the exact location and time it was being dropped off.

Driving up in a tinted black limousine. I had the person walk up to the fish hatchery. As I watched from a distance dressed up as a chauffeur. The package had been handed over; it had been Oliver who accepted and now I knew for certain. As my chosen hand off made his way back, we had taken off but not soon enough to miss the swearing and other profanity that followed. I had simply wrapped a doll quite well with a few water balloons taped to it giving it the feeling of being a real child. Pinned to the outside had been a personal note.

"Did you honestly think I would just hand the child over without knowing who all is involved? Shame on you for keeping secrets from me, I'm debating whether to let the rest of the council know what you're doing behind their back or quite frankly actually protect what now happens to be mine?"

Dropping off my helper, I now had a few plans of my own. From now on. I was going to find out what this power was that was so desperately wanted by Gerard, and to keep the child safe just as I would have with Drezin. He might have had a reason for keeping all of this from me, however, now there wasn't much of a choice other than to find out as much as I could. If he wanted her to be safe, then I would have to find out everything there was to know.

Chapter Three

Too Many in the Picture

I certainly wasn't going to be heading home or directly back to the child. Right now, I had far too many eyes on me. The last thing I wanted to do was lead them directly to her. Instead, I found an interesting way of amusing myself. Finding the most outrageous stores or unusual shops. I would go in and ask for the store owner to simply hand me a bag filled with dirt. As I would leave, those who followed me would go in to find out what I purchased, some asked rather well without raising suspicion while others even the shopkeeper knew what they were doing. They had been paid to inform them of all the strange items I would purchase, leaving them wondering what I was planning to do. It had given me something to do for a while and of course have them send back reports I knew would only worry and frustrate Gerard. I was sure only Lydia understood what I was doing. Except I only felt the need to keep this up for a short time. As the time passed there were fewer following. There hadn't been much to report other than my meeting a woman as I traveled and picking up rather strange items.

I knew if I were to simply kill the ones following me, I would end up with the entire council after me; most of the ones spying on me had been their messengers. However, if Gerard truly did not want the others to know it would be a good way to flush them out, and he would have to explain to them what was happening or make something up. Only problem I had with all of this, if the child was going to be as powerful as Gerard thought, they might consider her a risk to the council and simply want her killed only for that reason. Either way, rumors stay silent for only so long.

I hadn't wanted to let the others know where I was heading. Instead, pretending to be engrossed in a small town not that it really had any meaning to myself, other than the simple fact no one knew me here. Walking around keeping an eye on the other two who were not very good at hiding themselves from me. I looked up to find I had an old woman waving to me. Making my way across the street I had gone in following behind her to find out what she wanted. Still not saying anything she led me back to a far room away from her customers lowering the thick layers of lace and blankets covering the door opening. I hadn't felt she was a threat other than being curious what she needed my attention for. Then I found she was thinking the same thing I had been thinking for a while. The woman turned out to be a gypsy woman traveling through town using this back room waiting for me. She had seen me making my rounds and knew she needed to point me in the right direction.

"Sometimes we do not come to the conclusions or rather our heart has not caught up with us until it is meant to. Searching to hard can make the obvious disappear and we miss finding what we are truly meant to find. There are times we are tested and find out who our true friends are. When you do find the truth, it can and will change your entire life, yours is already changing. You could have had your freedom from the council years ago except you were too comfortable. I know you will choose well when the time comes. Just be careful, there are six who follow you except only two will catch up to you." Turning from me she lifted six small boxes all rather solid with a smaller plastic box inside.

"I take it you're supposed to be a true friend of mine.

Showing me what I need to know?" I was already feeling skeptical of whatever she was getting at.

Looking directly at me she had given me a rather strange gaze.

"No. I am neither friend nor foe, but certainly no friend of yours. If I were, it would show I have taken sides which I have not. These boxes are for your use; I will waste no time telling you a future that is not for you to know right now. In the envelope that is for you to read in two years. Do not open it before then and it is for your eyes only. There are ones who already know, however, that for you it is not necessary right now. I will not be around later to give it to you, so take it now." Glancing down at the envelope for a second, I had been tempted to open it right then, after all how was I to trust someone who I had never known before?

I never did get a chance to ask her another question. I never heard or saw her leave other than the fact of when I looked up, she was gone. Thinking about it for a second there had only been six that followed me now, I had wondered how she knew the exact number let alone I was followed unless she had been a true reader? Not wanting to stick around any longer. I grabbed a blanket that was draped across her chair and wrapped the boxes inside so that they would not be seen. Not forgetting the envelope, I folded it and set it inside of my jacket so that way I would not risk it being stolen from me when I was in my next fight.

It had been rather awkward carrying all these things, heading for a hotel room I had looked for some privacy. I knew right now it was a rarity with being followed all the time. I wanted to make my way back to the child to make sure she was safe. Except I felt if they were so busy following me, I was sure they had no clue where she was, or they believed I had removed and hidden the child myself. I found myself acting more cautiously, not sure if it had been because of the impending death the other members of the councils would inflict while I tried to figure out this child thing, or if it had simply been from learning patience finally? Letting out a light laugh to myself I knew it couldn't possibly be that.

If I wanted to speed things up, I knew what I had needed to do. Waiting in the motel room for the rest of the day until night fall, once it was dark enough, I sensed a few of the spies had moved themselves into the bar below in the same hotel. Flipping on the television to a children's cartoon. I had the television on a bit louder then I normally would have. As I had counted on the humans staying in the room next door had gone down to complain that a child had its program playing to loud. Receiving a phone call from the front desk, I assured them I would have my child turn her program down. It had not taken very long before the first made his way up to my room.

I wished I could have been there with Gerard to see his expression as he opened each box to find his only followers heads sent to him. Not wanting to leave the bodies for the motel maids to deal with. I simply threw them out the window. Leaving before anyone could ask any questions or any other spies could locate me, I took off in a shot still further away from my target area. I was definite the boxes hadn't been left to me for this reason, however, what they held didn't need that many boxes.

There were eight vials of either liquid or powder which I now carried in my pocket with the note. I wanted to make sure I was far enough away before I risked going anywhere familiar. First stopping at Drezin's home again, I hoped there still might be something I was missing. After setting off almost every trap in his home. I had not left any areas unsearched. The only thing I had found was a picture of a woman I had never seen before. At least I knew why others had not found Genevieve; no one assumed she lived this long believing she had been left human when the rest of us were changed. However, I was not sure who this woman had been. Sadly, she had not resembled anyone I was familiar with. I knew if I had started asking questions about this woman the same information would eventually spread back to Gerard, and he might start looking for her as well. Setting the picture in with the envelope I was ready to head back and see how Kendra was fairing.

I should have expected it since I had not warned her exactly when I would be back; I had been knocked flat on my back with another personally designed knife of Genevieve's grazing my neck as she stood over me. Smiling at me the second she realized who it was, she had stepped back walking away from me. I underestimated her over these last several years but then I had only learned she was still alive myself perhaps about eight years ago. The children had been out playing while a few of the older ones had taken off earlier to hang out with their friends. Kendra apparently felt like playing inside the house alone, which she did most of the time. She hadn't been very social but then she picked that up from her parents, they were rather private also. For the first time I had to admit time might not have mattered to me before except it was going to go by rather slow for once. I had been used to fighting fellow vampires and other special creatures, even those with unusual gifts always having to stay alert. Now the basic goal had been to keep a small child from drowning in a swamp, falling off from a cupboard or even bitten by a snake. Genevieve seemed to have her hands full except she handled it with much more patience then I had. Kendra had been playing with a toy next to me as I was reading; nothing irritated me so much until I heard the same noise repeatedly getting louder each time. I kept hoping for the toy to break or for her to lose interest except she kept playing without letup. Finally, I snapped, grabbing the toy and crushing it with my hand. Normally I never would have thought about my actions or felt guilty for them. Except the look on her face as a single tear went down her cheek, she was trying to hide the fact she was so hurt over her toy.

"I'm sorry. I grabbed it too hard; I'll either fix it or buy you a new one." I knew it hadn't taken care of the situation; this was not what I had seen myself spending my life doing watching over a child.

I barely had patience for me and now I certainly proved I had none for a child. I was a vampire; we weren't expected to have kids, so where would I have learned to handle this? All Kendra had done was nod her head as she walked out of the room into her bedroom. I had never felt guilty for any of my actions my entire life and yet this little kid complaining with a simple tear, not saying a word made me feel an emotion I thought I was incapable of. Throwing the paper I attempted to read onto the floor. I was getting more frustrated with myself now. Rushing off for the town, I knew which store would sell the items. I had planned on replacing it with another one when I wound up getting sidetracked by two strangers in the bar. Slipping her toy into my pocket I had known I better not show up at home empty handed after crushing her toy, except I had to find out what these two were doing here. Had they found out where Kendra was? Or had they managed to follow me undetected.

When I stepped out of the store, I took in every detail around me, only to realize that others were watching the strangers too. Those same strangers were watching me. Instead, I chose to go into the bar next door choosing my usual spot, I had thought of sitting at a table, but they might assume something was up and I didn't want to risk anyone joining me. I noticed the strangers went over immediately to a table in the corner no doubt to keep an eye on everyone that was there. Perhaps they were passing through trying to find something, or anything they could to clue them in on where I was, or Kendra had been taken to. This place was boring me as everyone watched each other doing nothing, even the bar tender wasn't serving drinks, so I took that as the time to leave. I was going to leave through the backdoor by the restrooms when I felt a tap on my shoulder, quickly grabbing the arm twisting it I shoved the person against the wall. Letting go right away thankful I hadn't decided to snap the arm now and ask questions later, I was sure Genevieve never would have forgiven me or worse killed me this time. Her son Tyler was against the wall while her daughter Lily was standing directly behind him. Motioning for me to follow them. I wondered what they were going to show me. What I needed to do was to keep an eye on the two who were in the tavern or at least

I thought I needed to until Lily pointed out something much more dangerous. There was one person standing alone in front of Genevieve's home looking it over, no doubt he had figured it out as I had. The only other person I ever considered a threat and there he was somewhat in the flesh, Jerome.

"Both of you know who that is?" I was curious how the kids knew who he was.

"We know from our mother teaching us who to watch out for. We can't seem to get home without anyone watching us. The youngest of our group took off north to our cabin since it's safer for them, they stay out of the way except we need to warn mom." As Lily spoke, I was looking around assessing the danger, as I did, I could see he was quite prepared.

He had his men stationed in various places around the town. I was surprised I hadn't seen him but then I might have just missed him as I entered town. I knew it would be too dangerous for me to risk heading back to the swamp right now except I knew how smart he was, and he would soon pick up on the small clues I had and eventually find them. I tried to eliminate as much as I could that would lead anyone to them, unfortunately there's always a chance I missed something myself.

"It would be best if you didn't split from your siblings, larger numbers are better when you're dealing with people like this, head north to the cabin and I'll make sure your mother and the little ones join you soon. How far up north is the cabin?" Just in case I had to come find them, it would help knowing.

"It's just a mile north, down slope from the Mezzy mines." Not having to convince either of the kids, they walked to the other end of town chatting with each other passing a tennis ball back and forth acting as if nothing was wrong and it had been another typical day for them.

At least Jerome and his group wouldn't associate them with who they were looking for assuming they were just general youngsters from the town. Losing interest in them. The watchers started patrolling around again, when they were far enough out of the way, both shot off as fast as they could heading for the family safe place.

Walking into one of the stores again the clerk had been watching me as I walked towards the back. I had seen another one of his men checking out the place. Standing behind one of the aisles. I kept my attention on him as he lifted a tiny little box that fit in his hand. Speaking low enough into it he announced there was nothing in here. Apparently, they hadn't figured out this was a town that consisted of only vampires. As he moved further, he went out the back door behind the shop, as he did, I kept close. Hoping there were not several more in the back as I caught his attention. Apparently, he was about to search the dumpster behind the store, Jerome had certainly been thorough except I had never seen him scour a place this much before.

"This should make things much easier; I should have guessed we are in the right place if you're here." Smiling rather assuredly to himself.

"I could just be here to collect a few things, after all why would I bring the child here? You know me better than that, risk hanging around and being seen by you if I intended on keeping the location of the child secret? Seems like a stupid move on my part if she was here and I made it that easy." Lifting his hand up I was sure he was about to report his latest finding.

Not hesitating for a second, I raced over as fast as I could knocking the little box out of his hand and onto the ground. Usually, I preferred my opponent to make the first move except this time I had to jump the gun a little. As he swung connecting with my stomach forcing me back, I was able to catch my balance turning into a roundhouse, kicking my opponent in the side of the head forcing him onto the ground. Before he had the chance to get up, I lunged at him only to have him quickly roll out of the way. Scrambling to catch him. I couldn't risk him getting away to alert Jerome except I had a feeling he wouldn't need to as there was a voice coming from the little box. As he made the mistake of reaching for it. No doubt calling for backup, it had given me enough time to do him in as I landed on top of him, he had the little box in his hand as I grabbed his neck not only snapping it but also separating it from his body. Not usually an easy task however, his gave way to easily leaving me with an unsettling feeling. The others knew he was in danger by now, pulling out my own cell phone I called Genevieve quickly. It had taken her a few rings when she answered. I was worried she might have already been found. I only had a few seconds to tell her not to come into town. There was a group here for her that she needed to join the kids at the safe spot. As I had said this the phone in my hand had been crushed as another came attacking me. Grabbing me by the waist as if I weighed nothing, he threw me into the side of the building.

Standing up quickly I was not alone. A I looked. There were fourteen of Jerome's men. I rarely had any of those who worked with me follow me anywhere. I had learned not to trust any of them and to only rely on myself. Besides, this way, if I get hurt or die, no one else pays the price for it. I didn't like feeling guilty for others when they died unless I caused it. I knew I could handle a lot however even this was more for one man to take care of. Even a vampire with strength still used side weapons when it was necessary. Reaching into my pockets. I pulled out my special made daggers as the others came racing at me. Throwing the two. I hit at least two of the vampires slowing them down, the knives, although a short steel serrated blade covered with titanium metal with a slight hook, once it entered the target it was extremely difficult to get out. Slowing those two down. I had no choice but to run for it. I knew they would be able to keep up as I weaved through a few buildings hoping to break the number of those who followed behind me. Jerome had never felt a vampire should use weapons feeling we were enough of one and that's one of the most important reasons we were different. I felt if it made us stronger or helped in any way, I would use both. Knocking dumpsters into the way as several of those simply leapt over them. I was sure the whole town was aware what was going on with all the noise we were making. As I ran, I had grabbed two more daggers out of my jacket pocket throwing them blindly behind me as I heard at least one vampire howl in pain as it struck him. If I didn't kill them at least I could slow them down. I was now out in the middle of town where all the townspeople would be able to see us. With nowhere else to run. I decided to stop and confront them. With only twelve following. I was ready for the worst. It helped that some were faster runners then others, those I could take out hopefully before the others caught up. At least I hadn't used my favorite weapon of choice yet, pulling it out of my pocket and tossing it out into the crowd. They stopped for a second looking at it rather confused.

"I guess it was a dud." Not giving them any expression to go off of as they were ready to attack again.

The little round ball on the ground split open showering them with a bright explosion of light, sulfur, and fire.

Catching majority of the group with my favorite personal made weapon. I could see Jerome out of the corner of my eyesight. Therefore, vampires were either burned, staked in the heart with an aspen or willow stake. He was the only vampire I ever knew who could repair himself this quickly, probably why he's survived so long. He showed no visible signs of coming after me or being in a hurry as he simply stood there watching his men getting beaten by me. The last two that had come after me were still rather determined as I kept dodging their movements. As soon as they would come after me, I would move back or ducking between the two as quickly as possible, hoping to confuse them enough getting them to strike at each other. Finally, the opportunity came as one was standing directly behind me. The other took a strike at me as I ducked, and he hit his partner snapping his neck. Not enough to kill a vampire however long enough to incapacitate him for now. The other I simply struck with my last handmade knife. Not wanting to lose this one. I pulled it back out of my assailant's chest and as I did, I could hear the ripping of his flesh.

"I see you still collect your personal weapons back." Jerome had made his way over to me.

"Yes, I do, it's a pain crafting these. Besides, I see you still lack loyalty." Jerome and I had served together a few times although we remained independent as well as preferring our own assignments.

"You know me, I hate being told to bring along lackeys, they only get in the way. So, what if I lose a few. Where is the kid? I was hired on a need-to-know basis by Gerard, he said you went rogue, kind of difficult for a man that was supposed to be dead?" We never did say much to each other, we were always direct and to the point.

"She's not here; I'm surprised you took a job by Gerard, especially since he's working separately from the council." The expression on Jerome's face hadn't changed.

"That's why I took the job; I wanted to find out why Gerard would risk going against the others. He's told me absolutely nothing about all of this and from my own research, apparently this kid is key to something larger than the council combined." I knew it wouldn't take him very long to figure it out.

"I'm surprised Gerard didn't ask you to kill me before looking for the child." I was surprised he seemed more relaxed than usual.

I only hope Genevieve had the kids out before any of them found out they were in the swamp and head there.

"The only reason I don't kill you myself is that it would take out all the challenge. As far as I could tell, if this kid had more power than vampires, it's putting us all at risk, I say she needs to be put to death regardless of what Gerard wants. If you're smart you will do the same." Pulling his cloak back over his shoulders Jerome was about to walk away.

"She's only a threat if the power is taken from her before she learns to use it. You do realize what she is. Don't you?" I knew this would get him interested.

"She's either vampire or some other creature; no human would have a power like that." Not moving, however, listening still for me to fill him in on what I was willing to.

Right now, she could probably walk right in front of him without anyone knowing that they should be looking for a human. At least I could find one more way of stalling them from finding her.

"You know how Drezin liked to experiment with things. She's mixed with so many different creatures she's just a hideous looking thing, why do you think I don't travel with it? I have it hidden in a safe spot until I can figure out how it uses its magic and yes, it has it now, not later when it hits sixteen the way Gerard explains. She's never been a risk before so why now suddenly?" Even if I hadn't given him accurate details, I wasn't about to tell him the one thing he wasn't assuming.

"It's a good thing at least one of us had a sense of humor or poor Drezin never would have had any friends. However, you should consider this especially if you consider yourself loyal at all to your own kind. The majority are more important than just the one." This is where we again had differed, and I had proven so on many occasions that the actions of one were at times much louder, stronger, and just as important as the majority.

"Who's to say the power of one is not to the benefit of the majority, after all, she may be what is needed in order to save our kind, there is much more then you realize to Gerard's intentions." Jerome had already walked quite a distance away although I knew he heard me, even as he said his parting words, 'never trust a man who has a weakness.'

I knew exactly what he meant. Gerard knew my weakness and it had been Lydia. Instead of hanging around while very few of his men started to get back up again, I left the town as quickly as I could. By passing the furthest side of the swamp to make it appear as though I was simply crossing through taking a short cut to the next town, I had to stop for a second as I could see a rather strange glow in the distance. Taking off for it. I had to be careful how much was allowed to be seen. I was sure I was still being watched by Jerome's men, it's not as if he was going to let me go entirely. He was a smart man and knew at some point I would return to the child, and he hoped to find her because of me. He always felt if you had a weakness then there was a flaw no matter how slight in everything you did.

As I came up closer to the swamp where the glow had

been off in the distance, I now knew what was burning. Genevieve must have set the swamp on fire creating a fume with the natural elements of the swamp mixed in with the fire. The straw house that they had lived in temporarily was already burnt to the ground, showing no signs of anyone ever being there. At least I had hoped it would be her. Heading to the next town over I needed to kill some time or distract at least two of those who were still following me before I could proceed again. Reaching into my pocket I still had the toy I had bought for Kendra. At least maybe this will cheer her up since they had to leave so quickly and for my destroying her toy from earlier. Now that Jerome was searching for her, it would be safer to get her out of the country entirely and perhaps get her to blend in with other humans. At least they had no idea what they were looking for. It might buy us more time as she grows up. Working my way north. I made a few stops along the way, as I did, Jerome's two men stayed far enough away making sure they did not repeat Gerard's spies' mistakes.

While I was in the area, I decided to pay a visit to a mutual friend of ours, he knew Drezin and Thea as well as I had. I never needed a map, I knew when I was up far enough north to find their place, they were surrounded by woods. Just like Drezin, Arthur preferred solitude away from the world which was slowly building up even around him. Lydia and I seemed to be the only ones who preferred to be directly in town. I could just barely make out his log cabin as I was getting closer until I heard a faint voice.

"I haven't seen you in ages, surprised you're not dead yet with your reputation." The voice seemed genuinely surprised.

"You're correct, I should be dead; I caught my second wind. Is Arthur still around?" Not sure where the voice was coming from.

I had always been good at locating the direction except Elizabeth had the special gift of speaking and making her voice echo from two different directions.

"He's at home and I'm sure he will be very happy to

see you, we were talking about you last night because of some events that have gone on, however I'll let him fill you in on that, I have to get going for now." Not seeing her once or hearing her leave, I could only guess she had been out of ear shot for me not to hear her move.

She might not have been able to sneak right up on me however she was always the best at staying hidden. All vampires learned some way of getting by for safety. Walking up to the house it had been painted a hunter green with gray streaks around it. A rather strange color for wanting to be hidden in the woods, but then it was hard to tell what was going through Arthur's mind until he explained himself and usually, he had a good reason for it. Arthur was already waiting for me at the door.

"It is good to see you….old friend, been far too long. I had a feeling you might show up soon. Come on in." Leaving the door open to me I closed it as I entered following Arthur to his living room, sitting down with his cigar now being placed in the ash tray.

"Elizabeth said you two were discussing me because of the events happening. What's been going on that I would be interesting enough to be topic of conversation?" Sitting back making me comfortable.

I was rather curious what would be going on here and that it would involve thoughts of me. I could think of much more interesting things to talk about.

"It has to do with Drezin, are you familiar with the fact he has a child? Or rather he had a couple of them, its unheard of for a vampire and not sure how it happened." Shaking his head, Arthur seemed rather perplexed by the thought.

"It's the main reason I'm even in this region of the country. I've met one of his children and she certainly takes after her father in personality, however, for looks. She's a spitting image of her mother.

"We've been hearing rumors and not quite sure which is accurate or not. However, apparently Drezin made a rather unique friendship with a magical creature, this is where the stories change quite a bit. Now mind you once someone is dead, they are dead and no bringing them back, however you and I died while we were still alive, very different circumstances. Supposedly this magic can bring to life things that were dead and make them human again. Whether we have or are a soul is debatable. But supposedly they would be as human as when they first started in life. It can supposedly control vampires making them too weak to fight or strong enough to annihilate. There is also the rumor that it gives vampires the gift that rare light walkers have. Rumors are that Gerard wants to take over and wipe out the council all together however no one believes it since they have apparently chosen to keep Gerard as a council member. It's hard to tell what is true and what is not." Taking a puff from his cigar Arthur placed it back in the ash tray.

"Are there any other rumors floating around? I don't think the rumors are that far off." Handing me one of his cigars I merely fiddled with it in my hand.

I never was into smoking; I loved the smell of a cigar however I could never get the smell out of my clothing. I wasn't exactly worried about cancer or anything else it could give me, after all technically. I was already dead.

"Supposedly the magic festers in the bloodstream until it is full growth causing its recipient the use of magical abilities which means it can either be shared or completely drained killing the victim. It could allow a vampire to take over the council and rewrite vampire laws leaving no one able to stop it. If they wished, they could wipe out humans or allow our world to be exposed trying to dominate both worlds. It affects humans as well deteriorating their muscles and other creatures, depending on which ones it will affect them also. That is of course only one of the theories. Drezin is capable of a lot of things however creating godlike magic isn't one of them. The other popular opinion is he found an actual god and as most myths, was gifted something powerful from it." Taking a few more puffs from his cigar Arthur stood now walking over to his bookcase taking down a book.

Flipping through it leaving it opened to a certain page and now handing it to me.

"What am I looking for?" Looking at the book, I wasn't sure what he wanted me to see.

Arthur had a way of teaching. He preferred for one to find the answer themselves except if he was in a hurry, he would point it out earlier. He had taught and been a mentor to Jerome, Drezin and I. There was a main picture on one side with a rather large Amish looking barn in the background with four women standing out front expressionless and a man standing off to the side almost trying not to get in the picture. I had been concentrating on the women which I had not recognized any of them until I finally realized who the man was, and it was Drezin.

"Are you sure you do not notice what's there? I trained you better than that. Besides, there are always hidden messages even from those we lost." Concentrating even more on the picture I knew there had to be something more to it.

I still couldn't place where the photo had been taken except, I did notice the woman resembled Drezin a little. Drezin had always been loyal to Thea however myself I had never been able to settle down with anyone for any longer then I was forced to. Even with Lydia I would disappear for years at a time just to get away.

"The women look as though they could be his family, I know he didn't have any siblings so they would have been distant relatives except the clothing looks modern and not from the time we were young. This looks rather recent." Still searching it was frustrating knowing whatever it was had been staring me in the face.

Simply sitting back down in his chair Arthur offered no words of advice giving me time to figure it out for myself. Looking off to the side of the barn it had been a small private cemetery. That's when it hit me, Drezin's grave was there. Now I remembered where the place had been, I was looking at it from an unfamiliar angle.

"Is he still alive?" I was stunned, not really surprised if

Drezin had felt there was a reason to do this, at least it would explain the rather bizarre death, but then why wouldn't he want to protect his child himself?

He had two other children then just Kendra. As I looked closer these two woman were younger then they appeared at first, they simply had makeup to make themselves look older and the woman on the side had changed her appearance was Thea herself.

"I knew you didn't need me to tell you. Having knowledge can either help or hinder you. He knew you would come after his daughter at some point except he trusts you as a brother. As Jerome would say you have a weakness, yourself. Drezin has five." Arthur didn't need to list them to know what they were.

This had been one more person that I needed to avoid otherwise others would find he was alive and use it to their advantage somehow. I almost forgot the envelope I had been carrying in my pocket. Oddly enough I still felt hesitant to read it, not that I was afraid of bad news. I wasn't sure I wanted to know. We started to discuss a few of the other pictures that had been taken, most appeared out of focus or blurry. Most would have thrown them out except this was the best there would be of us. We didn't exactly show up on photos or film of any kind. Mortals couldn't see us at all. At least with our eyesight it was clear enough, you needed a vampire's eyesight to see us in what would look like a blank photo. We talked for a few hours when Elizabeth came back home. She had started her own herbal shop in town and today was her usual day she replenished the shelves.

"Did you bring friends with you?" Setting down empty glass jars on the table as she now walked into the room.

Standing to be polite I hugged her; she had been a mother to us. She taught manners to us and even though I chose not to display them most of the time, I always did around her.

"No, those would be Jerome's men. They are hoping I'll lead them somewhere." Sitting back down in the chair Elizabeth had walked over to Arthur bending over giving him a kiss.

Through several centuries they were still very affectionate to each other, certainly not having any problems displaying it no matter who was around. One of the traits Drezin picked up from them, Elizabeth liked to say I did also, but I have not found the right person to be affectionate and loyal to yet.

"Oh well, I'm sure he can find more. Give my sympathies to Jerome then." She seemed rather unconcerned as she sat in her own chair pulling her yarn out of the basket that lay beside it.

A slight smile started on Arthur's face.

"I assume they gave you trouble?" Arthur looked at his wife curious why she would be sending Jerome condolences.

"No, not trouble or I would still be dealing with them. Jerome knows I won't deal with ill-mannered vampires; they searched my store making a mess and harassed my employees asking them questions, and then they had the nerve to curse and demand answers from me. No need to keep vampires around that are like that. They've lived long enough to have learned better." As soon as she said her piece, she started knitting whatever it was she was working on.

"What is that strange jingle sound I keep hearing from you Langston?" Arthur seemed a little confused.

I guess if I heard it, I would have been curious also, I never would have expected the sound to be coming from me. Pulling out the toy, both Arthur and Elizabeth gave me a rather strange look.

"I lost my temper and broke the kid's toy, so I replaced it; I just haven't had the chance to give it to her yet." Placing the toy back in my pocket I noticed the glance given between Arthur and Elizabeth.

"Should I be questioning that look you just gave each other or be glad I don't know?" There were times it was just private and other times it had been that they knew something I didn't.

"In due time. Right now, it would just confuse you. Perhaps you should get going before Jerome sends any more of his ill-mannered men to follow you." Elizabeth stood up giving me a goodbye hug before she went into the kitchen.

The smile she exchanged with Arthur was still there, even Arthur was still smiling.

"Yes, I think that would be a good idea, you're always welcome here, however; we know you have important things ahead of you." Standing up Arthur led me to the door.

Feeling a little confused, slightly grateful for leaving since I felt rather strange from the way they were acting but then I almost wanted to stick around to find out what the secret was. Leaving as asked. I knew better then to push to find out something. If either of them wanted me to know something, they would make sure I did know. I knew never to push them, or I would see a side I hoped never to see again.

At least I couldn't argue with their logic. If I was going to take off, it would be better before Jerome found out he had to send out more men to follow me. Taking off far north. I hadn't known where the cabin was other than to check ten different places, most had been close by while there were three that were rather isolated. Knowing Genevieve, I could easily eliminate the closer ones and choose the isolated ones further out. The first two mines I had come to were closed off with several warning signs of impending and possible danger. The third, which was rather far up north, much more difficult as the snow became deeper with no one traveling up this way. There were no active roads here or even tracks that I could follow. I was only hoping I was heading the right way; these were the only mines I could associate with her. We used to explore one of them when we were children, not that it was safe but then we were not exactly good about believing the signs warning of the dangers. Amazing how you can look at the same thing later and then realize what could have happened. We were lucky we hadn't died permanently when we were young. As I came closer to the site, I slowed down now looking around for any warning signs that Genevieve was about to pounce on me. There was a small cabin in the distance, at least it could be seen this far away and recognized, however leave it to Genevieve, she still liked to take me by surprise.

"What took you so long?" As I tried to turn, I didn't have a chance as she face planted me into the snow landing directly on top of me.

Apparently, she had been laying in the snow completely covered in white waiting to pounce up on me.

"I had a few complications except now that I'm here, I'll explain them in the cabin. Are all the kids here?" Standing up from the ground shaking the snow off my clothes, walking up to the cabin I could see Lily looking out the window.

"Lily and Tyler explained what happened while they were in town, except, they had explained you chose to stay in town. I assume the complication came right after they left. I burned the swamp to get rid of any evidence of us being there." Closing the door behind us we walked into the living room.

Looking over at Kendra. I could tell she hadn't trusted me with her toys, her doll she was holding she now held behind her back giving me a rather judgmental look.

"I told you I would get you a new toy to replace the old one." Taking the toy out of my pocket, I handed it to her.

Kendra's face lit up as soon as she saw the toy. Not risking it being broken again, she brought it to her room shutting the door, I could hear the toy making it's sounds as she played with it now.

"Wow? You felt bad? Kendra told me how you broke her toy. I never thought I would see the day that you felt guilty for upsetting someone, especially not a child." Laughing to herself she found it rather humorous how I had reacted.

"Don't read into it." I filled Genevieve in on the events in the town letting her know what Jerome's intentions were.

I also let her know I killed some time stopping by to see Arthur and Elizabeth except I left the part out about the possibility of Kendra's parents still being alive for now. She might have already known, just chosen not to share that information with me. If she was going to keep secrets, then I would keep a few. It was getting to be a pain hunting Genevieve and the kids down each time I had a new clue to search for. Even though I hadn't told her everything she usually knew when I was holding out on her, most of the time it was either habit or my being used to handling things on my own, not that I didn't trust her.

One thing I noticed after being with them for a few months had been the older children, and how they treated Kendra, they were always very loving towards her and even more patient with her knowing she was different from them. Never once had I heard them voice any negative comments or how they missed making friends. When they started going to school nearby, not once had they brought any new friends' home and neither had they mentioned making any. It wasn't hard to guess; it was difficult making friends only to lose them when you suddenly had to pick up and leave. I talked to Lily and Tyler about their past schools, which they had been well known at, except once they inherited Kendra it was easier to keep everyone together instead of risking attention by pulling them out of school all the time. This time when they went to school, they didn't risk getting excited over it. Instead, they smiled and just went. I suggested Genevieve take them all out of the country, anywhere but here. At least then, they wouldn't be under constant threat; no one would imagine they'd left, much less that they were with her.

"At least here I have places to go; I don't know anyone other than here. I haven't traveled the way you have; I've stayed simple by staying here." I understood her worry except I knew the benefits would be much healthier for the children as well as her.

"I have a place that you can stay at that no one knows about, it will be safe there and to make sure your transition is a smooth one. I'll send Brunswick with you to make sure everything is set up and ready. He'll work as your butler and when you need to get messages to me, or I need to speak to you, he will help with that also. For any reason you need to hide over there he will help you find a place to safely take the children. He's the rare person I trust." She had been listening to every word I was saying.

I knew she was nervous but also understood it would be

safer.

"I must speak with the children first. I'll let you know to-night." Standing up she had gone to round up the younger ones and speak with them before she had a private chat with the older ones.

As I figured the older ones were ready for it also. At least this way with them in another country. I would be able to concentrate better here without always worrying if I was leading others to them, or if something happened to them while I was gone. I knew Genevieve was perfectly fine taking care of them. She had done well so far on her own. I didn't always give her the credit she deserved.

Making sure everything appeared to be normal. Brunswick announced to others at the home he intended on taking his vacation. We were fortunate that this was around the time he usually did, even though he was still watched as he left for the airport. I knew they would still be watching him rather closely, after all, most knew I trusted him. I had sent Genevieve off with the kids first having them wait at a hotel once they were to arrive. That way Brunswick could be contacted in a neutral place, and he could check to see if anyone followed him before risking Kendra being found. After being watched for a while to make things a bit more bothersome, Brunswick switched two different airlines before leaving the country. Tired of waiting for all the delays and no signs of anyone joining him here, they stopped watching him as they guessed he was going on vacation. I made a point of letting others know I was still here in the states. It wasn't difficult leaving a few clues behind to have Jerome's men spread to the others; I was still around except this time I wanted them to know I was staying. I was extra careful making sure none of them stopped me. No one knew how to look for Genevieve, so she was able to fly safely with the children and not be noticed. Now I needed to do some investigating and find out if it was true or not whether my dear friend was alive or dead.

Chapter Four

Dead or Not

Now with the liabilities out of the way. I could start to research what I needed to know. If my friend had been indeed alive, I wanted to know why he hadn't contacted me himself or let me know he had children. We had confided everything in each other; I was still shocked I never knew about this. His kids are rather important even if I had never wanted any. At least I would have been supportive of his choice. I had always supported everything he did in his life regardless of whether I agreed with it or not. I was positive he would have his reasons. I was just curious what those were, especially to risk his daughter being killed and not there to protect her himself. While I made my way to the graveyard in the picture, I was hoping it would give me a clue to where he would be hiding. A few times I had to be careful and hide when I saw certain ones. I was positive they would not report me to them; however, they may say something to Gerard if they knew he was simply looking for me.

Halfway there I chose to stop at another place to see Lydia's sister. Not intending on keeping her around or for the reasons the rest of us had been changed, Lydia had been jealous of her sister growing up. Lydia might have changed some of her personality except her deep jealousy was always there, if she had known more when she was little, she would have preferred just letting her die naturally then gift her with such a long life. Lydia changed Nadine herself enjoying the temporary pain she had put her through. Her wish had been for her to live a long life alone, depressed watching all those around her that she loved die, never being able to share with anyone what happened to her or what she was. At first it had been difficult to deal with, and she had suffered from depression. What angered Lydia had been the fact she bounced back and became rather successful choosing not to let it hold her back. Personally, she had chosen not to date anyone in fear of getting attached. She had been able to make it appear her family line went way back just like many of us had done. I had always thought she was better off than the rest of us in the way she had to do her research, she learned from her own mistakes and not to make them again, she knew more than we did, which is why I was stopping to see her.

She had chosen to live in a rather beautiful place steeped in an extraordinary history as unique as its very own citizens. Living near the water with the strangest shaped trees her cabin blended in with the scenery. Her dog was sound asleep out on the front porch not bothering to see who it was. Either it was hot from the weather or just didn't care. Hopefully she wasn't using it as a guard dog to warn her of anything. Not that she needed it, our hearing was far better than a dog except I had to admit their nose for smell was still far superior. Knocking on the door the dog had yet to raise its head, looking down at it, the chest was still raising so at least it wasn't dead. There were no sounds coming from inside of the cabin, I began to wonder if she was still here. Maybe it wasn't even her dog? Stepping off the porch looking in the window. I could see the place had been decorated and I recognized a few items, especially the gift I had bought her. It was an early thirteenth century Renaissance oil painting that still hung on the wall. I purchased it during one of my trips to Italy. I knew she was an art collector not that it was the only thing she loved collecting, she also collected musical instruments.

"If it's not Jerome it's you." A sound of disgust came from the woman.

Maybe I really had been left out of it for a while. She looked so different.

"I take it you're not happy to see me then?" Not that I was that concerned.

I doubted she ever cared to see any of us let alone be reminded of us.

"Apparently Jerome thought you might have been here earlier, he wanted to know if you had spoken to me." Carrying a box, I tried to help her carry it as she turned to show she had no interest in my helping.

"What did you tell him?" Not that there was much left to say.

"I told him I hadn't seen you in years so there was nothing to tell, I take it there's a rift. I told him if he wanted to find you just find my sister. You were usually on top of her somewhere." Closing the door as she entered, I walked directly into it.

Reaching for the handle letting myself in frowning a bit I knew I wasn't exactly welcomed, and Nadine never had a problem letting others know when she didn't care they were around.

Walking over to the side wall there was a large table with several little wicker baskets each filled to the top with either herbs, dirt of some sort and other strange looking things. Even a few had plastic lining as slimy wet looking items were filled in those. From the smell I didn't want to know any more about the baskets. Moving away I looked in the living room where she seemed rather occupied with whatever she had in her hand. Not bothering to look up at me once she kept working on whatever project that seemed to be keeping her so occupied.

"I was hoping you might be able to help me. You were always good at coming up with alternative means." Sad, I hadn't thought about how to explain the situation or even what I was hoping to get help with.

"I want nothing to do with it; I've lived this long without help from the council or any others. I suggest you learn to do the same." Taking out a pestle and mortar, she started grinding a few things together before she placed them in a large glass bottle.

Repeating her actions, it looked as though she planned on filling the glass with the powder.

"I'm trying to figure out how to keep a child safe." As I said this, she looked up immediately.

I know it was rare I ever spoke of doing something for anyone else.

"Why is it up to you to keep it safe and from what?" At least now I had caught her attention.

"She happens to be Drezin's daughter, Gerard wants to kill and use her power to take over the council, and they are too blind to see it. If I point anything out to them right now he will only deny it, and he had others who will cover for him, even your sister would, she's working with him. I need to find something near a cemetery, a very particular one. I need to find information that will help prove what Gerard is after and the danger if he gets his hands on the power the little girl will have. He could gain control over all our kind and affect those of others. Jerome wants to kill her; he feels no one should have that power other than the council and I need to prove its safe if she is taught how to use and control it." She never once took her gaze from me.

"I venture a guess this is to prolong your own life to keep the council off your back as well as get even with Gerard and my sister?" Not raising the tone of her voice or showing reflection, I knew she was considering everything I was saying to her.

"I wish nothing of the sort. I was already prepared to accept my sentence of death when Gerard extended it already." I never would have gone through all of this or learned of Drezin's daughter if he hadn't, but then I almost wondered if Drezin knew this?

"That sounds more like you. I assume you wish to control the child?" Her one brow arched as she had asked this.

"No, there is already someone much more qualified than I am, trust me I've proven myself not to have enough patience."

The instant thought of crushing her toy oddly enough still bothered me.

I couldn't get over the look on her face.

"I don't think you've ever made that expression before; I think you actually felt something for this child." This was the first time she did not try to cover her surprise.

"Will you help me?" At least I hoped she would.

"What do you need me to do?" Smiling at her I knew at this point she was at least open and willing now.

"For now, we need to take it as it comes. I don't know what I'm looking for and sometimes it helps having two searching rather than one. You know I always worked with Drezin except this time he's not available and you're the only one outside of Brunswick that I would trust that won't go running to the council." I knew I was still holding back information however I felt I would share what I had to when it was necessary.

Besides I wasn't sure how to explain that someone who had died might still need to stay that way. Besides, the only other two I trusted were already busy since I had sent them off.

As I waited for her to get ready, she picked up a soft bag placing a few little plastic bags inside with different things in those, what looked like clothing and a few items to eat. Even I couldn't tell her how long we might be gone, even though I hoped to be done with this rather soon. I didn't want to drag this out any longer then I had to. Slinging the bag over her shoulder she had taken off to her neighbor's real quick leaving her dog there to be cared for.

Before we had a chance to leave, I could see someone standing on the front porch looking in the window at Nadine's home. Looking around to see if anyone was watching him, I could tell he wasn't very experienced otherwise he would know just by scent there was a vampire not too far. Forcing the door open attempting to enter was short lived. I had seen Nadine swiftly catch up from behind catching him unprepared, showing he was new.

"What do you think you're doing? Hasn't anyone taught

you not to enter a home unless you're invited?" Choking him so much he almost couldn't answer.

"I knew the council wanted to see inside your place in case there was any sign Langston had been here that you were not telling them. I thought if I found it, they would accept me as a messenger of theirs." After spilling the information so freely like that I already knew the council would never accept him.

"To start with, never tell the council how you caved telling me they were even interested in searching my place for him, even though I already know it. The simple fact you even found out and are not privileged to the information yet will get you killed, and anyone associated with you will be investigated to see who is leaking information out to non-council workers, then they get put to death.

"Are you going to kill me?" The kid was already shaking from being scared; Nadine had yet to let up on her grip not allowing him to move an inch.

"I should. If I had been anyone else you never would have made it this far, you would be dead already. I think you might be useful someday, I'll let you go but don't ever cross my path again or I will kill you. If I choose to warn it's only once, this is your only warning." As soon as she let him go, he fell to his feet taking off as fast as he could.

She was right, if it had been I, Jerome, or anyone else he would be dead on the ground right now.

"Are you ready to go? I'll need to know where we are heading to." Not even close to her, she knew I could hear her.

"I'm always ready." Catching up to her I handed her the picture as she now looked it over.

"I know exactly where this is, very few did, it was where he liked his privacy to experiment without the council getting nervous." Not having to wait long she took off in the direction we needed to go.

For as good as my memory was, even I couldn't remember every place Drezin, and I had been to, let alone the location. I knew the place in the picture looked familiar except if it was a place I had only been to once or not personally connected to. I would have dismissed it from my memory. Over the centuries I had enough to remember. Nadine on the other hand had a great way of remembering everything no matter how minor it was, but then it could be that she bothered to pay attention in the first place. There was no reason I would have thought this place had any significance, not that I remember being there. I had remembered seeing it somehow, perhaps another photo like the one I had found. Drezin had a few cabins in different locations he liked to visit and a few of them I had never been to. There wasn't a need to.

I would have brought Genevieve; she was always up for a good mystery however someone safe needed to take care of Kendra and I certainly didn't trust anyone else to do it. For now, Brunswick was added protection in case they needed it. Although I was able to travel in the daylight, I still preferred traveling at night and now with Nadine we had to. Unlike me, she was not a light walker. I had tried to figure it out many times out of the four of us. We had all been changed by the same person and yet I was the only one out of the group able to be out in the sunlight. Lydia might have changed her sister, however, the one who changed her was the same as ours and should have passed the traits onto all of us. Arthur and Elizabeth always felt just because you were changed by one and perhaps inherited certain gifts, it was only because of the way it mixed with your own personal physical makeup rather than random or simply inherited. I had to admit I was more apt to trust their opinion other than some of the other theories I had heard over the centuries.

While we traveled, I didn't have to stop once as Nadine kept up with me with no problems at all. If anyone had seen us, they would be left wondering if their eyes had played a joke on them as we were gone long before they could ever figure it out. Crossing several state lands until there was not much around other than flat open areas and more dirt then I had cared to see. The absence of trees had me missing other parts of the states. Recalling from memory where the picture would have been taken and heading the most direct route we could take. I had been surprised we hadn't run into any of Gerard or Jerome's men.

Off in the distance I wasn't sure if it had been a mirage or the actual barn until we were much closer to it. No house around for miles and certainly no dirt road heading out here other than a large red barn with crème tresses. Slowing down now as I walked to the other side with Nadine behind me, I had seen the four gravestones in the front. Drezin and his wife's name were listed on the first two along with two other girl's names on the remaining tomb stones. Behind theirs had been five others listed with similar family names, none of whom I had even recognized. He might have tried to make it appear his children had already died along with him, possibly only claiming having two.

Traditionally we would have had a ceremony for his death, except Drezin's body was never found and no one knew what happened to his wife. Most likely why I hadn't made any special trips out here before this and forgotten about it. When a vampire died, we performed a very special ceremony, so sacred it almost felt as if we were leaving a part of ourselves with the person to take with them.

"Langston, this is where you hope to find some sort of clue? It's pretty much just a family cemetery with an odd, shaped barn?" Nadine had been looking around amazed there was even anything out here.

"Oddly enough. This is the place, I know it might seem strange, but I know something must be out here and between the two of us. I doubt we will miss it." As soon as I had said that I started searching the graveyard looking through the mess on the ground, uncovering a few of the headstones.

Reading personal messages that had been left on each and searching as much of the ground outside as I could. Each grave including the older ones had strange symbols on either side of their name. At first, I thought these might be symbols representing the family name until I paid closer attention to each one. Starting from the far back to the front. I pieced most of it together, not that I understood it, however each had been a

Greek symbol. I should have known that Drezin would use Greek mythology, calling him fascinated on the subject was an understatement. I doubted any of them even had anyone buried in them. I was almost curious enough to dig one up.

On Drezin's headstone it had the simple message, "even though we are parted from our families and friends we will always remember them as they remember us." Giving a nod of my head I had to agree.

I could never forget either Drezin or Thea. Before heading in. I noticed the picture painted on the backside of the barn; it was of a particular lake we used to go to every summer as kids with our families. Heading into the barn I had hoped Nadine might have found something.

Nadine had gone inside to search while I was scouring the outside. She started in the upper loft, the high beams creaking beneath her feet as she looked down onto the first floor below. Beneath even that, as she'd mentioned, was a basement, its entrance boarded up, with no visible way to get down. But the way the air shifted made him wonder if someone had found one anyway.

Through a thin crack in the floor, she caught a glimpse of something that made her breath catch. It wasn't a basement at all, not anymore. The space below looked like a furnished room —clean, warm, lit by a faint, colorless glow. No dust. No decay. Just the quiet, waiting stillness of a place that shouldn't exist.

In each corner, where the heavy beams crossed or rose like pillars to hold the barn together, strange symbols had been carved. They were almost identical to the ones I'd seen etched into the headstones outside. No other marks appeared anywhere else, not over the doors, not along the walls.

The rest of the floor had been filled in long ago, the wood uneven and buried under years of hay and dust. As I looked around, Nadine was down on her knees, brushing the hay aside, searching for any loose board or hidden latch. When she cleared one corner, we saw it. A deep impression burned into the wood in the shape of a Greek god's symbol, with a small, perfect hole drilled into the center of its eye.

Searching each of the symbols in the barn none of them had been loose. Checking the gravestones again only one appeared different, exactly the right size of the impression on the barn floor, it had the same symbol only this one could be removed. Taking it inside. Nadine placed it in the impression on the floor as the tiny piece on the back fit the little hole in the floor perfectly. Motioning for me to come over she pressed down rather firmly as the whole symbol lowered itself.

Feeling slight shaking from the ground we stood back to see these wavy lines appearing on the floor. They had looked almost similar to those you would see on a road when it was extremely hot. Casting what appeared to be a mirage. Reaching forward I only meant to touch it to see if it had been a gas of some kind, if there was some sort of heat source creating it messing with the refraction of light passing along the ground. Instead, I felt my hand being pulled by a force much stronger then myself as the rest of my body went in after it. Nadine was unable to help keep me from being sucked in as she held on tight, trying to keep me out. It had pulled her in as well. Almost expecting to be in the small hollow room below that we had seen through the crack in the floor, instead, we were standing on a dirt path with dirt walls and vines creeping everywhere. Above us there was only dirt and no wood planks resembling a floor at all. The barn was gone and the room we had seen was only an illusion hiding this place down below, the best mirage I had ever been fooled by. We hoped we would find a way out along the path since there had been no physical way out from where we just came from. Feeling the roof, it was a solid dirt roof with clay filling in the cracks around a very nonflexible hard rock. Sadly, I never knew one rock from another; personally, they could have all been called the same thing. Following along the narrow pathway in front of us, we preceded with caution as I took the lead with Nadine not that far behind me.

Water started pooling at the end of the pathway. As we walked, we heard the usual slosh of the water as we walked except it was missing something that was normally associated with and a very fundamental element of water, neither of us were getting wet. The further we walked the deeper the water was getting until it rested at our necks. We had no problems walking through the water; we had only wondered if we would be able to breathe under it? Only one way to find out as we both bravely continued as the water was now far over our heads, leaving no opening in the tunnel that we now followed. Oddly enough we could still breathe in the water without needing to swim. It never felt wet however felt more like air. The further we went along the tunnel the deeper it was getting as we both could feel pressure from the oxygen change in the air rather than actual pressure from the strange water substance. Even the view ahead started getting a bit hazy that we couldn't see what we were about to walk into. We stepped out of the strange water into a large open cave style room fully decorated with furniture; there was a fainting couch, table with chairs and several paintings covering the wall. Someone had definitely lived in or used this room. If others could get in, then there was a way out. Looking around the room, each inch had been painted, the floor was a silver gray while one of the walls had been painted crème and the other two a light crystal blue that eventually blended in with the watery substance that took up the fourth wall.

Both of us started searching the walls, there had to be a way out that was either covered or a way of opening up. Not finding any cracks we started moving books on the bookshelf except none of those opened a hidden passageway, even behind the bookshelf had been a solid wall. Moving some of the chairs that covered the floor completely revealed nothing. Moving several pictures until one particular one had a medium size picture painted behind it directly on the wall. Setting the outside picture down to study the one behind it, there alone the painted outer line had been the actual crack. Pushing the wall, it started to slide in on the one side the same as a bank vault would have without all the locks. The picture had been up off the floor causing us to climb into it before we could drop down to the floor on the other side. Inside the new room, it was smaller, however, still decorated with several pictures lining the walls only with a small round table in the corner, a few books stacked on top of a hand crocheted lace doily. There were only two sitting chairs on either side. Another small hallway leading away with yet more watery substance in the distance, only this time it glistened with a dark blue hue to it. Walking towards it, we slowly entered the water still not getting wet from it, as we walked until we were out of it again, coming out the mouth of a cave alongside the lake we used to go every summer, the very same cave painted on the back of the barn. Normally if we had traveled here, it would have taken us two days travel except it had only taken a few minutes, but then it was rather difficult to judge when my watch stopped working in the water substance and it started working again the second we were out of the tunnels all together. Walking along the lakes edge. I could see the old summer house with the screened in porch facing the water. It looked as though whoever had been sitting on the porch stood rather quickly and walked into the house.

Nadine and I shared a glance as she went to the front of the summer house and I went to the back, either way if anyone tried to leave, we would see them unless there was another hidden passageway like the one we came out of? I wouldn't exactly be surprised since they obviously hadn't wanted to be found. Not worried about the lock on the screen porch. I had grabbed the door, almost pulling it off its hinges. The fact the doors were even locked sort of surprised me, not something a vampire would waste their time with, knowing other creatures would simply destroy or still be able to get in regardless unless it had been to keep other humans out? Opening the second door had been rather easy, it was not locked and neither of us had seen the occupant when we entered. Nadine had already come in from the front breaking the handle when she found it was locked.

"I'll take the upstairs; there's no basement so there are only a few places they can hide. There is a room off from the crawl space, I'm going to check that out first. It can be accessed from the first floor, and we might find something there." As I was about to turn Nadine caught my attention pointing out the window.

Whoever had been inside was now making a mad dash for the lake. Both of us ran through the house as quickly as we could, racing for the water hoping to catch whoever it was before they could get away. What we hadn't known, this person had left the cave area just before us no doubt noticing we were coming through. Not having a chance to do whatever they had come for in the house. They took off trying to conceal their face as much as they could. Racing for the lake, I wasn't thrilled with the aspect of having to swim since this water was real. Even though I could always swim fast enough and see in the water. I never did like actually getting wet. The figure ahead moved like a shadow come to life, gliding just out of reach. Nadine veered suddenly to the right, vanishing into the trees, her silhouette swallowed by the mist curling off the lake. I pushed harder, lungs burning, every heartbeat echoing louder than the slap of water against my skin. Whoever this person was, they knew this place. Each turn, each submerged stone beneath the dark surface. As if the lake itself belonged to them.

If it had been my friend, he would've called out, taunted me, something. But this one stayed silent. Mysterious. Almost... deliberate.

Then, without warning, they dove, cutting through the lake's mirrored surface like a blade. For a heartbeat, I froze, watching the ripples swallow the moonlight. And then I followed. The water closed over me, cold and sharp, stealing my breath.

When I broke the surface again, I was near land. I could hear the figure's breathing ahead of me ragged, possibly human, alive. Something in it pulled at me, inexplicably familiar.

They stumbled onto the muddy bank, and I surged forward in time to see them fall hard, a blur of motion knocking them off balance. Nadine.

She stood over them, fierce and triumphant, eyes glinting in the half-light. The stranger twisted beneath her, a dark hood slipping back just enough for me to catch a glimpse. Wet hair, pale skin, and eyes that found mine across the distance. For a second, everything stopped.

The world, the chase, even the cold air around us, gone. Just that look, electric and wrong and impossible.

Nadine's voice broke through the silence. "Got them."

But I already knew this was no ordinary intruder.

I was able to help hold down the person as they struggled to get free. Not able to escape the woman turned and spit in my face, not something I've had done in a while although I wasn't shocked. It certainly hadn't been the first time, and neither would it be the last.

"Where is Drezin?" Getting directly to the point I was hoping to let her know I was aware he could still be alive.

"I don't know anything by that name." She had said rather sternly

Not that I might believe her, she was the girl standing furthest from Drezin in the picture.

"I don't think he would appreciate being referenced to as a thing; however, I saw a picture with the two of you in it and there were two other girls and none of them were Thea. Why were you in their cabin? And if you had nothing to hide then why did you feel the need to run?" Now she was refusing to answer not that I could blame her.

If I was in her position and didn't know who was holding me down, I would refuse also, especially if I was trying to protect someone.

"We just need some answers; we don't intend on harming him, we happen to be friends of his." Nadine was trying to appeal to her sensitive side.

"Like I said. I don't know anyone by that name. I vacation here every year and it's owned by a friend of mine; she's back at college trying to catch up taking summer courses otherwise it's normally just the two of us. I never would have stayed here if I had known she would have so many creepy visitors." She seemed a bit calmer or as I would have guessed she might have hoped if she was nice enough, we would let her up.

"What's your friend's name?" Not that I had expected her to tell me but then maybe she might since she finally spoke a little.

"Tell you who she is so you can go harass her, the same you are with me? I highly doubt we know anything you would be the slightest bit interested in." Resting her forehead on the ground not bothering to pay much attention to us anymore.

"Your right. I doubt you know anything worth sharing, perhaps this will help, my name is Langston Jacobs, and this is Nadine Foster. Do our names sound familiar to you in anyway?" The expression on the girl's face had changed a bit; even if she had not wanted to admit it, she definitely recognized the names.

"Do you have any way to prove it?" She asked.

At least it was a fair enough question.

Nadine had given me a rather strange look. For years she hadn't bothered with a real identification card other than when she had to drive, and she changed last names and other information so many times to cover for the fact she was still alive after so many years.

"As a matter of fact, I do." Helping her stand up I knew exactly what I would show her to prove who I was.

Only those who had been around for centuries knew my passports were false, my driver's license and also my social security number had been inaccurate by this point. The only thing I had been lectured on from Drezin calling it egotistic, self-centered, conceited, vain, even self-involved, self-loving, and stuck-up. To be truthful I had heard this from quite a few people who had the privilege of seeing it, except I had yet to hear a complaint from the women I have been with about it. However, it had been the one main thing that would identify me to him. Taking off my shirt, I turned to show my back, as I did Nadine gasped, exactly the response I loved hearing from people. An exact replica of myself only a smaller version with my arms wrapped tightly around a naked angel crushing her lips with mine, down the side of her arm had my name 'Langston' in huge bold calligraphy. No longer struggling. She stood there as Nadine had. Looking at the tattoo, by now. I was used to others reaction to it especially when they would first see it, after a while it grows on you.

"I wasn't expecting him to be so accurate with his description. I honestly thought I was being told a wild story like so many of his other ones, they seem so farfetched that now I'm wondering about some of the other stories I've been told in the past by him." As she spoke, she never once took her glare from the tattoo.

"Is there a name you happen to go by, or should I keep calling you, "hey you…. that girl, or stop running girl?" Giving her a rather sly smile waiting for an answer.

Instead of answering Langston, she turned to face Nadine to give her an answer instead.

"My name is Lorah, we can't stay here for too long or we might be seen. There hadn't been anyone out here in a while, usually they look around for a bit then take off. However now that you're out here there may be those who start to search again." Not once had she turned to face Langston after being talked to rather rudely.

Taking off we followed her as I had hoped we might see the one person who had fooled us all. We hadn't taken off in the direction I would have assumed we would go. I almost expected to head back to the barn not that there were any traces of anyone living there other then perhaps for privacy, but then who would bother them if they truly thought they were dead?

Running much further away from the lake, there was another little pond out in front of us as we seemed to be running straight for it. At least now there were several trees around giving the pond a bit more protection from those who might be watching except it also gave much more covering for those who might be hiding and spying on us. As I looked upward looking for any possible threats, Nadine was already halfway in the water giving me that strange look before. How many places were like this? The first time we had ever encountered this had been back at the barn, and now this place out in the open like this. Wasn't the designer worried someone might want to cool off and find out it's not real water? Taking it slower this time when entering, running my hand over the surface the only difference that could be felt had been the temperature of the supposed water. Nothing stuck to my hand and neither had it become wet from the water other than to feel warmer as we entered. These water illusions had to be the best intentional created mirages I had ever seen. Directly at eye length I could both see under and above at the same time and still I couldn't figure out how this mirage was being made to deceive. The only deterrent I could think of for humans would be the color of the water itself. Instead of being a crystal blue or even dark blue showing it was deep water, it was a dark muddy brown color. Moving quicker to catch up to Nadine and Lorah, we walked much longer in this stuff then I expected, the other we were in and out of rather quickly.

This had been so much longer. I was beginning to wonder why we were walking instead of running through. Other than the two girls in front of me there was nothing else to look at, it was already hard enough to see through the dark brown water substance. I doubted anything else could have shown through. I noticed Lorah looking back a few times and I wondered if she thought the girl was leading us into a trap, but then she hadn't seemed tense or nervous. I was sure Nadine could take care of herself, or I would have to help out if something happened, which is why I preferred to be in the back, keeping an eye on anything that might slightly move. Eventually we came out of the water into a large oval room with nothing in it. It looked as if we were inside of a cave this time, perhaps a cave had been dug out and the water covered it? Except that would have been difficult since we had walked so far, we would have gone much further than the little pond, unless this was another allusion of some sort. Turning to face us. I wondered what she was about to say, not that she was looking at me. She looked more at Nadine as she told us.

"I'll be right back. I need to warn him we have company first." Before she had the chance to leave the room, I was instantly up by her side grabbing her arm preventing her from leaving.

"You don't leave our sight, if he needs to be warned, he can be warned with all three of us together." She smiled at me and I was curious what was going through her mind.

"What, you don't trust me yet? From all of the stories I've heard about you. I thought you would have been up for a little excitement?" Her tone of voice sounded like more of a challenge then anything.

"How do I know you're not setting us up for a trap? I don't remember you being around before, so how would you know Drezin? Your age doesn't fit." I was hoping to get an idea who she was.

"Amazing what vampires forget when they were once alive, Drezin has been very helpful to my family and my boss Valafar, which by the expression on your face, you know him well." Not asking, she continued to smile back at me as if she knew something I didn't.

Before I could respond the ground shook as she tried to steady herself, she slipped out of my grasp leaning against the wall disappearing instantly behind it. Both Nadine and I felt along the wall trying to find how she had gone through a solid object, without using any visible magic, not that we personally knew what it would have looked like. Now we were stuck waiting here hoping she would end up coming back, either way we would eventually find out. Nadine was already searching along the wall while I searched another one.

"I think I figured it out." Her voice sounded determined.

As I turned to face Nadine, I had only been able to catch a glimpse of her as she disappeared behind the wall. Quickly feeling along the wall where she had been standing, I still couldn't find what the others used to disappear. There had to be something I was missing until I had found it myself. There were cracks along the wall when followed they had gone along and formed extremely large letters that could barely be seen unless you were looking for them. Touching each letter as I found it, I wound up in the same spot as the other two, touching the last letter which was an 'N'. I hadn't stepped in as I planned, I was sucked in or rather controlled by the plasma, before there hadn't been anything to grab a hold of or anything to stick to the skin, and now whatever this was started to add a pressure around my arm completely encasing me pulling me in. I didn't have to wait long before I felt it recoiling away from me. I could see it now behind me as I was standing in a new room, not that anyone else was in here. Odd Nadine would have left this area but then perhaps she was taken to another room, or she was able to find Lorah right away and followed her? Moving around there was a narrow hallway that I started cautiously walking down keeping alert for any possible attack.

I hadn't anticipated the attack through the roof of the cave; I hadn't seen anything when I first looked up. Before I knew it, I had someone drop on top of me knocking me over, not that it took long for me to regain control twisting myself to confront my attacker. Sliding the knife from my sleeve quickly holding it against the neck. I stopped myself instantly from making a further move. Smiling rather coyly Drezin was staring right at me relaxed as if he wasn't even worried anything dangerous could have happened from surprising me. He knew what kind of control I had and that I could take over very quickly however he was always good at surprising me, still not as good as Genevieve.

"Sorry to have deceived you old friend, I had no other choice." Standing up lending a hand to Drezin pulling him to his feet, even though I was tempted to knock him back off his feet again.

I couldn't believe I was looking at him.

"No choice, I thought you weren't capable of keeping anything from me? There are some things I'm learning about you that makes me wonder where you found all of your free time?" Moving behind Drezin grabbing him by the shirt and putting him into a headlock which he was able to free himself from rather quickly.

Shoving me back into the wall knocking me repeatedly into it. Then grabbing my right arm, he was able to twist standing straight up he freed himself. Attempting to get me into a headlock which was pointless. Drezin had been the one who taught me to get out of them. I simply reached back pulling up with his legs lifting him causing him to let go catching his balance momentarily, then he caught my foot with his as he pulled trying to take me down as I hit the ground rolling knocking him over dropping him. Just like old times we used to practice fighting with each other. Even now nothing had changed bringing back some old memories.

"I had no other choice; besides. I was being watched far too close to let anything slip. I wasn't the only one being watched, you had eyes on you also. I didn't know how you would respond if you found out who was watching us, besides, if you knew I wasn't dead then you wouldn't have searched so hard, and the others knew if you couldn't find me then no one else would either. I knew I had hidden everything enough once you had given up. I was beginning to wonder if you ever would?" Shaking his head, he was right to wonder, I hadn't wanted to give up.

"It wasn't easy giving up; I never would have searched for you if I hadn't learned you had a daughter. Kendra is a rather interesting little thing. Why hide from her if you could fake your own death. Why not hers also? No one would have bothered looking for her then." There were so many questions I wanted to ask my old friend, however first I needed to know a few things that were more important.

"I hoped with her being human for so long and no one else knowing she was. She would blend in with the world around her. No one knew that Genevieve was alive, and she would be the safest to raise her," Drezin was choosing his words carefully, "I knew not to ask you for far too many reasons, not that I didn't think you would keep her safe, but who you were being watched by and the simple fact it's just not your thing." Following behind him as we moved along, I could hear Nadine talking to Lorah in the distance.

Oddly enough there was another voice that I recognized, I hadn't thought would be back from the grave also, it was Thea his wife. I had seen a lot of things in my life except when I had originally heard my friend was dead. I never once thought I would be seeing both of them alive again. She might have disappeared however I always assumed the worst.

"I should let you know the council is looking for your daughter or rather Gerard is. I'm not even sure the rest of the council knows about her; they've been trying to keep it rather hushed." His expression hadn't changed as he took in what I told him.

Thea looked worried for a moment but then relaxed rather quickly. They were either handling it rather well or there was something they were not sharing.

"Has she had any problems with the council so far?" Drezin asked in a far too relaxed voice.

"I would have to say yes, they have found her, both her regular home and the temporary one had been burned down. I still want to know how you faked your death to the council in the first place." As I asked, Thea motioned to take Nadine to another room to give us more privacy to talk.

Giving a nod of my head I wanted to let Nadine know it was alright.

"How are you and Lydia by the way?" I knew immediately he was testing me, not that he needed to.

"It's been a while since you were around, she's with Gerard now. You know my loyalty is with you, why ask me this way? I already know you're alive, what could you still possibly need to hide?" Getting comfortable in his chair he crossed his hands as he thought.

"You're not the only ones who had paid a visit to Elizabeth and Arthur. You never would have found us if I hadn't wanted you to. Your probably one of the only ones who can get past one of my traps and yet the night I supposedly died, my very own trap backfired on me. At least it's the way I wanted it to look. Gerard has been after me for years trying to harness a power that my daughter will have. All three should have had it except it only started with the one, I never planned on more other than having backups. Things don't always go the way you plan and at times it can turn out better. It happens to be a direct result from my experiments which was able to keep Thea pregnant. The children were able to grow and be nourished on their own without needing it from their mother. I won't go into the details right now other than to say, my youngest has a blood power that would allow vampires to walk during the daylight. That and among other things which I hadn't exactly planned on, most of it coming from a gift. We all know how much Katherine Hawthorne was addicted to the life stone but if she only knew how much came through that portal that Najee trusted me with." Letting out a strong sigh I knew my friend was troubled; however, he still had yet to answer my question.

"Are you even curious if Kendra is still alive?" Instead of waiting for Drezin to ask I had decided to.

"If she died, I would know. I have no doubts Genevieve will keep her alive. Have you actually seen her?" At least Arthur and Elizabeth always kept conversations private.

They felt if you were meant to know, it would be presented to you. It was not a matter for them to mess with. Probably why they never came right out and told me they knew Drezin was still alive.

"Yes, I have seen her, right now Brunswick is taking care of them at my private cabin. I would like to help more except it's difficult when you hold back, something you have never done with me before." As soon as I said that Drezin looked at me directly in the eyes.

"Yes brother, I know I have kept much from you and with reason. Gerard is planning on taking over the council, he has for a long time, and I don't know how to tell you this, however, Lydia plans on doing this with him. What she doesn't realize is he has no need of her once he gains control." At least now I knew why he was stepping around the issue of Lydia.

"I can't always protect her, she has made her own choices, and I don't like them however I don't have a choice. Is there anything I can do to help you?" Standing up quickly coming over near me, with a new vigor and a slight flash of light showing in his eyes, I knew immediately he was planning something.

"Over time her gifts will emerge, not all at once and as one is fully matured she will have another emerge, she can't perform any of it now as she is still quite young, she was meant to be older than she is. It was a gift from a demigod I helped, nothing I could have imagined but I was fortunate when it happened. I hoped no one would have found out, I wasn't sure how Gerard found out. She has potential for amazing abilities, many of which I don't fully understand, she might be considered a demigod herself because of the gift. Her main ability is slowing time, it might not seem like much however when time is slowed, there is much a person can do if planned right. We need to take Gerard out without the rest of the council knowing we killed him or knowing about my daughter." I liked the way he thought however there was a slight flaw to this particular plan.

"We would have to take out more than just Gerard; he hired Jerome to do the same mission when they realized I was no longer working for him. I hate to say it except we might have to tell the rest of the council what we suspect, show to them you are alive and whatever proof you have of who tried to kill you and present them your daughter. They usually stay neutral; we just have to hope they don't see her as a threat. Why didn't you contact me earlier? I might have been able to prevent this much earlier." There were so many things I could have done to prevent all of this.

"I tried. It wasn't safe with Lydia around, her loyalties are only to herself, it's too difficult to tell what she would have said or done. You were extremely involved with the council, I wasn't sure if you would be able to, besides it was far too much of a risk for you to take. It was difficult enough knowing when I started all of this that I might put my own family in danger before others found out. Besides, you were busy." Not wanting to look at me I knew what he had meant.

My own personal rampage to get the council to condemn me to death among many other personal demons I had to contend with.

"Right now, she is safe, however we will need to figure something out. I should test the council out and see what sort of support we will get from them if we need it. We need to prove to them what Gerard plans on doing. I can show he has already paid me for my involvement. All there is to do is show what he plans on doing to the council which will be more difficult." I wasn't exactly sure how we would do this, but I was sure with the two of us we could plan something.

"I'm rather limited what I can do, I have my other..... daughters that we are taking care of and besides due to my past indiscretions, I doubt I can approach the council too easily. I fear they would be far more worried if the Augustus family were to decide to be the only vampire clan in control of our kind again. They may worry that my daughter would be used against them as a weapon to take them out of power or possibly use her themselves." Even I knew what he meant.

Over the past century he had challenged the council quite a bit himself and now to show he was trying to protect them after supposedly being dead might look suspicious.

"Not to worry. I'll figure out something; I'm sure Genevieve might even have a few ideas of her own by now. I should get going and make my appearance elsewhere before they grow tired looking for me and start looking for Kendra again. I promise I'll keep her safe. I'll contact you as soon as we have a plan.

Although my visit was rather brief, I had so much more ahead of me to figure out. Now I actually had to stay alive to finish my new temporary purpose in life, and once that was fulfilled the council could do whatever they wished with me. Not that Drezin wanted to say it. I had a feeling Lydia played a much larger role when it came to Gerard trying to kill my best friend and his family. At least much more then I wanted to admit. I knew Lydia could be rather evil. Over the years she had become much worse. Sometimes being changed wasn't a bad thing except in her case it accentuated the situation. I knew this wasn't going to be easy, after all, my best friend who is a brother to me and a woman who no doubt had much more of an involvement of his supposed death, the woman who I never wanted to admit that I still wanted and loved could be the very person I may have to stand against. I would deal with that when it had become necessary. For now, I had to figure out a way to convince the council.

Chapter Five

Finding Allies

I knew it wasn't going to be easy especially since most of the council had ordered my death, if they were neutral as they liked to position themselves, then it would be the best bet to allow a child to be itself as long as they did not see her as a threat to them. Not that I wanted to deal with Lydia right now, sadly she was my main connection to get in to see the others. It was rare they would take a meeting and there was one main person I needed to speak with first. I wanted to find out how involved Lydia was with the supposed death of my friend, as well as what her plans were to get rid of Gerard once she laid her hands on the girl herself, not that Gerard wasn't planning the same fate for her. After all I doubted, she would bother with him if she had the power herself, why would she need him anymore? The main council member I needed to speak with was Sakarabru, he happened to be one of the few members on the council that was quite approachable and that would give a chance of listening before retaliating for being bothered.

Without him and Valafar, there would be no mercy dealt when they reached their decisions as a whole. Valafar was rarely around the council since he, as many other demons preferred to stay independent and as for him, he had his own life he chose to deal with.

For centuries the Augustus family ran things until it seemed as though they slipped out of existence, some thought they had been killed off, died naturally somehow or simply retreated into themselves. What most had no knowledge of other then those who worked for them like me, we had known they simply chose the life of solitude for a while before planning on coming back into power. There was very little need of them and for the most part they took care of the worst offenders still, however now they did it with much more silence so that no one even had any clue they were even dealing any injustice or offense. For a while there were smaller groups fighting for power, most did each other in or poorly calculated causing their own defeat. Only the council currently had still survived all the vampire wars in the past. The council was rather intricate with eight members in the higher council, 10 ambassadors' beneath them, this is where Gerard and Lydia were a part, and each ambassador could have a set amount of assistants to either aid or finish assignments for them that the council saw fit. Next came my very limited group, seditionist or as I preferred to call ourselves, personal assassins. There were only three of us and only three needed. Finally, the last group of followers who supported the council was known as the informants. There might have been a form of hierarchy in the Augustus family, if there was anything going on, they seemed to know.

The only reason we hadn't been wiped out by the Augustus family who rose to power again was the fact that a few of them were already buried deep in our ranks. their own had slipped in among us, hiding behind false names and quietly keeping watch.

Apparently, we were never a threat to them. At least not until they were challenged and forced to reappear many years ago and once again taking a high-profile place in the vampire world and yet not one questioned their authority when they had taken over yet again, their reputation preceded them. I wanted to check in with Genevieve to see how she was or even with

Brunswick except I knew if I did. My phone call would be traced by either the council, Gerard or even Lydia. Genevieve was to call immediately if they had any trouble, so for now I had to simply assume they were still safe and for now Nadine went home, if I had needed any help, I was to call her even though I rarely asked for help from anyone. I doubted I would call her again. Besides, most of the danger that could have possibly come before would only be searching for me, I couldn't possibly risk her life any further into this then I already had. She would have been excellent at figuring out the councils moves based on tendency and personality. Solving codes, behavior, even hiding was always her best talent. I knew it would be too difficult for her right now if she had to deal with her sister in this way, no matter how strained or destroyed their relationship had been.

Instead of choosing to go directly to my home. I hadn't wanted to get to close in the vicinity of the council quite yet, after all, I didn't know what Gerard had fully planned. Instead, staying a state away. I visited a few old friends to see if they heard any rumors going around. The best gossip in town also happened to be a very old friend of mine. I used to crash on her living room floor when I was younger and would drink until I dropped, it took a lot for a vampire to get drunk so you could imagine the mess I made until then. She lived within walking distance of the bar and since it was still early enough, at least she wouldn't be working as a waitress quite yet tonight. As much money as she had saved up over the centuries, I never understood why she liked working as a waitress, except it made her happy, at least it seemed to help her still feel human and part of the regular world around her. As much as she detested being human when she was, there was no hiding the fact that at times she still missed some aspects of it. The job, working around mortals and remembering her old life made her current one a bit more bearable. After all, if she wasn't happy with the present situation, she had enough experience to know eventually everything changes again. At least she was happy; I guess that's what should be important.

Her car was gone not that it meant much, she often lent her car out to her friends or would in fact be drunk herself and leave it preferring to walk home. There was nothing else like seeing a vampire drunk. One night in particular, she was there, swaying slightly, eyes too bright for someone who claimed to be sober. A drunk vampire was a sight to behold... beautiful and broken all at once. The kind of thing that branded itself into your memory, whether you wanted it to or not.

I yanked open the garage door, half-hoping she'd be passed out behind a stack of paint cans. No such luck. Just cobwebs, old beer bottles, and that faint smell of motor oil that always clung to her stuff.

"Perfect," I said to the emptiness, "she's either kidnapped, dead, or drunk off her ass. And I get to be the one to find out which."

I walked around the outside of the house a little more. I hadn't seen any movement inside or changes on the outside of the house. Not bothering to feel around the rim of the door or the usual fake rock which she had, except she never placed a key in it. She always hid a spare key in an interesting place. Walking over to her garage and lifting up the garbage can lid. I was almost overwhelmed by the smell that had come out. I highly doubted I wanted to know what she had been cooking lately, one of her many favorite hobbies. Lifting the garbage bag out and reaching to the bottom. I felt a small hard piece as I pulled it out, I definitely had the key but then my hand was also covered in something I wasn't sure I wanted to know what it was. Placing it in the door and letting the door swing open I saw three shuriken's thrown at different levels at the door frame. It was a good thing I knew never to try to enter a friend's home immediately or in some way I would be assaulted by something. We might have had an advantage over mortals however we never trusted other vampires. I rarely knew a vampire who hadn't installed some sort of self-security system. Waiting a few minutes there still hadn't been any sounds or signs anyone was inside, not that I expected anything.

"Avalon, are you here?" Waiting for a moment to get a response, I stepped inside ready for whatever might be thrown at me.

Looking in the direction the shuriken's had come in. I saw her standing there looking rather angry. Whatever reason she was angry it could almost be over anything; I had a talent for making her angry.

"Apparently you have a death wish." Stating it as a fact more than a question, even though I had to admit she wasn't that far off.

"There's no one else I would rather see more then you." I did my best to sound sincere.

"It's a good thing your job doesn't rely on your lying, you never have been good at it. What do you want? I hear the council is looking for you?" At least the conversation was already started up in the direction I was hoping for.

"How bad does it sound?" I was curious if they would be after me or not.

"Not as severe as it should be, however if it were up to me, you would get instant death the moment you're spotted." Whatever I did the last time we spoke to piss her off I couldn't remember, I had done so many things.

"You're losing your touch a little. I guess the sedentary life of a vampire has set in. You don't normally miss." I never was good at behaving to get information that I wanted.

"Don't worry, I never miss. You might want to check your back." Smiling at me she came down from the stairs now walking into the living room.

I hadn't felt anything when I came in, reaching back and feeling around quickly there was a small hard piece, almost the size of a small button. Pulling it straight out there was an extremely thin needle attached to it. Totally caught off guard paying attention to the obvious and I miss the hidden.

"Sneaky, I judged you wrong. Apparently, you've been improving your technique. So, am I to assume you are on the side of the council?" After all the dangerous situations I had been able to get out of, this very simple move could have done me in.

"If I wanted you finished you wouldn't still be speaking with me, let's just say later tonight, you and I will finally be even." Leaning against the banister, I had to admire her style.

It's what had attracted me to her in the first place. Oddly enough I couldn't remember why we had broken up a century ago unless it was my idiocy because of Lydia.

"If I'm not going to die then I need to get a better idea who exactly might still be after me. Any rumors will help me form some sort of idea." Trying not to pay any attention to it my back was already feeling sore.

"Not sure how you made it this far without them seeing you or at least a spy reporting that your nearby, little creatures seem to be everywhere lately. They could order my death along with yours if they knew I had you here." Smiling at me I knew she would always be up for a challenge.

"Any particular names attached with the order? Perhaps Gerard? I wasn't sure if there would be any others involved along with him or if it had just been Gerard working on his own using Lydia to get to me." As soon as I had said her name Avalon frowned.

"Only Gerard and Stephen, hard to tell if he knows what's going on, it always seemed as if he was more of a follower then a leader. Far too easily swayed or rather manipulated, the details are extremely limited. You know the routine, whoever needs to know has the full details." Looking a bit skeptical Avalon sat down in her chair still watching me.

"I knew Gerard would be; he hired me for one last job except I think he knows by now I'm not going to finish it the way he wants. I have to admit I am surprised that Stephen is a part of this." I couldn't figure why Gerard would want to include him, even if he were to trick or use him somehow.

"I need to see Sakarabru, not sure how I'm going to make it past all the guards or other members. I can't exactly trust Lydia enough to get me in, and I haven't heard from Valafar yet." Rubbing the end of my chin, the idea was easy however now that I was planning it, I knew it was going to be so much harder not that I didn't mind a challenge.

"I think the rumors are true; you have lost your mind. Not sure who started it except I highly doubt you will make it past everyone to get to Sakarabru. After all, he's rather protected, even more so then the others." Leaning forward she was no doubt curious now about my plans.

"Either way I have to do this, it's my only option. Otherwise, I'll be living in hiding for the rest of my life with a few others." I could do it except I hated to see Genevieve give up so much of her life, let alone her children.

Every child needs a childhood at least once.

"There are only two guards at the gate during the daylight hours. That would be the best time to try to get in. It wouldn't be that difficult to distract them but then it would help much more if we could take the private entrance, only council members can enter that way." Resting her head on her hand as Avalon contemplated their choices.

"I take it you're going to help?" Smiling at her I knew she couldn't pass up a challenge anymore then I could.

"It's not going to be easy. Especially the way its guarded like a fortress." As she spoke she staired out the window.

Unfortunately, every inch was either monitored by a follower or guard. The building itself had been an old state hospital with an underground tunnel linking two of the buildings. The tunnels had been falling apart, making sure they were strengthened extending them out even further into underground self-made caverns many feet below the surface. Something that was very popular for vampires who could not walk in the light. To persuade anyone curious that might be walking on the outside, all of the windows had been darkly tinted. It helped keep the light out and those from looking in. From a distance I had to admit it was menacing looking even though it had a slight bit of an artistic flair to it. It had helped there were a few sculptures out front which prevented mortals from thinking it was anything other than a place involved somehow with the arts.

"I need to get this done now. There isn't very much time. Let's hope we get this right on the first try." Still not moving Avalon had something on her mind.

"Meet me at the back entrance where the council members enter, there's even fewer guarding it. I think I might know a way in, if not we can still go for the front. I'll be there in an hour." Avalon still had a serious expression on her face as she was thinking her plan through.

Standing up she had gone over to her cupboard pulling something out from what looked like a ceramic container containing sugar. Whatever it was it had shined and looked like a small hard chunk of stone or something, too difficult to tell from my angle. Not waiting for my response, she went out the back door of her house taking off while it was still dark out. The sun should be coming up soon, which would limit which council members could go out in the light, meaning more of them would actually be in their personal rooms. I would have preferred fewer members being there but then it also limited just how many could actually follow me out into the light if any were to catch me.

Making sure her house wasn't being watched. I left the same way I came. If they had been watching they would have seen me enter in the first place. Most were not patient which meant they would have made their presence known by now. I knew my own home would be heavily watched, being careful not to come in from that direction. I had to come in from the side of the lake. I was hoping to enter from the south side lot used for the personal cars of the council only, followers or anyone else that might have used a vehicle for any reason would have parked on the north side. Unfortunately, there were a few in the lot talking to each other. The lot had been shaded rather well with weeping willow trees, however, from the inside I would easily be noticed moving along, on the outside tree line it was far to open and also easily noticed. The only choice left had been to swim in the water to get to the building. At least coming out there were reeds of tall grass making it easier not to be noticed.

I hated getting wet, nothing to do with being a vampire, just a personal disgust. Squeezing out my clothes as soon as I had finished swimming across. At least I would be on the side with the private door. Staying close to the trees temporarily until I was sure the area was safe enough to get closer. I wasn't sure how long I would have to wait for Avalon; I was sure it would depend on her plan. Making sure my clothing were no longer dripping. I had moved in closer to the building thrusting myself up above the door into the tiny little alcove that housed a small gargoyle statue above the door.

The dark shadow of the night started as the sun began to come out. It was still slightly shaded but now it would start being much more difficult for nonlight walkers. Wondering how much longer it was going to take. I had held my breath as the door swung open with four people quickly walking out and around to the side lot. The first had been Gerard's personal guard, than followed by Gerard himself and then two more guards. Gerard had been fully covered from head to toe not risking being badly burned by the sunlight. Apparently, he was distracted by something of extreme importance, otherwise normally he would have been paranoid wondering if he was being watched and perhaps seen me sitting up here. Before the door could fully close, I slipped off my shoe using it to hold open the upper half of the door as it closed on my shoe. Jumping down to the ground. I pulled at the door letting my shoe drop to the ground. Putting it back on I looked inside where the hallways were dark with no one walking them at the moment. I had smelled a very sweet lilac scent which I knew had been Avalon, her skin was burning red. Letting her in ahead of me I knew she risked quite a bit being in the sun. I hadn't planned on her coming along just in case I did get caught; I had hoped she would have found a safe exit for herself.

"I couldn't let you have all the fun; besides I'm intrigued now. I'm curious what Gerard is up to. I stopped by your place quick to see what workers would be there; a few were cleaning no doubt snooping more than cleaning. I asked the one to put the stone on your dresser, that you needed it at the house for some reason." Waiting for a moment I realized what she was getting at.

"Was Gerard heading for my house then? Who did you tell there?" I was curious if there were new workers being set up there or if they had been one of the old ones that had been assigned to me.

"Definitely an old one, it was Gertrude. The one that has a face that's difficult to forget no matter how badly you wanted to. She seemed rather eager to be told you were nearby. I gave them the address of a bar you usually frequent; she said she wasn't surprised by your bold attitude of showing up like that. I even mentioned you had a kid with you saying it shocked me when I saw it. Definitely not like you. I tried to pretend that I wasn't aware of anything, but then it's difficult not to since rumors have a way of getting around." Not waiting for my response, she already started walking down the hallway with me.

Making no sounds as we walked along always listening for any hints someone might be coming. We had almost made it all the way to Sakarabru's private quarters. No one thought anything of Avalon being here. Except they would notice me. With my size it was rather difficult to hide myself. Stepping into the shared library quickly. I tried to shield my face as Avalon stood in front of me trying to hide my muscular size. Only one of the two who had been passing looked in with a curious look on his face, no doubt wondering why we were in there. Only those who had permission would have been this far in, no doubt not wanting to cause a problem they continued on their way. As their voices began to get faint, we still waited a moment before taking off in case they had only pretended to leave, or anyone else was coming we hadn't heard earlier. Just from the feeling and the scent I knew someone else was standing behind me. Doing my best not to turn around, Avalon quickly acquired their attention.

"We were here to pick up some books." Avalon stated without mentioning who they were for.

"These are the books Sakarabru requested be brought to

him, sorry I had you wait. Was he interested in any other books; I noticed you both looking at those?" Her voice was very sincere sounding however curious.

"No, these are fine; we were just looking while we waited." Taking the books from her, I had placed mine back into its place hoping I wouldn't have to turn around, or I would still be caught.

Leading the way out, hoping not to walk into anyone in the hallway. Avalon kept her voice steady as she thanked the girl and made our way out of the shared library.

Normally only four privileged servants would know the exact location and details for each room associated with the council and their private chambers. These would dispense information to the next level of council members down or fetch and retrieve things as needed. I was fortunate that Lydia wanted to brag that she had known the entire layout, later I found out it was because of Gerard. He had the previous plans of the old building when they first purchased the place, and he helped with the renovations. Apparently, he still kept the plans and adjusted them as the renovations were being done. Simply keeping track for personal memory, I hadn't forgotten what the blueprints looked like. Only difference had been seeing the detail in person now that we were almost outside his chamber door. Taking a deep breath in. I hoped he hadn't sided with the others over my fate quite yet. Before I could even get the chance to knock at the door it swung open with Sakarabru standing there with a rather distressed look on his face.

"You better come in before the others figure out you're here. Hello Avalon, I see you're along for the adventure?" As we stepped in, he closed the door behind us.

"You don't exactly seem surprised to see me here?" I was feeling skeptical but then he was the only one I had felt might help sway the others with reasoning.

"I had a feeling you would show up. I knew about the assignment that Gerard sent you on, something none of the others approved of. However, because of my own helpers. I also know you were set up to fail, which Gerard was planning on. I've been doing my own investigations only they are limited since I cannot afford to be caught questioning another without solid proof. I had to find out first." Sakarabru started pacing the floor no doubt figuring out how much he wanted to share with us.

"How many of the council know what Gerard is up to?" As I asked, he stopped for a moment.

"Gerard had done quite well covering his tracks. Any blame would lay with his followers no doubt keeping him in a position of power still. Lydia is no better; the only reason I caught wind of any of this had been an argument I overheard between Gerard and Lydia. I was compelled to find out if it was even possible." Shaking his head, he seemed rather troubled.

"If he were to gain physical power, how could he take over the council? The Augustus family would destroy him along with the council and all their followers." This had been the only part, if he were under attack from everyone he could only hide so long.

Even I knew I couldn't hide forever if they wanted me badly enough. Even with a power at some point, he has to be either caught off guard or not able to fight all off at once. He was never a fighter; his gift was getting those who fought well to do the dirty jobs for him. He was more of a planner.

"It is wise never to think you're too powerful or infallible. I know the amazing things you have accomplished. It seems Gerard is going to single out a few eventually pitting our own against each other. Order in chaos is very difficult to control. As for the Augustus family, I'm not sure how he plans on handling them?" Moving over to his chair sitting down now focusing his attention on Avalon, looking directly at the books she held in her hands.

"I assume you're here about the child. The books you hold in your hands Avalon are ones I am studying, trying to find a way to prove the child is safe to let live. There is a reason so many live in hiding, so that greedy or evil ones do not control them for their power. This is going to be difficult for one so young." Shaking his head in frustration.

"Are you curious where the child is?" I wanted to know if he would assume I would have her or would produce her if he asked.

"It's best for now that I do not know. Wherever she is being hidden is best. I already assume you know where that is. After all, Gerard hired you to do the job, if you had done what he asked you would not be standing in front of me right now."

One of the reasons Sakarabru seemed so wise. I rarely could tell him something he hadn't already thought through.

"I take it before we can even prove the child is safe and not harmful to the council or the Augustus family, we have to prove Gerard as dangerous. Showing what he's up to?" Avalon had been the first to point out what we hadn't wanted to admit, something much more difficult.

"If I say anything it's simply my word against his. At least this is the way the council would take it. This is something he has already been working on far longer then I realized. Unfortunately, I do not know how much he has affected the council, if the decision were to be made right now by the Augustus family; the entire council would be wiped out. There are several who do not deserve to be eliminated because of Gerard's mistakes. Many of the council are much more untrusting and paranoid then they used to be." Sakarabru seemed less interested in the books Avalon was still holding.

"So, the Augustus family is aware of what's going on?" If they had known why they didn't just stop Gerard.

"That is what I had wondered until I spoke with my family, they want to know who all is involved, in other words, who is supporting and helping Gerard. They know he wants to take power; they know an unusual power exists however they do not know how he can use this or how much he already has to use." Scratching his chin Sakarabru seemed to be thinking something over.

"Would it make any difference if I were to stop Gerard?" It was something I would have to get to immediately before to many died because of him.

"If they already plan on taking Gerard out when they find out who else is involved, then why wait so long, usually they take care of things before anyone ever has an idea anything is going on. Anyone involved gets found out later; why not take out the problem now?" Avalon again spoke what we were thinking.

"Sad to think I once believed all I had to do was keep this little girl safe." I still felt there was more going on then what he was given information for.

Sakarabru might have felt it was unnecessary for us to know right now.

"You won't have to worry about the Augustus family interfering unless things get out of control; it's why many of us are here. It's up to the council to regulate their own unless it starts to reveal itself, something you know a little too well Langston. They do know your loyalties do not lie with Gerard; however, they do wonder if you are working for yourself as he is. At least now I can correct that part." Setting the books aside he motioned for us to follow him.

Walking through his study to his own private chambers, it wasn't exactly the way I would have thought he would have his room look like. Almost as if no one even lived in here, just a few basic things in case he was to get bored. There was a dresser at the far end of the room that he pulled away from the wall. As we entered. The dresser slowly slid back on its own concealing the entry. We continued to walk through what looked like a hollowed-out tunnel, not that the dark bothered us, however I was curious if the others had exits similar to this one. Soon we came to an open area that had three other tunnels leading to the same spot. In the far end there was a single door. Opening it, it looked like a walk out basement to a very average looking house.

"We use this for the possibility of an emergency. At least the family members of the Augustus family have these. You two are the only ones who know I am part of the Augustus family. Gerard and anyone following him must be stopped, it's not just the council they are after. If Gerard can knock one down for power, the next step is to take out the Augustus family, which is the only reason they are paying attention now. I must stay here however I expect you two to keep me posted." As we stepped out, Sakarabru closed the door behind us.

We were only a few blocks from the council's main building. Not wanting to get caught we left immediately to figure out what we could do next. I was beginning to wonder how much planning Drezin put into creating his original experimental family and the risks involved.

Chapter Six

Seven Daughters

I had counted down to this moment, and now the last day of school was finally here, summer at last. I couldn't wait until I could lay out on the beach hanging out with friends. Throwing on my skinny jeans with white t-shirt. I hadn't taken very long to get ready. I had already beat my sister Rachelle to the car and she's usually the faster one. She had worn her red lace t-shirt and cream skirt for her last day with her yearbook in her hand. We hadn't been the only ones in a hurry for our last day; we both graduated a year early. Carrying our ceremony gown and hat, we had gone off to find our friends. The ceremony had been rather typical except for the kid who decided to streak the very last day. As the others had thrown their caps up into the air I simply looked around at the sea of black and white gowns watching as the caps slowly fell back down, I will never forget this sight. It was difficult to believe school was over until we were to leave for college. My sister and I had always been inseparable, the fact we both graduated early together proved that. The only thing we had separate was a few different friends. I was feeling sadder then excited, Rachelle was planning on going to the university of California while I was going to head to Ferris in Michigan. I could fake being happy all I wanted. I knew Rachelle could still tell; she always knew how I felt without saying a word.

A graduation gift we had both been given from our art teacher Mrs. Thea McAllister was a bottle of Lilac perfume; I had the exact same bottle in a shape of a glass tear drop from my favorite science teacher Mr. Drezin McAllister.

"Willow, pay attention or you'll get trampled." My best friend Craig pulled me aside as a few excited students rushed by.

"Are you going to Kimmy's party?" Not that I needed to ask, he had a crush on her since kindergarten so why refuse to accept an invite from her now?

"Why do you need a ride?" He tried sounding sarcastic.

"I have my own car; you're the one who still needs a ride." Giving him a jab in the ribs as I was now being pulled away by other friends.

"We're stealing her for now." Aliesha had never been tactful waiting for a conversation to end even though I already knew the answer.

"How about learning a few manners?" I had known Aliesha since we were in preschool, and I highly doubted she would change now.

"Manners are not exactly what won me prom queen. Besides, you could learn a few, your boyfriend hates Craig. If you want to keep him around after graduation you need to pay more attention to him." Waving over at Alex, he only waved and then turned his attention back to his football team.

Alex and I had always been in the popular group, while he played football, I had been the cheerleader. I never thought about us dating after school. For some reason I had been busy either thinking how I would keep up with friends or the simple fact I wanted a change. It hadn't included him. On paper we seemed like a perfect couple except we would argue so often. He never liked any of my friends, if Aliesha even knew some of the things he said about her, which is why I found so many ways not to spend any time around him anymore. I didn't know how to stop dating him; it felt more like a social date then anything and certainly not personal. Aliesha thought it would be great that since we were childhood sweethearts that we get married when we graduated, thankfully the subject had never come up again. I had so many plans, and marriage wasn't one of them, especially not to Alex. Not that I'm against marriage. I wanted to accomplish a few other things first on my own. Even Rachelle knew how I felt telling me after graduation it probably wouldn't be a bad idea if I had gone far enough away to get distance from him. That neither would even give it another thought that we had dated. It would be much easier since he did have a temper when he was opposed or didn't get his way, thankfully he was planning on going to Madison Wisconsin.

Most had gone to the birthday party right after graduation, even Rachelle had gone with her friends. We had both brought a change of clothes with us. Being at the party hadn't made things any easier either; I picked up Craig since I knew he needed a ride. Apparently, he already had a ride home so I didn't have to wait for him, even though I would have waited years, it felt as if I already had. I never said a word to him since he only wanted to be close friends, I had a crush on him as long as I could remember. Watching him talk to his own crush wasn't easy, so I did what I normally would do, daydream. I only had to last so long during this party and then I could leave. Rachelle had come over after watching me daydream on my own in the corner for a while.

"I see you're at your pastime again?" Rachelle had given a slight laugh.

"I should be somewhere else; I don't know where. I feel like I'm forgetting or missing something?" As long as I could remember I felt there was something else.

A dream. It felt so real it was far away and too hard to forget especially when Rachelle had the same dream on the same night.

"Let's get our birthday over, everyone is waiting and then we can slip out after." Rachelle would have preferred staying at home just hanging out with a few friends instead of such a huge group.

It looked as if the entire school had shown up for our friends graduation mixed birthday party, last one we would be throwing while we were in school. Our birthday was always just as school ended and for how extravagant it gets; we blended our graduation party with it this year. The football team had carried out the large cake setting it on the table, it had been ablaze with candles, at least enough for both of us. Every year it was the same theme for our cake, something our parents understood and a few friends. From our favorite book Alice in Wonderland, the mad hatter cake changed every year only getting larger and more extravagant that it became an event all on its own. This year it was ten layers high with several little hats around it, no doubt to help support the weight. Everyone stood around us watching, even Aliesha reminding us to make a birthday wish. Rachelle and I looked at each other smiling knowing exactly what we would wish for; we only shared it with each other and wished it since we were five. We were finally turning eighteen.

Our friends always waited to see if it would happen again, it happened every year on our birthday, it was almost a sign of good luck in a way, or at least it's what we had been told. There was always a shooting star extremely bright. As soon as we had blown out our candles it would shoot overhead. This time it was different. After looking at each other smiling we had looked at the cake, blowing out the candles. A rumble that had shook the ground slightly and lit up the entire sky with lightening. A huge crash of sound echoed through the air as a giant downpour of rain came. The players grabbed the cake rushing it into the house. Everyone panicked racing inside trying not to get wet. For some reason Rachelle and I lingered to feel the cool water dropping on us. It felt good getting drenched; it had been incredibly hot out. Making our way into the house, dripping water on the ground, we only stayed for another few hours, at least until three in the morning until we were tired and left for home. I barely touched my pillow after laying down and fell asleep.

Only an hour passed and certainly not the way I would have preferred waking up, even though it was still extremely early, and I should still be dreaming. With a loud crash from the window, I could barely see anything. My eyes were still blurry. The next thing I had known was someone was yelling at me from the side, pulling at me telling me to get out of my room. As I jumped up, I slipped my loafers on. Leaving my room as I realized my sister was the one making me leave the house. This would have been the first time we had been left on our own without adult supervision. Our parents were on vacation and our neighbors who usually watched us were left in charge, except this time we were the only ones in the house. It was our parents' way of saying we were old enough to take care of ourselves, although if we needed them, they wouldn't be far, and we had our neighbors. This summer was supposed to be our first real taste of independence. It wasn't that we'd never been left home alone before; this was just the first time we were responsible for the house by ourselves for two whole weeks. After this I was sure that would never happen again. As we stood outside looking at the house, I could hear the fire trucks pulling up to the house trying to control the blaze. I don't know how I missed all of the smoke when we went through the hallways. The entire house was engulfed with flames and oddly enough our neighbors were nowhere to be seen. What had been stranger had been the fact that no one seemed to see or notice us.

"Am I the only one losing it, people are walking past us as if we are not even here." Grabbing Willow's hand, I did not want to risk losing my sister even if it turned out to just be a nightmare.

"I don't think anyone sees us, I'm positive we're alive, but they act as if they can't see us." Waving our hands in front of everyone we realized another problem.

No one heard us speaking. Looking back at the house I noticed one other person left the house through the front door, which no one else was paying attention to. He was holding a large suitcase of our fathers walking away with no one even stopping him, and then we saw something I never believed would happen. Another person we thought was going to stop him hadn't; they simply walked right through him. Both Willow and I were thinking the same thing when we had seen it, almost as if he knew. He turned to face us.

"You should be dead." He seemed rather angry as he yelled this at us.

Still, no one around even heard him yell at us. Turning to run, we ran as fast as we could. Not that we were sure where we were going other than to get away from him until we could figure out where or what we were doing. At least we had this to our advantage; we knew our neighborhood better than he did. We raced through neighbor's yards but then as we thought we might have slowed him down with the fence being in the way, we found he simply ran through it with no problems. Not bothering to look back, we kept running, darting around buildings heading for the water and then Willow came up with the best idea, at least I hoped it would be the right choice. We ran for the graveyard and as we had, the ground started covering in almost a strange hazy fog. As soon as we passed the gates the man stopped immediately. He was yelling something in another language that we had no clue what he was saying. Standing behind the large building in the center, we watched as he was screaming at us, he had barely made it past the iron fencing when smoke billowed out around him, then as quickly as it had appeared there was a small ring of red fire that surrounded him swallowing him whole taking him into the ground no longer to be seen.

"I must still be asleep. There is no way that just happened." Willow was still in shock.

"Are dreams supposed to hurt?" My sister looked at me.

Something I hadn't noticed until we stopped, a piece of glass still sticking out of my arm.

"Stand still Rachelle, this might hurt, we can't keep that in there, if it were larger, I would leave it in since it could cause more bleeding, but this looks small." I kept hoping it was a dream.

Looking at my arm, she looked queasy. Pulling out the piece of glass had hurt; I couldn't help but whimper when she pulled it. She was wearing a soft cloth decorative belt that served no purpose until now. Wrapping it tightly around my arm it helped slow down the blood. Feeling dizzy I sat down next to the building. Just our luck, it had started to hail turning the dirt on the ground into slippery cold mud. Even though no one could see us or hear us, we were still getting wet. Sitting as close to the mausoleum we tried to stay out of the hail. Sitting close to each other we wanted to make sure neither of us was separated from each other.

"How do you think he saw us when no one else did? If we are like him then how did he pick up dad's suitcase?" Shaking my head, I couldn't figure this out.

Far too much was happening and no way of finding out answers or at least we thought there wasn't.

"I don't know but somehow, we will figure out something, remember mom always said no matter what happens in life we always have each other. We can figure this out. I just don't know how yet." Willow was always good at staying calm while I tended to panic.

Watching the rain, it seemed to thicken as we watched lightening streaks shoot across the sky. Then as everything else had been going tonight just about four feet in front of us, the lightning struck the ground five times in the same spot. As we watched there were so many colors illuminating from the lightening as it hit the ground. Once it stopped, we expected the dirt to almost turn to glass or possibly next we would be its next target, however, it never struck again. Watching the glassy sheen on the top of the dirt it started to rise and form into a building. Pressing against the wall of the building behind us as if we could have gone any further, both of our eyes were fixed on it. The sand from all around slid along the ground grouping up in this one spot as windows, doors and a roof appeared out of nowhere. The haze in the graveyard had yet to go away. It was still very warm outside with no natural fog except it was forming even more so to the point we could no longer see our feet. Once the building stopped forming. The front door started creaking as it slowly opened. At first, we hadn't seen anyone. Stepping out of the shadow had been a man dressed all in black, black jeans with a black shirt. He had been the most terrifying person I had ever seen. So far, we had felt safe in the graveyard since our parents always referred to a cemetery as holy ground, except if this person could form like that there was no way or hope of getting out of here. Holding onto my sister tighter. I think she had the same thought.

"Rachelle and Willow, I presume?" All we could manage to do was nod our head in agreement.

His voice was such a deep tone it echoed on the ground as he spoke our names.

"How do you know our names?" I never did know where Willow summoned her courage.

"I know everything about you, especially what you do not know about yourselves." Smiling at us he opened the door wider as if he had expected us to follow.

"Why can you and that other guy see us where no one else can? Are you going to kill us?" Willow tried keeping her voice from wavering.

I knew she was scared however if you did not know her, you would assume she was fearless.

"At some point, yes, I will kill you and if you do not come with me then you will die much earlier. Just enter through the door when you're ready, however, do not delay too long. Your time will run out." Before he could disappear, Willow stood up and he hesitated thinking she was going to follow.

I had grabbed her arm since I was worried myself that she might.

"You didn't answer the rest of my question, besides, that's not very enticing if you want us to come with you." Getting bolder by the moment I backed her up by keeping my eyes intently on the man in case he tried to pull anything.

We had been in scrapes before and defended each other. Not that we could always explain it however the smallest things seemed to happen to us. Almost magical, not that I believed in it too much other than the fact I wasn't going to ignore it either in case I was wrong. Willow, however, fully believed in the supernatural so this I was sure was scaring her much less. But then mom always used the saying that just because you believe in it, things are quite different when you actually see it.

"Yes, at some point I will kill you, however for now it does me no good to have you dead. You're under a protection spell, an extreme one. There are few that have figured out how to see through it now that they have killed those who were meant to protect you." As he walked away from the girls, he made a statement, not a question.

"Roger and Eden, our neighbors." As I said this, he barely needed to say anything even though not looking at us as he kept walking into the building and out of sight, we could still hear his booming voice.

"They were simply a consequence, protecting the natural children of Drezin. Once you come with you can meet your other sisters Hannah and Dahlia, not everyone is together yet." Disappearing into the darkness we no longer saw or heard him.

Looking at each other neither of us knew what to do. Then we looked at the entrance of the gate. There was a man standing there again except this time he was there with four others who also saw us. They were what I assumed a zombie apocalypse would look like.

"You can't stay in there forever; there are others who wish to kill you, they do have people who can go on holy land." He waited for us to make our choice.

As he said that, one of the men at the gate stepped right through the entrance very slowly, even though he looked as though he was in extreme pain, he was making his way over to us. Still holding onto my sister's hand, we made a dash for the door. Even if it hadn't promised the best ending, at least it delayed it. We were sure if we stayed here our lives would have ended much earlier. Besides, I was curious what he meant there were more sisters. We had only known of us unless he was lying which could be possible.

Immediately the doors closed behind us with a loud bang. The last sight we had seen was of the man trying to prevent the doors closing when his hand was between the doors, it simply cut it in half as part of it now laid on the ground, limp in front of us. We couldn't see a thing; it looked as though there were windows except no light came through them. There was no way of telling the walls or the floor were even there, other than reaching out and touching them. I knew Willow was standing next to me, I had yet to let go of her hand, which I hadn't planned on doing. I couldn't see her, and she couldn't see me. Then a light blue beam materialized in the center of the room. Enough to see in the direction it had come from. Moving along, we followed the beam hoping it would lead us in the direction we were expected to go.

"I feel as if I woke up in the middle of a horror movie." I barely whispered it.

"I know, I feel the same way. My bed started to shake, and I jumped off from it, when the glass from my window and dresser was crashing into my room. I ran out as fast as I could. I almost didn't expect to find you in your room. Hopefully we will find out something. Either way we make sure we never separate from each other." Not that it needed to be worded, it was a simple given with us.

The light pulled us onward until the ground suddenly slanted downward, almost sending us sprawling. We clutched each other as the floor became steps, descending at an uneasy angle. Blindly, we felt our way down until the stairs finally ended and the ground leveled beneath our feet. The darkness stayed complete, thick and heavy until a strange, unnatural glow at the far end of the hallway.

Walking towards it, we could hear two light sounding voices that sounded as equally concerned as we were. Going into the room there were two girls standing rather close to each other at the far end of the room. The man we thought we would see in here wasn't here at all. Turning to step out for a second to see if the pathway showed better now that the room was light brightly, I couldn't even step out of the room now. It was as if we were trapped. Looking back into the room both of the girls were still looking at us.

"I'm Dahlia and this is my sister Hannah; we were told you might join us." Her voice was rather low however assertive.

I assumed she was the more outgoing sister of the two since the other stood rather protectively beside her just as I was with mine.

"My name is Willow, and this is my sister Rachelle. How long have you two been here? Do you know when that guy that spoke to us will be back or what he plans on doing with us?" We were hoping they might know more not that it looked very promising.

"We haven't been here very long ourselves. We just know we can't leave; we can see out except we can't walk back through the door. I don't know why he wants us here; we found out our parents are not our biological parents. We were being attacked when a lightning storm kicked in and this building appeared right in the middle of town, I don't know how no one else saw it, it was large enough." It hadn't exactly been the exact same as our experience, however, not that far off with the lightning storm.

We explained what happened with us that led us here. I had to admit we all did look very similar as if we could be family. They had been born as twins just like we were. The only difference had been we knew we were not biologically related to our mother even though she gave birth to us. We were raised with the idea that our parents could not get pregnant, they had been donated fertilized eggs.

There were books left in case we were bored, food in the refrigerator and a bathroom in a separate room slightly closed off. There were seven beds in the room, each set up and ready as if they expected us to be here a while. We assumed once he found the other girls, we would find out what he wanted or would die. Not that we were looking forward to that. There were no other rooms leading out of here, just the one we first came through. We talked with the other girls for quite a while, as we did, we found we had much more in common. The main thing had been the simple fact we had unusual or unexplained situations that would happen to us. Hannah could make her hands smoke after saying a few words. She explained if she really concentrated on it, she could shoot a straight line of fire from her palm, but it still burned a bit. Her sister Dahlia hasn't had too much happen other than when she would get upset, lights would flicker, or glass burst if she was angry enough.

Dahlia showed how she could make the lights flicker in the room we were standing in. As they did, Willow concentrated on one of the books, the wind had swept past her pushing the book. All I could do was rush from one side of the room or the other rather quickly before they could see me go. I could physical see everything slow down around me as if I was racing against objects in slow motion., I never felt fast but felt everything else became abnormally slow. Willow always told me I over thought this. I rarely ran very fast since I was usually keeping at my sister's pace.

The other two girls had no idea how much time had passed since they had been picked up, or how much longer we would be here. Feeling tired. I sat down and slept while Willow stayed awake to keep watch. After a while we all took turns almost as a precaution not that there was much we could do, however with all of us combined, we could at least do enough damage hopefully to find a way out if he came in or tried to kill us. It seemed strange they would want all of us in the same room together unless they wanted to get us to do something for them.

If they wanted to kill us, they would have let the others who were coming after us do that. With us combined just for a moment. I thought we might out damage our captors but then who knows what they are capable of if they don't fear us together?

Eventually, there was a change, we had seen the doorway light up brightly. Dahlia and Hannah let us know last time it had done that was before we came in. We were almost expecting to see two more girls or possibly three. The original told the first two girls here that there would be seven sisters total that they were collecting. We still were not sure if it was a matter of individual sisters who did not have anything in common with each other, if we were supposedly related to each other, or if it happened to be sisters who had special gifts. As we watched, a girl had walked in rather slowly, we could watch the door itself seal around her as she stepped in on her own.

"Do you have a sister?" Hannah had been the first to ask the question we were all curious about.

"Yes, I do but she wasn't home when I was attacked. She was spending the night at a friend's house, so I don't know where she is, I don't even know where I am." She was keeping her arms protectively crossed in front of her rather tightly from being so nervous.

"We don't know where here is either. Other then it was safer coming in here then where we were before this." We didn't have to wait too long before the mysterious man came walking in as he looked at the young girl.

We all stood next to her; we had decided we were all in this together then we would do our best to protect each other.

"Where is your sister? She should have been with you." His voice boomed making the little room we were in tremble.

"I already told you. I don't know where she is, she was spending the night at a friend's house, and I don't know all of her friends. We have always had separate friends, it was to give us our own identity, our parents were always separating us trying to get us to socialize with others instead of just sticking together." Grumbling not happy with her response, he walked through the closed barrier leaving all of us there again.

Apparently, he was having a hard time locating her sister. Sitting on the edge of the bed with Dahlia, she looked rather afraid.

"Do you think they will hurt her if they find her?" Closing her eyes, she seemed to be concentrating on something, almost blocking us out for a bit.

We just stood nearby watching and wondered what she

was doing.

"What is it that you're doing?" We were curious if it happened to be a twin connection?

We always knew if our sister was in pain or needed us, however we never actually concentrated on it before.

"We have an unusual bond. I've been able to talk to my sister before; except I can't seem to get to her. I've never been this far apart from her before. All I can tell is that she's frustrated. So at least I know she's safe, but then I don't know for how long." We all knew that worried look she had on her face.

We had the same feeling for each other. The new girl with us was Piper. Her sister Taylor was still out there somewhere and alone.

"How old are you and what day were you born on?" We had already discussed the strangeness about this earlier which made us think if someone could mess with life like this, it could be possible that we were biologically related.

After all, how often does this happen? Millions could be born on the same day; however, how many were the same age, with gifts, found out their birth parents are not related to them, and end up here?

"My sister and I are eighteen years old, and we were born on October thirteenth, why?" She seemed rather curious why we would ask her day of birth.

We all looked at each other noticing much of it rested on numbers.

"We are all born on the same day and the same age as well." Dahlia supplied the new girl the information.

We also discovered that we had all been born in the same hospital on the same day within only a few hours of each other. That alone was unsettling enough. Then the room reacted.

One of the stone walls began to slide sideways with a low grinding sound, revealing a narrow hallway beyond it. The same pale blue light we'd followed before reappeared, glowing softly along the floor like a path waiting for us to step onto it.

This wasn't the door we'd come through. That one had

vanished the moment we entered, leaving no trace behind. And this time, there was no stranger guiding us, no reassurance that stepping forward was safe.

We hesitated, clustered together, unsure if following the light was what it wanted… or what it needed from us.

But the room gave us no other options. There was nowhere else to go, and staying put felt worse than moving forward.

So, we stepped into the hallway, sticking close, our shoulders brushing as if contact alone might keep us grounded. The moment we crossed the threshold, the stone behind us slid shut, sealing us in and cutting off any chance of turning back.

It felt less like escape and more like being guided through a maze, one we hadn't agreed to enter.

At the end of the hallway, the space opened into a large chamber. Two figures stood waiting for us there, already aware we would come.

"Do any of you know why you are here?" The woman asked us first.

We looked at each other not sure how to respond or if we wanted to share the information, we were sure they had already known.

Willow was the first to speak, "we were hoping someone might be able to tell us why we are here?"

"We have great things planned for all of you once everyone is here. We have new rooms for everyone to stay in; we had to rush the emergency room. When we first set out looking for you girls, we had only been looking for three girls until we found out there were actually seven of you. For now, I'll be your temporary mother until you either refuse to help us, or you're no longer needed." She certainly had a way letting you know we were limited and removable.

"What my partner means is that you have gifts we need in order to protect others, I'm sure you girls like to help or do good for others? We are new at dealing with mortals or at least we assume you are mortal still. My name is Gerard, and this is

Lydia, if you need anything, let us know. Now follow us." As he spoke the woman was already heading down another hallway.

Slowly we followed them still close to each other for protection. As we did there were several other rooms that went off from the hallway and they no longer closed in behind us.

Opening one of the doors to a room there were only two beds in it. We all had looked immediately at Piper as we knew we would have been scared staying alone, we didn't want to risk leaving her behind either let alone splitting up from each other.

"We would like it if we all could stay in the same room. It's kind of a teenage girl thing especially since we are not familiar with this place. It helps us relax more." I tried to sound convincing hoping if they were calling us mortals, they might not think anything of it, that we wanted to stay together.

Gerard and Lydia momentarily glanced at each other as she nodded her head in agreement.

"That would be fine, we will have the other beds moved in for now and if you change your mind or want privacy, the other rooms will still be available. We have books we would like each of you girls to read and practice, perhaps in your separate rooms later. For now, feel free to be teenagers and get comfortable in this room. We will be gone for a while; we are still locating Taylor and Kendra, the last two girls." I was usually good at thinking immediately, so I was thankful they had agreed to my request.

The rest of the girls were also happy they agreed with it. Willow giving my hand a bit of a squeeze. I knew she was proud of me for coming up with it. Closing the door behind us, we all looked around the room inspecting the decorations on the walls, the pictures, books covering the entire side wall by the door. It had looked as though it was decorated for a witch and definitely not as they would have put it, mortal teenagers. There were even vials in the corner on a table with several little jars filled and labeled with rather strange names, nothing any of us recognized other than a few symbols Hannah recognized but did not remember what exactly they meant other than knowing they had been in one of her supernatural books.

"I wish I had my books. I could look up the symbols to find out what they all mean." Looking as if she was concentrating trying hard to remember she stopped feeling frustrated.

"Willow, take a look at this symbol. I think the alternative bookstore downtown had this same symbol." As I pointed it out, she shrugged, not sure if it had been the same or not.

Picking up the book next to all the strange looking jars it had several ingredients listed in a rather unique handwriting. I couldn't tell what all of it was for. However, it certainly wasn't a recipe for food. Looking over the rest of the room, there had been little pictures and in each one had a single shot of us. None of us together and it looked as though they took the photos from a distance. It felt strange someone would have been watching us for a while. The picture of myself, I knew exactly where I was when they had taken it. I was reading a book outside during free period; willow was in the corner talking with a couple of her friends barely in the picture. Our picture was the only one that came the closest to having both in it. They must have had a hard time getting a picture with us alone since we were so close, we rarely left each other's side.

The rest of the beds had been moved in rather promptly for us. Then Piper seemed rather shocked as she was holding a piece of paper. It was a mini calendar with the dates marked off and our names were written in certain boxes when we had been collected. Hannah and Dahlia had already been here for about a month before we joined them, after us, Piper joined us three weeks later. I was beginning to wonder what our parents would do once they found the house burned to the ground and no signs of us around. Even with the neighbors gone, hopefully they hadn't thought they would kidnap us; it was depressing thinking of the kind couple as being killed because of us. We wished we had known they were there to protect us, that is, if we were being told the truth.

Chapter Seven

Discovering

Touching the door handle, it hadn't been locked at all. Not that we knew where to go, we walked out into the hallway out of curiosity to see where we would end up. Each of the doors we tried opened up other than the door that was at the far end. They made sure there was no way of escaping. We couldn't tell what the weather had been like outside. One of the rooms had a television in it. As we sat down, we watched in horror as the news was announcing how either some of us had died or disappeared. They even listed Taylor even though she wasn't with us yet and her sister was positive that if she had died, she would know. There wasn't any local news, or it would have given us an idea where we had been.

If we wanted to explore this would be the time to do it without Lydia or Gerard wondering what we were doing. Still agreeing not to separate from each other, we walked cautiously almost expecting the door to the room to either seal or lock behind us. There were several rooms that didn't have very much in them or at least not anything that would have given us a clue what they wanted with us. We also noticed there hadn't been any other way out of this place guessing the end of the hallway that was closed off was the only way out. Dahlia was touching everything almost hoping that something might trigger the door leading out or at least open a secret room or something. The only thing that had been unusual was the room that had been locked.

"I wonder what they're hiding in there, can't see through the lock it's so small." Willow was trying to find any crack in the door possible that might give her the slightest glint through.

"I could try opening it." Not sounding too sure if she could.

Looking into the tiny lock she could see where the notches the key would fit into. Concentrating and blocking everything else around her, Rachelle gusted up wind shoving against the notches trying to trick it into moving. The first attempt had only pushed them in slightly almost unlocking the door. Attempting a second time concentrating much harder she almost blew the door open. No one had made any moves to go in yet almost too afraid to find out what was on the other side of the door. Both Willow and Hannah were the first to walk in with the rest following. While all of the other rooms had been pure white in color almost having an antiseptic appearance to them. This one was completely different. The walls were black with black lace hanging down from each one. Almost the most feminine-looking room possible, only all in black giving it more of a gothic steampunk style. The room looked extremely large compared to the other ones we looked in. This one had little tables with black cloth and a silver star design on the top with lots of little vials, very similar to the ones in each of our rooms. There were a few books on the walls, none that Dahlia had been familiar with other then the fact they had spells or other incantations handwritten inside of them.

In the center of the room there had been a long bed, it looked more like an early renaissance chamber bed. There was a serving tray in the center of the bed with four large jars. There was no way of knowing what was inside the jars without looking. They looked as if they were made of porcelain. Willow opened the one jar to peak in, not sure what it was, she took a whiff. The look on her face let us all know it wasn't something pleasant. It looked like simple water except the smell was far worse almost causing her eyes to tear up after smelling it. Piper opened the second jar finding what looked like dirt. Shifting it around a little by moving the jar the substance reacted like dirt.

"I wonder what they need these things for?" I wondered what it had to do with this room or if it had anything to do with us.

"Not sure sis, all of these items are strange. I have a bad feeling it can't be for anything good. They might be telling us we are sacrificing our lives to help others; I have a feeling it's to further help their own, not something we want to be doing." Everyone picked up on the tone in willow's voice.

We were all coming to similar conclusions. This might have been a way to escape whatever was after us at the moment, but now we wondered if we stepped into something even worse? Perhaps it wouldn't have been as bad if we let the others catch us, not that we knew if they would have killed us or not. We made our decision quickly not knowing what would happen to us either way. We were going to have to wait to find out what they were planning with us and hopefully find a way out somehow. Making sure to put everything back the way it was before, locking the door behind us, we made our way back to our room. Not too long after we could hear the two talking in the hallway. Their voices were muffled; we hoped to hear what they were saying. We didn't have to wait very long to find out what they wanted, at least what they were going to start with. For a few seconds their voices were silenced before the door opened. Expecting to see one of the three we had talked to, there was a new person standing there that hadn't looked as intimidating as the others. She was bright and cheerful looking with a huge smile on her face, even her voice matched her appearance.

"My name is Amber and I'm here to help you with your training. We know you don't have very much experience using your gifts, that's why I'm here to help you get stronger with them. It will help you learn better on your own, so you're not distracted by anything around you. Willow, you're first." Standing back out of the doorway expecting Willow to follow.

"I'll let you know what it's like as soon as I'm back, I don't think they will do anything to us this soon." I knew from the sound of her voice she was trying to be brave so that the others wouldn't be afraid, after all, it wasn't as if we had a choice.

Walking out of the room we were all watching her walk out with her head held up straight not showing any sign of fear or hesitancy. One of these days I wanted to be more like my sister. As soon as the door closed leaving the girls waiting to find out what they were doing, Amber hadn't waited as she was already walking down the hallway. Almost having to run to keep up, Amber seemed rather fast when she walked, or it was an illusion. Not walking down to far from their room, they turned into one of the empty purely white looking rooms that had no furniture in it. Following her to what looked like a closet had been rather deceptive. There was a staircase leading downward into a dark area. Almost unable to see now walking slower not sure if she would trip over something, slightly feeling along the way with her foot, hoping not to run into the woman ahead of her.

"Sorry Willow, I forgot mortals don't see very well in the dark." As soon as she had said this, she lightly whispered the word, "lights."

"Thank you." I hadn't wanted to sound rude, but when the lights had come on it made it much easier to see and the fact she was already so far ahead of me.

"This is the room we will be in, later on, when you get better and are doing much more complicated exercises. I'll be watching from the adjoining room." Amber waited for me to walk past her into the room.

"What kind of exercises are we doing?" Trying to figure out the whole thing I was hoping it wasn't real exercising.

I used to fake being sick in gym class so I wouldn't have to do anything.

"Trust me; these exercises will actually be fun for you." Walking over to a desk at the far corner of the room, she placed a vase on the table.

"Sorry if I show a lack of enthusiasm but knowing that we are going to die at the end of it kind of takes away the fun aspect of it." There was no point in hiding the fact we either knew or disliked the only option being given to us.

"Yes, I have heard about that, too bad since you could be quite useful later on as well. I can't say why he wouldn't want to keep you. Not that I know why myself, it's something they are keeping to themselves." Even Amber seemed confused by the choice except she was obviously willing to go along with it.

"What exactly are we doing?" I was hoping to find out instead of being thrown into something.

"First we need to find out how much control you have. I want you to knock that vase off from the desk as hard as you can." I was standing in the middle of the room wondering how was I supposed to do that?

I never managed to do anything on purpose. It either happened or Rachelle would do something accidentally. Amber seemed incredibly patient, I felt as if a long time passed while I tried to focus on the object picturing it moving. I hoped what I watched in the movies might work but nothing was happening. I even swung my hand in the air almost as if I was slapping it off the desk and it hadn't worked. Eventually she walked over to the vase, Amber picked it up looking it over. I was curious why she was looking the vase over unless she thought it might have been stuck to the table? Without warning, she turned and hurled the vase at me. As she had I did the only thing I could think of. Closing my eyes and raising my hands to block the vase from hitting me. I waited for it to hit me until I heard it smash on the ground.

"Next time keep your eyes open." Amber made herself rather clear.

"Why? So, I can see what's about to hit me?" I still felt nervous from her throwing the vase at me.

"Did it hit you? No...it didn't...so keep your eyes open." Amber walked over to the desk picking up something to the side of it not seen well in the shadow.

Holding an object that looked round, shiny, and black in appearance, I tried to figure out what she had. Then she turned the object slightly and I could see the three finger holes. She intended on throwing a bowling ball at me. Taking her time before she moved at all, she was building the suspense making me even more nervous by the second. I could feel my hands shaking and a bit of sweat from my forehead.

Rachelle was worried. I knew it the instant fear surged through me. It slipped past every wall I tried to hold up and rushed along the bond between us, raw and unfiltered. Somewhere beyond the room, she would have felt it like a sudden drop in her chest.

'What happened?'

The thought wasn't a question spoken aloud, just a flash of her voice brushing the edge of my mind before vanishing again. She hadn't meant to reach for me; fear had pulled her in the same way it had pushed me apart.

Amber's smile never wavered, her voice bright as she guided me through the rest of the training, but the fear she'd stirred was still coiled tight inside me. She'd needed it, needed me off balance to force my gift to surface. I'd survived it, barely, but the damage was already done.

Rachelle wouldn't know the details. She wouldn't see Amber's too-cheerful grin or understand why the training felt more like a test of endurance than control. She'd only know that something had scared me badly enough to crack our bond open. And she wouldn't stop worrying until she saw me again.

Then as quickly she turned and hurled the bowling ball into the air directly at me. As she had this time, I kept my eyes open almost too afraid to shut them if I wanted to, holding my hands up expecting to hopefully catch it even though I knew it would still hurt quite a bit. The fear alone from not wanting to get hit. I could feel myself flinch just a little, a slight prickling feeling from my hands and the bowling ball went flying back at her. Moving out of the way the bowling ball embedded itself into the wall behind her. Smiling at me, I was sure she was accomplishing whatever she had planned. Not that I was sure if I was actually doing anything other than acting out of self-preservation.

"How do you feel?" Amber was still smiling at me.

"How do you think I feel? You threw a bowling ball at me? How am I supposed to feel?" I wasn't getting the point of this.

"Think about how you felt the instant you thought either of the objects were going to hit you. The body has a remarkable way of healing itself no matter how minor, or the fact it even functions the way it does on a daily basis. Then when it's either weak or sick it needs help handling its normal everyday functions. Just like the body. You need a little bit of help getting your natural ability to function right. It's not a matter of thinking but feeling." Amber grabbed a broom sweeping up the broken vase.

If I had ever been scared in the past it was never for very long. I was rarely in a position for anything to happen except maybe three times that I could remember. Once when I thought a certain bully was about to attack me and flew back a few feet away from me. The other time when I realized a driver was drunk driving up onto the sidewalk that almost ran me over until the car screeched to a halt. The third time happened when I was angry, I was sleeping over at a friend's house until I found out I was only invited there on a dare, every glass in the house along with the windows and mirrors broke all at once. Up until now I thought it was a creepy coincidence. I wasn't sure if she was finished or not, but I could still feel that panic feeling swelling up and as I looked at the desk it flew back against the wall.

"I guess we should teach you control or how to relax afterward?" Amber watched as the desk that had been moved forcefully broke to pieces on the floor.

"Am I doing that?" It was still difficult for me to believe.

"Yes, that is all you. Actually, it's you who use the air around you to do it. The vase smashed because of the force against it as it came at you, the bowling ball had more mass and handled the air current you sent at it causing it to retreat from you. From the looks of it, you are rather strong but need more practice so you can do this with intention and not out of fear. I want you to practice with this little ball, just moving it around your room." Not bothering to move the desk back, Amber made her way to the door opening it up waiting for me.

"Are we going to do this again?" I felt strange that we were only in here for a little while unless my concept of time was off.

"For now, yes, we are finished. Each day I will train one of the other girls. When I teach Hannah and Dahlia I want to be better protected physically, I may have been burned at the stake a few times, but it never gets easier to handle." Almost sounding as if she meant it to be a joke I wondered if she had been burned before?

Walking back down the same hallway we made our way to our room. All the girls had been intently staring at me as I walked in, and Amber waved goodbye to us all shutting the door behind me. Not that we would be able to explore anymore, maybe they found out we had been in the one room, but she had locked the door behind me. Unless of course for a short time they wanted to keep us in here, either way I was happy that my training was over for the day, and I could explain to the others what we did. At least now that Rachelle could see me, she knew I was alright so far.

"Willow, did she hurt you at all? I could tell you panicked for a while; you look fine, but what did they do?" Rachelle desperately waited for an answer.

"It's the way she teaches, I'm not sure if she could have explained it better without it. It's one of those feelings and quick reactions that helped me use my gift intentionally. It's something she will be doing with all of us. I'm not sure how my gift will actually help them with anything?" I kept running this through my mind trying to figure it out.

"Maybe they want to use us as an army of sorts? We would be useful as a group instead of separately?" Dahlia and Rachelle had been discussing why they would be using us while I was gone being trained.

"The only problem with that is the loyalty factor, why

should we be loyal and actually do what they want if they only intend on killing us? They must not fear us at all if they know we will get strong with our gifts. If they keep calling us mortals and don't have experience dealing with us, then what are they?" Rachelle looked at each of us hoping one of us might have figured out what they were.

"I'm not sure what they are. They look human, same as we are other than the first guy who collected us. He looked rather scary, like a warmed-up corpse. None of them have done anything to stand out, even our trainer when she was teaching me. The only thing she was concerned about would be teaching Dahlia and Hannah because apparently, she's been set on fire before. She didn't look like she had been burned, so not sure what she is." I wasn't sure if we would find out or not, hopefully they would at least give us some sort of idea.

No one else was being tested tonight. Tomorrow they will have a full day of testing. I assumed my testing was short because I wasn't as dangerous as some of the other girls' gifts could be, and mine was strong as it was pointed out except, I needed more control. At least all of us knew as long as they needed us, we would be alive. For the rest of the night none of us had talked, all of us were worn out physically and mentally. None of us stayed awake to keep guard. We hadn't felt it was needed since our lives wouldn't be in danger quite yet. Not that I slept very well, I kept having this image creep into my dreams. A woman screaming at the top of her lungs looking directly at me, the other girls were standing around me at the same time. As she came into view, her body seemed to materialize even more until I had seen this woman who looked more like a dark silhouette then an actual person. It wasn't until she walked over to me and began to speak that I wondered if I wasn't dreaming but picking up on something about to happen. I wasn't able to move away from her, the faster she spoke the more I was immobile and could not control my body. Looking off to the side I could see Gerard and Lydia watching as if what they planned was coming true. That was also the instant we all died very quickly turning into dust.

Each time I had this dream I would wake up quickly to find I wasn't the only one having problems sleeping. I could see that Piper was having problems also, Rachelle was next to me slightly stirring but never fully woke up, Piper would look directly at me before turning over and went back to sleep. There were nights we would see each other wake up several times throughout the night except we had never once talked about our nightmares together. Not that there was ever enough from my dream to discuss other than the fact it felt so real. I had a hard time telling if I was dreaming or not. The dream wasn't always the same other than the woman who would eventually approach me. Looking over at Piper. I could tell this dream of hers was different, as she sat up, she looked more disoriented then anything. For a second, I was trying to figure out if she was still dreaming or coming out of one slower than normal.

Making sure I hadn't made any noise. I walked halfway across the room to Piper to find out what had spooked her so bad this time. Not saying a word, she had gotten out of bed also walking to the corner of the room furthest away from the beds. No doubt she didn't want to risk waking the others. Sitting down on the floor with her I waited for her to speak.

"I realized something; My nightmares are not just dreams. I feel we are being tested to see how we are best suited for the others use. We react more realistically especially when it comes to loyalty, they know what we would truthfully choose over what we say verbally when we are awake. If it were one hundred percent real, we would all be dead right now. The dreams are to real, look at my arm." As she said this, she turned her wrist showing the veins which had turned almost black.

"Does it hurt at all?" From the looks of it made me shiver.

"No, it doesn't hurt except when I started having these dreams my veins started to get dark. I wish we knew what our birth parents were like. Gerard kept referring to us as the seven sisters. We found out we were adopted, and you and your sister already knew that you were. How could they know we were all related? You and Rachelle definitely look related but not identical, Hannah and Dahlia are identical twins, so is my sister Taylor and me. I can only assume Kendra looks similar to us. If we were created, were they trying to create twins or was it an accident. I'm starting to think all of this was planned out a long time ago by someone." At least I wasn't the only one still fixated on figuring out our connection.

"The fact we had separate mothers who physically gave birth to us, born on the exact same day at the same hospital. My gift isn't the only thing that makes my sister and I different from each other. We don't look similar at all; we look more like distant cousins at the most." There were many differences between Rachelle and me.

Rachelle and I had never looked very much the same. Obviously, we hadn't taken after our parents, we always knew right from the beginning they were not our biological parents. Not that it mattered to us much growing up. They were there for us, raised us, loved, and looked after us. I always wondered where Rachelle inherited her dark red hair from. My own hair was also dark, black as night which made me worry about my connection with the woman I kept seeing in my dreams. She had the same hair color and looked very similar to me.

"I've wondered the same thing, my sister Taylor and I are identical physically but that's where our similarities end, even our gifts are different, we look a little more similar then the others, but we don't match the rest. How could we be related unless there's something they know and how would they know us? I've never seen either of them before?" We talked quite a bit until Rachelle started to stir.

Not wanting to wake the others, we made our way back to our beds quietly hoping to not only get answers to our questions, but also to find a way out. The next day came quickly; our mentor had chosen Piper. While she was gone most of us were still trying to figure out what they wanted with us, and to find a way out. Looking around in the simple room we had been sleeping in, there wasn't a sign of a crack or anything, not even a window.

While the others talked, I practiced with the little ball our mentor had given me. Knowing what the feeling was like helped me control the ball rather than hope it would kick in from sudden fear. Over the next couple of weeks, we were all getting stronger with controlling our gifts. None of us ever wanted to call them powers since it felt strange saying it, it had too much of a superhero vibe. One of the evenings they let us have a television in our room. We were not allowed to watch outside news or any other program; they had left several DVD's they thought we might like as mortals. We were watching one of the old movies when Piper sat up right away walking quickly over to the far wall that had a desk in case any of us felt like writing or to sit at. Sliding it to the side almost as our mentor had. We watched wondering if she was going to practice in our room. Something none of us had done yet other than my playing with a simple ball.

"Willow. When you were learning from our mentor, and she threw the bowling ball at you. You said that you lodged it into the wall, can you do that with the little boll you practice with?" All of us could hear the hope in her voice.

Even if I had been able to, it would have been a rather small hole.

"I don't know, it's a tiny ball. I can definitely hit it against the wall." I wasn't sure if it would even break the wall or indent since it was such a soft ball.

Probably why she gave me this. It would be safer to practice with in case I bounced off the wall and hit me or the other girls.

"If a hurricane can send a stick through a brick wall, then you should be able to send that ball through this wall if you get enough force behind it. Try it." Piper was rather excited, standing back waiting to find out.

There was enough air coming through the ventilation duct to the room so I could pull up enough air to start making the wind whip extremely hard. I knew I was forcing it rather roughly when the other girls were plastered to the walls waiting for me to send the ball at the wall. I fixed my attention on the bare wall where the desk had been and unleashed the wind. The tiny ball rocketed forward, struck the wall, and disappeared in a burst of dust and debris. I hadn't been the only one concentrating on it. Hannah was concentrating on the wall itself heating it up while Piper did her best to freeze the wall. With the wall's temperature being affected back and forth so much and the force of the little ball, the wall fractured until it shattered about the size of a small hula hoop even though the ball itself was rather small. Looking through it, we were amazed that it worked. Just from the loud noise we were worried the others might come and check on us. So far no one came. Piper was the first to squeeze through the hole and look around. There was light coming from the other side. It looked like a long tunnel, nothing like we had come through before, since the walls had no cement on them at all. There was only a hardpan floor and rock shaped walls with Caliche ceiling. After the last of us was through the wall we stuck closely together following the tunnel, not sure where it would lead us but if it was a chance to escape, we had to take it.

The tunnel as we found wasn't that much of a secret since there was a door at the end of the tunnel. Opening the unlocked door, we stepped into a large, round chamber, and immediately the air felt wrong. Icy water covered the floor, curling around our ankles, while a raised stone platform loomed at the center. Dry, smooth, and waiting. None of us spoke, but we all felt it: whatever the platform was for, it wasn't meant to be kind. The water crept toward a narrow opening in the floor, draining away with a slow, hollow sound that echoed through the room. There wasn't anything else in the room other than us and one other door which opened. Gerard, Lydia, and Amber our mentor had come in. Standing still not able to move we knew we were caught.

"At least I don't have to wonder if they will be able to use their powers well enough. Move them to the other room for now, it's much better until we get the last two girls and then we should be ready." Gerard's voice was rather rough sounding.

"Taylor and Kendra won't be as effective as the rest of the

girls without enough training." Amber seemed worried.

"Kendra doesn't need to control her power and Taylor should learn quickly enough since these have." Lydia looked angrily at Amber questioning their ability to decide if we were ready or not.

As the two exited, we were left with Amber. Following her into another room and this time it didn't have a bed or anything else in it. She closed the door behind her not looking to happy as she glanced over at us.

"I was hoping when you reached this point, they would be kind enough to allow you beds to sleep in still. We don't know how long it will take them to find the last two?" Not an expression we were used to seeing on Amber's face, she looked very concerned.

"Amber, do you know what we are expected to do if they do find the other two? Have they let you know anything about this?" I hoped she might know something by this point.

"I still don't know anything. Usually all I do is errands for them or if the council needs someone trained to better use their gifts, then I mentor them. No one is to know any of this is going on or where we are. I don't even know where we are since I'm stuck inside along with you." As soon as she spoke, she realized she said more than she should have.

"What's the council you work for? We thought you worked for Gerard and Lydia?" I knew I had to ask while she might still be willing to fill us in.

"At least it won't hurt that you know, at some point you will need to learn to give loyalty to Gerard and Lydia as I have. The council makes the final rules for us; the only ones who could possibly change those rules are the Augustus family, which is above the council. The members of the council are allowed to have their own private dealings as long as it's not conflicting with the council." Not wanting to give us too much information, I knew we would have to keep asking questions to get it out of her.

"How did you start working for Gerard and Lydia?" I

hoped she wouldn't stop answering questions once she started.

"I've worked with them only for the last twenty years so not very long at all. I worked for the council after my change; I was about your age. They felt I was loyal enough to put in the investment and time with me." Still keeping it short I had to think of more questions to ask.

"Why do you keep calling us mortals? What change did you have to do, is it the same for us? Do we have to change?" Perhaps we will find out something important.

"This isn't something you need to know and no you won't be changed the way I was. We might not always agree with what the individual members do independently of the council. However, as long as it does not conflict with the best interests of the council and its followers. A rule cannot be made for the sake of being made; it has to benefit our kind as a whole. Apparently, Gerard and Lydia feel this fits that and I am not to question them." Before we could ask her another question, Amber let herself out the door leaving us standing there.

The only benefit I could see would be the fact she was different from the others. She wasn't as cold-hearted, I wasn't sure if we would be able to get her to help us if she was incredibly loyal as she said to this council, Gerard, and Lydia. They definitely left this room empty; there wasn't anything to even sit on. We assumed they were no doubt worried we would use any item to escape again. We even tried to manipulate the wall except it hadn't worked this time. Apparently, they expected us to get to this point and put us in a very well protected room.

Apparently, their plan was to continue with our lessons until the other two were found. We no longer trained separately or left the room when we trained. It was hard getting used to sleeping on the floor, usually leaning against the wall or each other. Each day Gerard and Lydia were getting angrier that they were this difficult to find. Many times, Gerard and Lydia stared at Piper angrily, leading us to believe they thought she still knew where her sister was. Amber had come into the room with a few chairs setting them almost in a full circle. Not sure what she was doing since we hadn't spoken other than very few words regarding training. This time she seemed more relaxed then she had been even though Gerard and Lydia were getting much worse. Pointing to the chairs. Amber sat down in one expecting us to sit in the others around her.

"I'm sure you're wondering why we have the chairs in here. We need to discuss a few things, at least a few things that we are allowed. I'm going to ask a few questions, and I want you to answer them the best that you can." Apparently, she was a good mentor however not so good at teaching loyalty.

"If you work for the council, and even Gerard and Lydia are not supposed to go against them for the best interest of your kind and humanity, last we checked we were part of humanity. How can it be in the best interest of anyone if we get killed when we can help others with our gifts?" I decided I would ask before she asked us anything.

Amber looked rather stern except she hadn't answered my question. No doubt she was expecting it.

Ignoring my question, she went on to ask herself, "have any of you heard the names Drezin, or Langston?" Not paying attention to my comment she looked at the other girls to see what their expression was.

"Doesn't sound familiar, at least I've never heard it." Piper had spoken up not that any of us felt we would have said if we had known.

"Are you saying you don't know because you don't know or don't want to tell me?" Amber still spoke very calmly and slowly as she asked.

"When they changed you, did you do everything, and I mean everything they asked, on command or did you question any of it?" I knew I was pushing it but one of us had to.

"My life changed so drastically I had no other choice then to follow them. I questioned a lot but there was always a reason for everything they did regardless of if I agreed with them. It's why they are in charge, and I am not." Her voice rose slightly before she calmed it down.

"If something they do is against the council, would you stand against them?" I wanted to find out exactly what kind of power they had.

"I doubt I would even get the chance." Looking frustrated answering before she had the chance to think over her answer.

"Even if we do have control over our gifts, how are we supposed to know what to do or if we are doing it right if no one ever tells us what it is that's expected from us?" Rachelle asked Amber.

"When the time comes each of you will be given orders when you are needed, telling you exactly what you need to be doing. Are any of you familiar with castings?" Again, Amber waited for an answer.

"I've read about them, but I've never performed or seen one." Piper had always been interested in the supernatural.

"All of you might not like your fate, it's something that probably shouldn't have been shared with you and this would have been made much easier for all of you. Unfortunately, Gerard and Lydia don't know how to deal with mortals. If I were in your place, I would be eager to help save millions which is what you will be doing by cooperating." It almost sounded as if Amber was about to get patriotic sounding the way she spoke of Gerard and Lydia.

If this was that important, it seems as if there should be no problem or hesitancy for them to share what was going to happen to us, and what we were supposedly doing that would save millions of lives. Personally, I knew that Rachelle and I had heard of Drezin, I wasn't sure if it was the same person, but he was our substitute teacher. Now thinking about it there was something special about him, especially when my sister had given herself away with her gift the day she was angry, and he covered for her saying the heat made it appear as if she was running faster. At first the others hadn't wanted to believe it until he explained her running past the wall with the heat sending ripples up can make objects appear quicker, even odd shaped at times, similar to a water mirage on cement until you get closer and find out there is no water. He showed this by running faster himself by the wall. No one else questioned it anymore other than us. Rachelle and I talked about it later. After that none of the races were held so close to the school to keep us from being viewed by too many. If the others had ever heard of him, I doubted they would say anything either. Especially since he was always available to any of us if we needed him, he was not only our best teacher but also had an interesting way of teaching. At this point if we were to be loyal to anyone, he already earned our loyalty.

"Unfortunately, this is taking much longer then we have time for. We need to know if you have any idea where Taylor might be. I would ask about Kendra except you barely knew about each other and she was born several years later." Even Amber seemed to be getting frustrated at this point.

"Hopefully you can at least answer this, what do we have in common with each other? We keep hearing Gerard and Lydia referring to us as the seven sisters. We know our birth parents but not our biological parents. It is strange we were all born as twins." I hoped she would at least answer something as simple as that since they hadn't seemed worried about us hearing it.

"I can at least answer that." Amber at least seemed to know about this information.

As she explained it, most of us were shocked to find out we had been nothing more than an experiment. As she stated our biological parents were never supposed to be capable of having children, for reasons she still kept quiet. Our birth parents and protectors had been hand chosen, spreading us out to separate parents feeling we would be safer from those who would exploit our gifts for the wrong reasons. Also, our biological parents were not even sure we would all live if we were birthed by the same mother, which is why they enlisted the others, as Amber guessed most likely friends or people they knew and felt they trusted. Our biological father worked for the council at one time, however, leaving to pursue his own inventions. Our gifts were simply a mutation for most of us, what we happened to be predisposed to, adding to that, someone he knew added a special power no creature on earth could create. Not something that our father apparently was trying for when he created us.

"How can you be positive that the seventh girl, who is supposed to be our sister, is actually related to all of us. We were all born at the same hospital on the same night born not that long after each other within a short few hours. If Kendra was born considerably later than the rest of us or even at the same hospital, she might be no different than any other random person out there?" Piper was the first to ask.

"There were only four eggs, three of the eggs split giving natural twins and one singleton, she would have been the same age only they gave birth to her much later. Her gift is rather different from the rest of you, at least we've never seen any of you display the same expected gifts she will. All six of you naturally relate to the four elements in one way or another, she is almost similar to the guardian of the four corners, a deity or God. She is able to reanimate the dead, not those who have simply died but the living that are already dead. A gift that would have died out however was given to her. After this ceremony it will no longer be a lost gift but shared among many." Amber smiled rather excitedly about this bit of news.

"Will our gifts be shared also or is it the last ones that are wanted?" If many of my questions hadn't been answered before, she might answer this one and we can slowly put them together later.

"Not that your gifts are worth any less. None of us know how to replicate yours and they would be quite useful, however our main goal is your youngest sister, which is why she is so vital to this. Shades can control wind. And live a long life, so do guardians of an old life-stone. However, shades can control only so far, guardians without the stone being fully intact can only use the elements around them, Willow, you can pull all the oxygen from around the world and through several dimensions. Basic M theory or string theory." Amber slowed as she spoke for a moment almost as if she was listening for something." It sounded like we were going to be given a science lesson but then she stopped speaking immediately.

"Are you alright?" Rachelle asked in a light voice towards Amber.

"Yes, I'm fine, I thought I heard something. I believe I'm finished here. It won't hurt anything leaving the chairs here with you." Still looking at Rachelle almost as if she wasn't used to someone caring if she was alright or not, she stood and left the room.

Not one of us made a move from our chairs no doubt thinking the same thing. I had always wondered about our biological parents; however, I never once thought I might have been part of an experiment. Did we have mad scientists as parents?

"How could we be a part of an experiment and never know? My parents loved Willow and I, why would they keep something like this from us if they were supposed to protect us?" Rachelle was deeply upset by the news.

"Sis, there are always two sides to a story, we don't know if this is what they had planned or if it's the truth at all. It might be said to confuse us and possibly get us to go along with a plan that was never meant to be, or I could be wrong, and it's what everyone wanted all along. We won't know until we find out the truth and we will only find that out from our parents." Unfortunately, I wasn't sure if we would ever find that information out.

Piper sat rather quietly during this entire event doing nothing more than staring at the floor almost in a deep concentration. We knew that Piper was still concerned for her missing sister Taylor, that she would be out there alone and frightened but at worst, she worried if the others who came after us had caught her. Dahlia usually spoke up from time to time but this time she stayed silent. Finally, the silence was broken between the two as they spoke to each other as if the silence had only existed to us but now, we were hearing their conversation to each other. Feeling nervous, not one of us spoke out loud listening to the other two speak.

"We might have a chance." Faintly speaking, it was Piper.

"It's going to be close but as long as we are together, we can do this." Dahlia seemed positive of their plans.

"How will we get Gerard and Lydia to believe us?" Piper asked her.

""This shouldn't be difficult," Dahlia declared. "They don't share our connection. As long as they can't reach us the way we reach each other, our plans are protected."

"As soon as one of them comes in, even if it's Amber. I'll start up. We will appear to support them as much as possible, and then we do what we need to." Piper was laying out the plans as we all listened.

"I still can't believe you took the ashes when we were in that one room. What made you think of it?" Dahlia asked as we all looked at Piper.

"I wanted something to bargain with. I thought it might be important, so I took our pepper and replaced it. Apparently, they don't check it since they haven't said or made any comments about it to us yet. I'm sure if it had been important, they would have done something by now if they had known." Piper at least was trying to think ahead.

We all knew we needed the truth and the only way to find that out would be to escape from here somehow, and both Piper and Dahlia had been discussing it to each other while Amber had been in the room. Even though I had my private discussion with Piper that night, apparently the two had found they were able to speak to each other privately without the rest of us knowing and now opening up for us to listen since we were involved. However, the rest of us were not sure how they were doing it to speak to them also. None of us knew when they would come in other then to possibly train us. When the next day had come and gone not seeing Amber, we assumed our training was over. Some of us wondered if maybe Amber had told us too much? All we could do for now was sit here and wait for our opportunity, which all of us were nervous but definitely ready.

Chapter Eight

Running

If they were afraid of us using our gifts against them, they could have separated us, except for some reason they wanted us to work together. For the next few weeks, we simply sat in the room waiting for one of them to check on us. It was almost what I would expect from solitary confinement, our food was delivered through a small slit in the door, so we never actually saw who dropped it off and they certainly never spoke. The only way we learned time passed had been from Piper's watch. Apparently, she had taken it off when she slept but kept it in her pocket expecting to put it back on. It was something that hadn't bothered the Gerard, Lydia or Amber that we had.

Hearing footsteps on the other side, it almost sounded like an elephant making its way through the hallway. As the door burst open, we almost expected to be finished right there. Amber made her way into the room motioning for us to follow her. Standing up and doing as she was expecting of us for now, we were surprised with the way she had looked. Her clothes looked ripped possibly getting caught on something. Blood stains were all over her shirt and legs. Her face had the same equal look only with a few dark spots, not bruises but something I couldn't tell what it was, almost as if she had been burned. She even smelled of fire. Not questioning why, she hadn't spoken a word to us, yet we followed her down the hallway past our old room and out the way we had first come in, except this time we took a turn instead of going up the steps leading to the cemetery. The hallway was extremely dark. The floor and walls no longer showed. We each reached out for a hand helping each other through the darkness. Even Piper, who had been in the front of the line held onto Amber's hand as she assisted us out.

There was a light at the end of the tunnel where we could see a very old-looking door, the same style we had come in from. Not sure if we would end up at the same spot since we had all come through the same door in different locations. This door must have a habit of bringing on the worst weather possible. As we ran out still following Amber, it was storming with lightning bolts off in the distance raining almost too thick to see anything. We almost wondered if this was the time to make a break for it since we were all outside and at first it had only looked like Amber with us. At least until Piper looked around telling the rest of us, she hadn't felt it was safe yet. Not sure what was moving in the shadows, all of us noticed them following us but keeping a safe distance. After running for a while, we were able to take in our surroundings. None of us were familiar with this place but then with it as dark out and raining it could have almost been anywhere. The only thing we had to dodge for now was all the trees. We were running through the woods somewhere and we could hear the sloshing from under our feet as the ground seemed to be flooding. The water covered our feet as we ran.

Not far from view there was a little cabin, nothing special looking but large enough to see in the distance. At this point we were all happy to be getting out of the rain. Almost expecting to see Gerard and Lydia inside, there was no one waiting for us. The place hadn't even been decorated with furniture or anything. The rooms were empty with cobwebs and dust all over. The only thing that had been in the room was a pile of clothing. Amber slowly handed a piece from the pile to each of us.

"Is this the place we will be staying at for now?" Not sure

if she should whisper or not, Piper kept her voice low.

"We are only staying here for a little while, we need all of you to change your clothes, and it's much too difficult to keep you hidden when your clothing stands out in the dark." Amber finished handing out our new clothes.

The items were nothing like what we had on. Piper had been the trendiest out of all of us. We were now expected to put on simple black blousy jumpsuits that slid over top with no buttons, only a simple zipper on the back. Most of us had worn jeans and different types of tank tops with designs or bright short sleeve blouse except for Dahlia who had been wearing a bright yellow sundress. Since Rachelle and I had been sleeping at the time, we had grabbed our clothes on the way out not wanting to be stuck in our sleepers. Thank goodness we did since we had no idea how long we would be gone or the fact we couldn't go back. Amber collected our clothes putting them into a black cloth burlap sack. Sitting down on the floor where she pointed to, she came over and joined us.

" "This place is temporary. We'll stay until I'm told to move you again. The ones we're protecting you from discovered our last hideout and staying there wasn't an option." Amber kept her eyes on the door also listening for anything that might possibly make a sound.

She seemed too nervous and jittery as she spoke.

"Would they be the same ones that chased Rachelle and I to the graveyard?" The thought of it made me cringe not that I liked the idea of something following us that I couldn't see in the dark.

"Yes, they are the same. Whoever it is they follow has given them orders to find and kill you. The council and the Augustus family have many enemies, except most do not risk causing trouble. Unfortunately, because of your gifts some feel you are a danger against others, that you could be turned evil and harm humanity and our kind. Others simply feel it is not right for mortals to possess gifts such as yours and my kind is limited with the gifts they possibly pass down. We are trying to change that." As legitimate her explanation sounded, the last part still bothered us, and Amber hadn't looked at us once when she explained it.

We were curious how they could have found us when Amber hadn't even known where we were. The doorway must have been for special use and perhaps led to an actual physical location? None of us were sure even though still curious about it ourselves. Amber hadn't said much to us other than to pace back and forth never once looking outside. Every time she brought up the wording, "our kind" made us wonder if she wasn't considered mortal then what was she?

One thought we had heard once from Piper was how much she missed taking a hot shower, that after all of this she planned on soaking in the hot water as long as she could. It was something we all missed and apparently not something Amber ever seemed to be worried about. Thankfully they supplied a bathroom for us except all it had was the toilette. Apparently, they were not aware mortals liked to stay clean. Only a day had passed while we stayed here leaving again once it was dark out. In the distance covered by the dark we were followed again by who we assumed were guards that helped Amber escort us. They were either there to make sure we did not escape, possibly use our gifts against her now that we were in the outdoors or to actually keep us safe from others attacking us, either way we were not sure yet. Piper's thoughts became rather loud to the rest of us as we were approaching a very nice-looking neighborhood.

"I know where this is; we used to vacation here when we were little. Only a month in the summer and then we would go back home." As soon as she said this we wondered if they had found Taylor.

Where could she be hiding all this time?

"We've been here also, usually in the fall before school would start." Dahlia answered.

Somehow, we had all come here at some point, so why would they bring us to a place that we had been, where others would obviously look to find us or assume we would go? There has to be something that ties this place in. Were we being watched when we were here? Following Amber into the house, the inside looked the exact same as we all had last seen it.

"I'm sure all of you know where your rooms are. I have someone to speak with before we do anything else. We have watchers outside so do not go outside for any reason unless I am with you." Not waiting for a response, she walked out of the room and into the separated kitchen.

Without having to discuss it we had all gone up the stairs and to the end room where we had always stayed before. The one place that always felt safe and comfortable for the first time felt scary. Not wanting to get locked into the room we left the door wide open. Rachelle had gone over to the old cast iron heater. Kneeling down she reached behind searching for something. Smiling as she had found it, pulling out a small cell phone.

"When we last stayed here, I hid it back here except when we left that last time it was rather quick, so I never had the chance to get it. My spare money is still back there." Happy to have her things, Rachelle looked for a pocket which there hadn't been one.

"I have a pocket that detaches; it's where I've kept the ashes." Lifting the bottom of the black pant leg and taking the safety pin off, the pocket came right out.

"If any of the rest of us have spare change we should all pool it together and have Piper put it in her pocket. We might need it if we get a chance to take off." Piper was already raiding her secret spot where she kept her money.

For all of us staying here at different times it's interesting how we never once came across the others hiding spot. It seemed we all have saved money on the side keeping it somewhere. Not sure why, but I had never once thought about who else might have stayed here the other months our own family had not used it. Even if I had personally found someone else's things. I know I never would have touched it. Taking out my own personal storage of cash. I handed it over to Piper as did my sister Rachelle. Making room for the money, we had taken the ashes out and used Taylor's favorite spot for hiding it. Taking off the cover to the wall socket, it had been a normal one. The cover had never been held in very tightly by the nails; just pulling on the outer shell it came off the wall. Putting the little shaker that held the ashes into the hole past the wires and to the side so it would not be seen, we felt it would be safe leaving it there, even if we had to come back and get it later. At least this way, whoever it was they couldn't use it unless we chose to. For coming out of an urn it wasn't very much ashes, not that we had ever had a reason to measure someone's ashes before.

Putting the money away we realized we hadn't heard one sound from downstairs. Who would Amber be speaking to if there were no voices? We could always hear our parents talking in the kitchen, even looking out the window we could still see the shadows moving around. Slowly we all walked down the stairs. Our excuse if we were caught coming down would be to ask when Amber was going to be coming upstairs to talk with us. At least it sounded like a legitimate enough reason. Down at the bottom of the stairs, we still heard no footsteps or voices. The room was completely empty. Making our way to the kitchen where she had gone, the room was empty also. There had only been a living room, dining room, family room, bedroom and bathroom left on this floor, and all were empty. No sign of Amber even though we could still see the shadows outside watching over the house. The closet door in the bathroom had been left slightly open; it was always difficult to close unless you slammed it shut. We were always told it would be fixed but every year it was still the same, so we never bothered using it. Opening it up to peak in there was only a bath towel, hand towel and a half-used ladies red nail polish that seemed stuck to the counter in the corner.

Dahlia pulled at the nail polish which refused to move only tipping with a bit of a snap to the side. Letting go instantly thinking she had broken part of the counter trying to take it off, all the boards slid to the side moving out of the way making space for a person to almost stand in their place. That is if there hadn't been a huge hole that was now below. Neither of us could tell what was at the bottom of the dark hole. Apparently, who ever put this here didn't see any need for lighting. While we debated if we wanted to check it out, Dahlia had gone to the kitchen drawer grabbing a flashlight. The owners who leased the place out always kept flashlights in case the power went out. It had many times; the wind would get rather strong and cold being so close to the water. Dahlia decided to go down first, shining her flashlight downward there were little stakes sticking out of the wall. Not exactly the best to be using to climb down except there was nothing else to use other than to drop down and none of us wanted to risk that without being able to see the bottom.

The stakes were embedded firmly in the wall, much like railroad spikes, though they didn't extend far. We moved slowly and carefully from one to the next, afraid to lose our footing and just as afraid that someone might come up and catch us before we escaped.

Piper was the last one who was coming down; before she had she closed the closet door behind her in case anyone would look around the house for us. This way if they knew about the secret hole, they would only look because of that. As soon as we were all on the ground, we had the same expression. The stench made me feel like throwing up. Trying to control my stomach.

"Willow, I can barely breathe." Rachelle looked panicked.

"Pull your shirt over your nose and mouth, hopefully that makes it bearable." I wasn't sure but hoped it would work.

I pulled the front of the shirt up and over my nose hoping it would at least help a little. I could still smell it. The air was thick with rot and sewage, like something dead had melted into the walls. I gagged as the taste of it settled on my tongue, bitter and oily, refusing to go away. We didn't need light to tell us we were in a sewer. The walls and rooms looked like large pipes, far too many to decide or really to know what direction to go in. Randomly choosing a direction, we all decided to follow it wherever it led us. After a while we started wishing we had gone down one of the other directions. The stench was getting much worse the further we went. Eventually we came to the end of the tunnel only to find the worst site we had ever witnessed. I could no longer handle it, turning around so I wouldn't keep looking at the site, not that it helped since it was now permanently etched inside my brain. I finally threw up and wasn't the only one. Piper was the only one who was able to handle it, she was more curious then afraid. As she walked across the crackling bones. Piper took a look at the few bodies that had been left intact. After she was done, we all walked very quickly back the way we had come. As soon as we were far enough away Piper stopped us.

"We can't risk going back upstairs, we need to find a way out of here. If it's truly a sewer system, there has to be an exit. I've figured out what they are." Piper's voice quivered slightly.

None of us wanted to challenge what she found out. Her inner thoughts loud and clear, we kept hearing the words "vampires" over and over again. Picking random tunnels to go down, we wanted to make sure we didn't get to lost, not that it was easy. Each tunnel looked to be the same except for size. A few were rather large we could walk down with no problem other than the water running along the ground, only a few areas were really bad. Then there were the small tunnels we had to get on our hands and knees and crawl through the horrible stench. At least we hadn't run into any more bodies, the only problem had been the tunnels, they felt endless as if we would never find the end again. By now we were sure they knew we were missing and probably looking for us. Something we didn't want to risk is someone catching us no matter who they were.

Willow asked silently to Piper, "how can you be sure they are vampires?" Even though we were all thinking it made sense.

Without speaking a word out loud Taylor answered, "there were two puncture wounds on the side of the neck directly over the vein. It's the same with the other four bodies that are down there. Same place and same puncture wounds." As she spoke the last word, her voice trailed off a little.

We had been walking around in the pipes for several hours that it would almost be daylight outside. Only once had we thought we were caught when we heard sounds coming to-wards our same direction except it turned out to be a rather large rat. Finally, we came to a center room in the shape of a square with each wall marked by the street name. There was also a small cage protecting a generator, at least we assumed that was what it had been from the looks and sound. Directly above it had been regular steps leading upward to the street above. Hoisting each other up to get to the top of the generator, we reached down to help the last one to get up, each taking the steps upward we were hoping the manhole covering wouldn't be too difficult. The cover hadn't wanted to budge an inch. Trying to climb past Taylor as she moved downward out of the way on the steps, I focused the best I could. As gross as it was, I couldn't stop if I had wanted to get us out bad enough. Forcing the wind to whip around us strong enough, we wound up getting doused by the sewage water. Forcing as much wind as I could. The manhole cover shot off almost blowing us up and out with it. Stepping foot on pavement, dripping wet and smelling like the sewer, we could take a much-needed deep breath.

"If they are vampires, we would be slightly safe as long as we stay in the light, but we are going to need a safer place to hide at night, not sure about the rest of you, but I desperately need a shower now!" Piper was still fixated on the shower but then now we all were.

"I think I know of a place we can go to. Rachelle and I had a substitute teacher for a year while our regular teacher was gone on maternity leave. He was always willing to help with anything, almost like family. Our parents liked him, and I know we can trust him." It was the only choice I could think of unless one of the other girls could think of something.

"Sounds good enough to me, as long as he has a shower." Piper was all ready to go.

Being careful walking along the sidewalk we had a couple people walk past us giving us rather strange looks. If I hadn't known where we'd been, I would've been thinking the same thing and making the same face. And if they *had* known, the smell wouldn't be the strangest part. They'd be wondering what kind of girls crawled out of a sewer and thought it was normal. At least we were not under a spell anymore to keep us cloaked from others seeing us. Unfortunately, we were being seen now at our worst.

Not wanting to stay out in the open for too long, we stopped and paid for a bus trip to our teacher's house. Most would smell us getting on and move away to another seat. The only good thing about the doorway Amber and the others used had been the distance it covered. At least the summer house was only an hour away. Rachelle and I lived an hour from our teacher's home and two hours from the summer house. As soon as we were there, the bus driver stood up announcing our stop no doubt thankful not to smell us anymore. As we had passed him, we could see the fabric spray he held in his hand along with a washcloth. Normally I would feel incredibly embarrassed but not this time, it was worth it to escape. At least the one we were going to see only lived about two miles from the bus stop and there was plenty of daylight left. However, his home wasn't exactly in the shape we were expecting. Instead of being welcomed by the overwhelming scent of lilac, it had been extremely light as if they hadn't been here in a while.

"Do you think it's just coincidence or do you think they did this to everyone we know?" Rachelle was looking over the place stunned.

"Either way, hopefully his shower is still working, and they have some clothes left intact, I doubt anyone would expect us to go in with it looking like this." Piper was much more eager than we were to walk in.

Following behind her looking everything over, the place had been completely trashed. The cushions of the chairs and couch were torn to shreds along with the stuffing falling all over the floor. Mirrors, table, chairs, banister to the staircase was smashed. Checking out each room there was a lot of things left behind so whoever did this obviously hadn't found what they were looking for. There were no signs left behind what had happened to him. Even his wife's clothing was spread all over the room. Each of us grabbing an outfit, we had used the two showers they had, taking turns either showering or keeping watch in case anyone had come into the house. The entire time we had been here there was no one around outside. It felt so good to get cleaned up and new clothes. The most we could find was either jogging suits or sundresses. Apparently, she had also preferred darker clothing, not black like the jumpsuits we had been stuck wearing but more jewel tone colors.

"It's so sad to see the house like this; Thea had given me piano lessons here in the living room." Piper was very depressed looking around the room, especially to see the piano destroyed.

"I know what you mean; she gave me lessons here also." I wished I knew the reason behind the destruction.

"Willow, I know we haven't been here before, but what was your teacher's name? Thea sounds familiar, the owners of the summer house we stayed in was owned by an older couple and the woman's name was Thea." Hannah seemed rather surprised to hear the name.

"The names were Thea and Drezin." Rachelle had taken a breath before saying Drezin's name.

"We know them also then, Hannah and I would, and they had babysat us when we were little when our parents would go out at night during our summer vacation." Dahlia smiled, knowing who we were talking about this whole time even though a look of sadness had taken over.

"Taylor and I know who they were also; they had also watched us when we were little. Last time we had seen them was about four years ago." Piper seemed rather sad when she spoke.

We all missed them wondering what had happened to them, even though it did feel strange we all knew them. It was almost as if they were our missing link that connected us all in one way or another. At least there wasn't any blood around to show they had been killed, but then there wasn't much left in one full piece. The closest thing had been the bed; it was mainly on the floor since the springs had been broken. Straightening out the bed and putting some bed sheets on it, we planned on sleeping here for tonight and hopefully we would be able to think what to do next. It was difficult to know what to do when you didn't know who to trust or where it was safe anymore. The world was suddenly looking very different. It felt strange snooping around their house without them at home, but then it even felt stranger looking through their personal things. The rock collection she had was gone, even though the case was still here. We searched every inch of the house and found nothing. It was already getting dark and none of us wanted to risk being seen inside walking around. Keeping the flashlights with us and all the lights in the house were turned off, we hoped to keep it looking as if we were never here.

For a moment of panic, we heard footsteps. It had been in the hallway behind us before we heard a door close. We all looked at each other wondering if we should find out if it was Thea and Drezin or leave hoping to find a safer place to hide. Who else would be coming in here but then they seemed like they were being rather quiet?

Piper chose to check it out asking we stay hidden in one of the side rooms, she didn't want to risk all of us if she was caught. She felt it was easier for one to escape or at least worth only one and not everyone. We stayed close in case she needed us; we would help her. Watching Piper walk closer to the door, listening by pressing her ear on the door, she hadn't heard anything moving around. Turning the knob slowly hoping no one on the other side would see it, she slowly opened the door. We had already searched this room before; it looked like it had at one time been an office before it was destroyed. Walking halfway into the room and almost jumping out of her skin, Piper had arms wrap around her pulling her in and hugging her tight.

"I can't believe you found me." Taylor squealed out of delight of seeing her sister.

"Have you been here the whole time? Did you see who did this? I have so many questions, but I can't believe your actually standing here. I finally have you back.

The door swung open as the rest of us were worried what the squeal was from and the shuffling noise. At least until we had seen Piper crying holding another girl, we assumed to be her sister. She certainly looked like the rest of us, especially Piper.

"If your Taylor, do you know who Kendra is? Have you seen anyone here?" Rachelle was curious how she found the place.

"I thought it would be a safe place. I was at a friend's house when they had people break into the house, and with the huge storm that started creating a tremendous noise, lightning, rain, and fog, I took off running. I hoped they wouldn't see me; I could barely see through the fog. There was a strange door that showed up in the middle of the road, but I hopped into the first car that was going by. I had an intense feeling I needed to get away from there. I've had people find me occasionally, it's how I have this scar on my arm. I made my way here, but someone already trashed it before I got here. Since I've been here, I haven't seen anyone. I've kept all the lights off so no one passing by would know I was here. This was the home of our old babysitter and family friend. When mom and dad were not answering their phones, I came here." Taylor explained quickly not letting go of her sister once.

After talking for a while explaining what has happened so far and what we learned, we were all yawning. Instead of staying in the room we first picked, Taylor showed us the bedroom she was staying in, it looked like a hallway closet but instead it opened up to a larger untouched bedroom. The bed was comfortable and most of us couldn't wait to fall asleep.

Closing the bedroom door, we had all laid rather close to each other almost feeling a little safer. Only Piper had taken the longest to fall asleep. For the first time she could feel herself feel afraid to sleep, hoping this whole thing wasn't a dream and we were back in those white empty disinfected looking rooms. Watching Rachelle and her sister Willow hold hands as they slept, Taylor slept with her head on Piper's shoulder. Even Dahlia, who happened to fall asleep first, was squished in rather close to Hannah. Finally, feeling tired enough where my eye lids were fighting to stay awake was when I finally gave in and fell asleep also.

As the night went on no one bothered us or appeared to be in the house. What had woken us all up, pretty much at the same time had been the bright light coming in from the window. We made sure all the windows were closed and covered before we went to sleep so no one would be able to look in and see us. Almost jumping to our feet, we knew it was daylight, but who would have opened the window? Was Drezin or Thea here? The only hint that someone had even been in the same room with us had been the curtains on the windows were pulled back and someone placed warm blankets on each of us. Ready for the worst, we carefully looked into the hallway. No one was waiting there for us and neither had anyone been waiting in the other rooms, almost as if we were not what they were looking for, so they either left or knew who we were and felt we were safe being left there.

"Someone knows we are here, and we need to leave right away." Taylor had been right unfortunately none of us knew where to go.

"I wonder who it was, if it had been Gerard and Lydia, they would have grabbed us again. Who would have been nice enough to leave blankets on us when we couldn't find them ourselves, unless it was someone who didn't realize what was going on here? That's generally an act of kindness, not of someone who wants to hurt us." Piper was no doubt trying to sound positive.

"How could someone not realize this isn't the safest or a normal situation to find a bunch of girls in? If something happened to Drezin and Thea, then we could be held accountable since we are here and don't know what happened to them." Dahlia brought up another problem we hadn't wanted to face.

It was a common thought we were all having. If something did happen to them, if we were caught here, we could be held accountable for it.

"Sorry to interrupt your conversation but we had a couple

questions we would like to ask all of you." The voice was rather calming.

Turning quickly, we all looked at him almost frozen in our tracks not sure if we should run or stay put. Trying to act as if we were not afraid even though we had no idea if this person could be trusted or not. For now, he wasn't making any sudden moves, he actually sat down on part of the broken chair with his hands relaxed on his legs showing no signs of a threat at all.

"What can we help you with?" Sounding kind, acting as if nothing was out of the ordinary, Rachelle put on a rather good act.

"My name is Charley, and I was hoping you would know what happened to my brother since you're in his house. Rumors have a way of spreading that he got himself into trouble beyond what he can handle. After seeing the condition of his house and a few other places leads us to believe the rumors are true. Sophie, my wife is checking on a few friends in the area right now." Charley sat still, sensing the girls were nervous, not wanting to make them feel worse but to put them at ease.

"My name is Rachelle, and this is my sister Willow. These are my other sisters Dahlia, Hannah, Piper, and Taylor. We needed his help, so we came here looking for him also, but we found his place like this. None of us have any idea where he is or how to find him." Rachelle pointed out each of us then softly explained why we were here and what we had been running from.

Before speaking again or answering us, he seemed to be thinking it over. Shaking his head a few times as he thought made us all curious what he was thinking. The front door had opened slowly; he hadn't made one move as he was still considering what Rachelle told him. A young-looking woman walked through the door carefully stepping over the objects as she made her way over to the gentleman we had been speaking with. We assumed she was Sophie his wife he had just told us about.

"Sorry, where are my manners, I guess this mess threw me off just a little more than I expected. I'm not used to the messes my older brother seems to get himself into. I realize you don't have any reason to trust us, especially after what you have been through. Except it's not safe to stay here, whoever did this will no doubt come again if they think they might have possibly missed anything or connect why all of you might be here. Our family isn't too far and you're welcome to come with us. We can protect you. You won't be stuck with us and can leave at any time." Charley tried to sound as reassuring as he could even though he was still troubled with what was happening with his brother.

"There are a few safe places we can stop at if you need to make any phone calls before we get to our home?" Sophie tried to relax us letting us know we were not being rushed.

"There isn't anyone to call, Drezin was our only person to contact, we weren't sure if he could actually help us, we were just hoping he would know what to do. We think that Gerard and Lydia might have had our parents killed. Or as they kept saying our protectors, there's been so much going on, we didn't know who to trust and what they have actually done or are trying to use to scare us." Taylor sounded depressed when she spoke.

"We will do everything we can to help you. For some reason I have a feeling Drezin is in the middle of all of this and as soon as we find him, we might get some answers. The sun is much lighter right now and it would be best if we left now before the sun is to bright out." Sophie's voice was so soothing we almost felt completely relaxed.

Charley seemed quite a bit like Drezin in personality, just the way he held himself, the way he spoke and even his mannerisms.

"How far is your home from here?" Taylor wondered if we would need a bus or if they had a car that would fit us all.

"For us it's not very far at all, it might be difficult for you to walk, and we didn't exactly bring a vehicle this time. We were not expecting to stay long enough for others to be up and around to notice." Sophie looked at Charley almost as if she was looking for an answer.

"I think if they are going to feel comfortable with us and trust us, then we need to be upfront about a few things. I'm not sure how they are going to take it?" This was the first time Charley actually seemed uncomfortable.

"We understand certain things can be a bit scary when you're first introduced to it, especially when you are not familiar and might have certain ideas in your head about it from either movies or stories you might have heard." Sophie had spoken softly and slowly for all of us to follow along. We had an idea we might not like what we heard.

"How well did you know Drezin? I'm guessing enough to at least trust him. How would you feel if you found out he had a massive secret he was keeping from those around him?" Charley asked a few questions fielding how we would respond before they told us something else.

"I've known him my entire life, what has been going on for the past few months has never been like anything we have experienced or been introduced to before. It's the first time I've ever known the supernatural to be real. I've read books before, but they all say different things, some are similar, but I guess I never took it that seriously." Taylor was the only one who was capable of speaking at the moment.

"We don't exactly care for the term ourselves, however, it's something society has labeled us with. Personally, I like the term immortal. We do everything we can to blend in and not to stand out, we do everything we can never to harm anyone." Sophie's explanation had us paying attention waiting for the bomb she was about to drop on us.

"To put it short, we can definitely keep you safe from anyone that would wish to harm you. We want to find my brother Drezin to make sure he and his wife Thea are safe also. However, we are not mortal like the rest of you, and neither is Drezin. in term we are vampires, and we can move you around rather quickly before anyone can catch up to us except, we want to make sure we let you know what you are getting into and not shock you with it." Charley was the first to break the big news to us as we stood there not sure what to say now.

"We won't be locked up and can leave at any time?" Taylor was thinking over the options.

"How do we know we're not falling for another trap like we did the first time? We only went with the creepy guy because he was the only one at the time not trying to kill us. At least until we were locked up and they told us they were going to kill us anyway once they were done with us." Rachelle spoke her concerns that we were all thinking.

"We don't have anything to give you to relieve your fears, we only have our word that we can help and won't harm you. If we intended on kidnapping, killing or doing anything harmful to you, we could have done that while you were sleeping." Taking a picture out of his pocket, Charley handed it to Rachelle.

Looking the picture over, Rachelle passed it around until we had all taken a look at it. It was a picture of Charley when he was much younger, Drezin no matter what age he looked the same. Then there were several others in the picture that Charley described as their younger and older siblings.

"You said we would travel much faster? What way did you mean? The others had a door that showed up and brought us to wherever they wanted us." I was curious if they had something similar.

"We don't have anything like that. It would be by piggyback and lots of wind in your face. Most seem to enjoy it unless of course you have motion sickness, then it's not so great. We have a couple other family members here that would help us move you to the house where you would be safe." Charley had smiled when he said this.

Not waiting too long there were three more people that came into the room. Lorah had introduced herself as Charley's sister; the other had been Lucian his grandson, even though when the two stood next to each other it was difficult to believe Charley was actually older. They looked to be the exact same age. The third had been Nichole, Charley's daughter, and Lucian's mother, she looked younger then Lucian. The last one standing there was Anthony, we all had instant crushes on him and were thankful he couldn't read our thoughts. He was Nichole's husband and Lucians father. All of us had gone to the backyard; Lorah made it clear the path home would be open for now and still under enough shade to make it safely. Something we all intended on asking when we were back, why they avoided the light if they were visiting us during the day. We had so many questions we wanted to ask and hoped they might feel comfortable and willing enough to answer them for us. They could have been lying to us for all we knew but at least they were much more relaxed, willing to do anything to make us comfortable and if they had wanted to kill or control us, Charley was right, they could have done it while we were sleeping.

It did feel strange at our age climbing up on someone's back, holding on around their neck. They let us know to hold on as tight as we could, and they would also hold us as much as they could. We were not to let go and not to worry about choking them since we couldn't possibly hold on tight enough for that. Before we knew it, we were off and sailing through the woods out back, trees were passing so fast it was more of a blur. I hated to admit but it was a little more fun than I thought it would be. We had even heard in her thoughts how excited Hannah and Dahlia were enjoying it. They were even going to try to help us find our missing sister Kendra and find out information about her and if she needed help. Charley had a feeling that Drezin was securing hiding places, it might have been the last thing Drezin was working on before he had a chance to get to the rest of us.

Chapter Nine

Temporary Homes

Charley had been correct; it hadn't taken us long to get there. It was difficult taking in anything as everything shot past us so quickly, occasionally there was a bright color that would stand out. Growing up, I had an idea in my head about vampires, zombies and other creatures and how they would live. I'd imagined stone towers and echoing halls, something dark and holy and terrifying all at once. Instead, the house was warm and calm, more like the homes back where Rachelle and I lived. The normalcy of it loosened something tight in my chest.

I guess if you wait long enough, eventually everything comes back into style. I always loved the older Victorian style homes. We lived in a newer subdivision, however, most of the homes looked the same even though they had some character to them. Charley opened the door waiting for us as Sophie, Nichole, Anthony, Lorah and Lucian had already walked in leaving the five of us to take our time. No one ever tried to rush us in.

The only hint the house would have been old had been from the furniture and paintings that hung on the wall. We weren't sure how many would be inside except it was much more than we thought there would be. Drezin always seemed like a very soft-spoken person who was laid back but not into crowds. He was more of a loner then socializing with the other teachers or students. The times he came out of his shyness seemed to be when he had us working on a project or a subject he was passionate about. Science was really his love, and everyone had picked up on it. His brother Charley reminded us of him the way he spoke; I couldn't wait to see what the rest of his family was like. There were quite a few people in the room that had been talking until we walked in silencing the room. Not sure if it was a good thing or if they were curious who we were.

"Feel free to sit down and relax." Charley pointed out the couches and chairs for us.

"Thank you." Barely squeaked out as we sat down in different places all trying to at least stick together if we could.

"It's always nice to have guests." Aiden seemed unsure since they had been discussing Drezin and wasn't sure if he could continue with the new guests.

"They are here because of Drezin. At least they are looking for him. I believe for the same reason we are." Sophie had spoken rather calmly letting Aiden know it was alright to continue.

"To catch our guests up on what we know so far, all of Drezin's houses, summer homes or hobby spots have either been stripped down, destroyed, searched through to one degree or another. Apparently, he has a huge experiment that he's been working on, and a few members of the council want their hands on it and the Augustus family is now starting to get involved which is never a good sign." Aiden spoke rather clearly but quickly.

"Most of the family hadn't even known he was still alive until a few years ago, personally I had but then it was because I worked for Valafar and he's part of the Augustus family. Drezin thought he was keeping his family safe by not letting the rest of us know he was still around." Lorah filled the girls in a little more about their family connection.

"Since everyone else is summing up their connections, most of us knew we were adopted. For Piper it was a surprise to find out, especially to have it confirmed. We were all born on the same day and same hospital, we all have different gifts that apparently Gerard and Lydia wanted us to do something with except they never did explain it. The only thing we found out was from another woman named Amber, she said we were experiments. We hid some ashes; we were not sure if they were important or not but figured it would be hard to do anything with them if those two couldn't find them. After being locked up for so long we all thought of Drezin and Thea and felt they would be the safest people to try to get help from. They were always involved with our families in one way or another." Rachelle had spoken for the rest of us.

"We told the girls as long as they wanted to stay here, we could keep them safe. Not sure where else to look right now, last, I had known Drezin was alive and then rumors started floating that he had died... again. It could be a rumor, or it could be true but if it was a rumor it doesn't seem like so many would be searching for him." Charley seemed rather frustrated.

While the rest of the family discussed Drezin and his wife more, four members of Charley's family took Taylor back to the last house we were hiding at with Amber, careful in case anyone was following. Showing them where the ashes had been hidden, Lewis took the ashes and took off to have a friend to determine who's they belonged to, even vampires at some point have had their DNA or blood drawn somewhere. It was almost our odd way of keeping track of family lines and who was the next generation or the original. Carefully heading back to the house, we all waited as patiently as we could to find out who exactly they had found.

Over the next two days there were several family members and a few friends coming and going at times reporting on the Augustus family and what they were up to. The family tried to keep us busy with either art projects which Nichole taught or letting us try to grow something in Sophie's garden. The time had gone rather quickly as they kept us busy, and our minds occupied. It was beginning to feel as if we had gone off to camp, even spending a few hours by the pool in the sun felt so good after the nightmare we had been through. The family was extremely kind always looking for any way to make us feel more comfortable. Unfortunately, they hadn't seen, heard or found our sister Kendra yet.

The council seemed to be rather silent, not being active at all. Lorah's boss made an appearance; he was the most impressive looking man we had ever seen. Not a matter of being tall, however he had such broad shoulders that he not only dwarfed us in size, but he could also have taken on a polar bear. Dressed in a black double-breasted suit he could have walked off a cover of a magazine. Valafar looked at us rather strangely shaking his head a bit. He hadn't looked angry he looked confused when he saw us. Charley spoke quietly to him when he had first come in. After he made his way over to us pulling a chair to sit on.

"Not exactly what I was expecting when I heard Drezin was messing around with experiments again. Usually, his experiments look as if they are out of control, he seems to handle them just fine, it's usually why we don't bother him. Honestly. I was prepared for deformed. Hideous, even. This is… not that…. Charley told me that all of you have mainly dealt with Amber. Kind of surprised they have her working for them since she's so loyal to the council; they must be keeping her in the dark about what they are working on. Otherwise, she would have turned them into the council." Sitting back relaxed, Valafar seemed to be looking all of us over.

"Has he done experiments like us before?" Taylor was hoping she might get an answer.

"Nothing like you, usually it's either chemical or technical. Always messing around with computers and creating gadgets that most of the time are harmless or have little use. Occasionally he comes up with a good one that my family will use." Valafar hadn't exactly answered her question but at least he didn't seem opposed to answering anything.

"I can't help it, but Drezin seems so different from the way everyone here talks about him. If he has all these places, then why did he teach?" Rachelle asked.

"Most likely to keep an eye on you, he hadn't needed another summer home. Which is why he no doubt made them available for your families. They would rent it out for different times in the summer making it easier for Drezin to keep an eye on you but low attention so no one else would notice." Valafar was very clear and to the point.

While we had been talking, not only Valafar, but the rest of the family had stopped talking as everyone looked at the front door almost expecting someone to come through it at any moment. We tensed up feeling we might be attacked if they were paying this much attention, but then we had wondered how they always knew someone was coming before we had? Not having to wait very long. Lewis walked in the door with the rest of the family members who had gone out earlier. The expression on their faces let us know before words, it wasn't going to be good news. Standing in the center of the room as everyone watched him, Lewis seemed like he was at a loss for words until Charley told him to hurry and spit out the news. Taking a deep breath, he said it.

"The ashes you found, they belong to Katherine, curse and all." Lewis said as his voice was rather heavy sounding and the rest of the family gasped at the same time.

"How exactly did you find these?" Everyone looked at us making us a bit nervous, especially after they said, 'curse and all.'

"It's when we looked around our first day before they started locking us in a single room. I had kept the pepper shaker from the first room. It was empty and I thought if they had one less item to use against us or at least it would slow down whatever they were doing we would live longer." Taylor's usually forceful voice came out rather low and almost shaky.

"I highly doubt Drezin had any of this in mind when he started this, for once I think he was doing something personal, and it wound up getting planned by others for the wrong reason. He might already have Kendra; he is great at hiding." Lorah didn't like the idea the girls were being treated as an experiment and not as people, for once she was disappointed hoping to be proven wrong by Drezin.

"Hard to believe the curse put on her was the inability to die, seems more of a curse to everyone else. I don't get how they thought using the girls would reanimate her? She needs the right elements and all her ashes together; these are not all of them even though it's a significant piece. I thought she wanted death if she didn't have complete power, why would they try to bring her back if she would only wipe them out?" Lucian asked curious why someone would try to recreate something that would mean their final end.

"They might be trying to get something from her, or they don't realize how dangerous she is. I think with their plans they are starting to feel more invincible then they are, hard to believe they would think she would help them." Even Charley seemed surprised they would try to bring her back.

"We have a more serious problem to deal with; it would be better if we moved to a more secure area since they know the girls are gone along with the ashes." Anthony had been the last one to get back from his rounds.

"Too many know we live here and if they find out we have the girls and the ashes. We could be an easy target. Besides, we all know how ruthless Gerard gets when he's after something, he'll kill whatever is in his way to get what he wants. He certainly earned his reputation; the only reason he lets someone live is if there's something he wants from them." Lucian made it clear he agreed with Anthony and the need to move to another area.

The McAllister family was used to moving for many different reasons. Not taking long to pack, Nichole grabbed extra sweaters for us to wear telling us what direction we were going, we would need them. Apparently, there was a place they rented from another family much further north, further than we were expecting. We were beginning to wonder if there were any other people living up here at all. Eventually we passed a few towns, the sparse little homes along the way until the woods were getting thicker. There were times I could feel the branches of trees whip against my legs as they ran so fast. I was positive that I would either have cuts from the branches or at least bruises, but then if we stayed behind and were found, they would be doing far worse to us than a few bruises.

As soon as we stopped, I had to catch my breath, not just from the wind whipping in my face making it difficult to breath, but also from holding my breath so often, something I tend to do when I get nervous. As I looked at the other girls, I noticed I wasn't the only one. We stopped at a rather modest-looking house, a little small to fit all of us but then that might have made it safer for now. The rest of the McAllister family had gone in leaving us to trail behind. Every time something changed, I felt more nervous. Our entire lives changed; none of us even had the time to grieve losing our families that we had known. We had to keep moving simply because we had no idea if we even had a future left. The house was definitely packed tight with so many people, not that everyone stayed. Quite a few would leave every so often, many times for reasons we were not sure of. After a few days it was only Charley, Sophie, and our group. The others were only going to come back if they heard any news or to warn us if we needed to move again. The family felt it would be safer if there were less of us here to attract attention while the others were still careful in case there was an attempt to use them to find us.

Over a period of a week, we found out more about Drezin and what he was working on, possibly that Lorah thought she might have located him. At least this gave us some sort of hope to find out what he originally planned for us. Sophie had taken dahlia, Piper, and Taylor to the waterfall. Even if there wasn't very much to do around here at least it was a fun spot to go. There was a small cave underneath the waterfall, walking in quite a ways there were little streams of water coming out of the rock and at the halfway point of the tunnel there was a large natural pool. You could feel the water draining or if you swam to the bottom, you would see the small hole the water left through. The pool was constantly filling up from another stream. Outside the water would have been far too cold to swim in accept the water in the cave was much warmer and felt great swimming in.

Rachelle and I had already spent every day for the last week there; so, for the next week, instead, we stayed behind at the house. Charley left for a little while with Lucian and Lorah leaving us alone in the house. After having so many around and always heading to one place or the other, constantly having them feel as if they have to entertain us, it was nice to sit down and relax. Rachelle grabbed a book to read while I was still looking through the rest. Nothing was catching my attention other than a quick blur outside. Walking near the window to see if they made it back already. I hadn't seen anyone and if it had been them, they would have entered the door already. Not having to say a word or try to pass a silent thought to Rachelle, she had already set her book down on the couch looking over at me concerned.

Being careful not to stand directly in sight of the window. I had drawn the shade closed. Something was out there, and it wasn't making itself known. Rachelle was already standing next to me. Leaving the living room and walking for the laundry room. There was a door leading outside from the pantry, we made sure it was locked not that it could keep out vampires or anything else that might be strong. if anything, we could join Sophie, at least it would be safer instead of it being just two of us. Before we could even get to the back door it was being opened not that anyone showed in the window. Taking a quick step back holding onto my sister's hand, we waited for someone to come into the house. There still wasn't anything other than a small can that now was letting out smoke; the front door now burst open having a few cans expelling the same black smoke. The ground started to shake, using each other we were able to keep our footing without falling to the ground. Pulling our shirts over our nose making sure not to breathe in whatever they had filled the room with, we felt along the wall for the nearest window. Opening it up. There was so much dirt flying around outside, neither of us could figure it out other than it was concentrated around the house only, there were such small glimpses past that were clear enough to see, not that we knew what was causing the heavy sandstorm that was swarming the house along with violent tremors. Neither of us wanted to risk staying in the house but it also didn't look safe to go out into that mess. The ground shook again as the rest of the windows in the house had now burst. Something shot past the window quickly.

Sitting down on the floor making sure whatever it was hadn't seen us as the ground continued to tremble. It had been rather bright, and Sophie hadn't planned on coming back until the evening, around the same time as Charley, Lorah and Lucian had. We didn't expect anyone this soon. Now it was pitch black outside. Far too dark to even see the trees that surrounded the house. Making our way back into the kitchen we opened the cupboard door below the sink. It had the most space, squeezing in the best we could. We held the door closed hoping no one would either find us in here or think to look here for us. We could feel the house continue to shake, that's when the loud crashing came. Loud sounds we had never heard before as if the house was being torn apart by a tornado.

After a while the loudest of the sounds had stopped with only a few pieces of glass still breaking or a board dropping. Shoving our feet against the cupboard door we could barely open it except enough to look out. There were shingles from the roof in the kitchen and the light from outside was shining in again, the darkness had disappeared. Now we could smell smoke. Someone set the house on fire. The pieces of the house that had fallen in were shoving against the cupboard so hard making it difficult to get out. No matter how hard we pushed, it wasn't going to budge. The smell of smoke was coming even closer until we could see the flames shadow in the distance; slight orange pieces would spark out from the wood burning. Now getting sprayed with water the sink suddenly shot straight up and thrown away from us. Aiden had been leaning over us giving us a hand pulling us out of our tight squeeze. Once we were out, we looked around. There was barely anything left of the house. If we had stayed by the window, we definitely would have been dead.

"This is Emma, she's my wife. We are going to move both of you out of here as quickly as possible before they realize anyone lived." Without waiting for a response Aiden whisked Rachelle up onto his back as Emma stood in front of me waiting for me to put my arms around her neck and get secure.

"Who do you think attacked the house??" I was curious if they knew.

"A few members of the council have found out what Gerard and Lydia are up to. There is a war between council members who are for or against and the Augustus family is now involved. They've sent out searchers to find you, them and the half apparition of Katherine." Not taking another moment to speak another word they were off and running.

Staying in the shade the majority of the time they tried to avoid towns as much as possible. Otherwise, we were stuck walking, keeping an eye out for spy's and any other danger that might notice us. We hadn't gone to another house as I thought we would, instead we were stopping inside of a cave for the night. We traveled all day and even crossed a large body of water. After traveling so much and not knowing where we were, neither of us had any idea what body of water we had passed other than it had started to get warmer. At first, I felt a wave of panic when I had seen the water, except it hadn't felt as cold as I was expecting, it was still chilly but bearable. Emma had a change of clothes for us in the cave; setting up the screen we had some privacy while we changed. We hadn't felt cold until we stopped long enough to notice. Sitting down against the wall of blankets, Emma handed us both a cup of hot cocoa. It looked as if we would be camping for the night with the pot being hung over a light fire and only a few items in the cave with no tent or sleeping bag.

"We won't be staying here long. One of the other girls sensed you were scared, and they took precautions before they felt the ground moving. Right now, they are safe and will join up with us in a few days." Emma tried to sound reassuring.

"Lorah also found Drezin and Thea; they will be joining us

in a few days once we get to the safe spot. We have to take care of the problem with Katherine once and for all, otherwise, we may never have a chance with the Augustus family. There's no way of hiding from them forever." Aiden hadn't sounded to reassuring even though we would prefer to know the truth then have it sugar coated and find out we had little chance.

"Rachelle and willow, if either of you are hungry, we do have food in the basket here for you." Aiden pointed out the small basket in the corner.

"Thank you." Rachelle replied first.

"Do you know where we are heading to?" I wondered since we were not there and already traveled quite a distance.

"Yes, we do except we would rather not say yet in case we get overheard. It's easier to change our course and drop someone if they are following rather than let the others know they have to relocate again." Aiden had made sense even though I was beginning to feel lost not knowing.

"Not to worry, both of you will find out soon enough." Emma's soft voice was reassuring.

When we had been traveling here, Emma was out in front of Aiden most likely since she was able to run faster. I could smell her perfume; it was the same scent our mother wore, and Thea had always worn. I was beginning to think it was a family scent. Not feeling like talking, we sat leaning against the rock wall letting what happened today sink in. It was incredibly faint but both of us could recognize who exactly the voice was coming from. Dahlia was reassuring us they were alright and were almost on their way there. She explained how they were swimming and Piper felt a huge swell of panic, realizing it was coming from both of us. Telling Sophie right away they had taken off to the furthest end of the tunnel. By the time they reached the end the tunnel, it started to cave in from all the ground tremors. Aiden and Emma had already been on the way to visit and now were there to make sure we were alive since they hadn't known if the attack was directed at us. There was a body lying outside the tunnels they had come out of, a member of Gerard's guard.

The second body belonged to one of the council member's guard. Even though the McAllister family could not read our thoughts, a few of them could converse with each other letting them know the conditions. The other girls had been terrified hearing the condition of the house wondering if we were inside when it had been attacked. It sounded as if there was a war going on outside and the house happened to get caught in the middle of it, no doubt they were after us while we were still in there except, they had been ambushed themselves.

Aiden and Emma had been used to sleeping during the day instead of at night, even though they could walk in the light as long as it wasn't overly strong. Rachelle and I had taken a while to fall asleep. It wasn't exactly comfortable leaning against the wall but then no worse than when we had slept in the white room with no chairs and on a hard floor. Gently being nudged we were off again for quite a distance. The landscape was very unfamiliar, and we hadn't run into any towns along the way. We seemed to follow the coast until they turned inward and down a rather steep hill, not even bothering to slow down their speed we raced across a meadow and down to a crowd of others who were waiting for us, behind the majority of the crowd had been the other girls. There had been a few people we hadn't met yet who seemed rather curious about us. First person both of us noticed was Drezin and Thea, they hadn't changed one bit since the last time we had seen them, both were smiling excited to see us. I almost choked when they said we would finish talking inside the home. Looking at the home it hadn't looked like a home at all, it resembled more of a castle then anything. At least it would be far more secure then the house we were in earlier. One thing we all agreed on is that they were certainly not broke.

Charley's family almost immediately stood to the far side with Drezin in the middle with Thea and on the other side had been the few none of us had known. Apparently, Drezin and Thea tried to locate the rest of us except we were already gone. They knew who we were with except they hadn't known if we were still alive. Drezin was thrilled when he found out his brother Charley had found us, not that he wanted to involve his family anymore then he had. The only reason we were all split up had been to preserve our lives for something that was about to come.

When we first came through the door we were excited to see Drezin and Thea that we almost ran to them with Rachelle in the lead being faster, hugging both of them it felt as if we took them off guard, but then they might have thought we would be angry at them for what we had been through. For now, we were just happy to see them. The only thing I noticed was Thea, she wasn't wearing her signature scent that I loved smelling, the smell of lilac and she had stepped back slightly after we let go from our hug.

"It's been about two years since I've seen all of you." Drezin had been looking at us except Charley gave him a rather strange glance.

"Yes, I meant the girls; I haven't kept up with my own family either." Drezin's voice lightened for a moment.

Drezin hadn't looked up right away, not wanting to have eye contact with his family. Even though they were still close, they still felt hurt not knowing he was alive all this time except with their recent encounter and even then, they hadn't had the chance to get to know him and what had been going on in his life other then what Lorah had been able to fill them in on. Lewis and Evangeline were sitting down on the couch with their daughter Amanda. Drezin had known she was his sister except this was the first time he had even seen her since she also disappeared when she was a baby, although she had been handed away where the family couldn't find her. The rest of the family that had been there in support, along with the mysterious guardians who were thought to be myth was now standing there and real as everyone else had been.

Before we had started to talk, Drezin was hugging several of his family members, only a few he had been able to see before and the others this was the first time seeing him since they were rather young.

"Even if we haven't been in contact, family is always here to protect each other when we need it." Charley made it rather clear how he felt even though his own family had always known this.

"I should probably introduce the others here; I had a rather difficult time finding them once they started looking for me. I had to start leaving clues around. This is Langston, a friend who I had been changed with and grew up with as family." Not wanting to word it any other way since Langston had been like a brother, Drezin felt bad for alienated his own family for so long even though it was with reason.

Avalon introduced herself without waiting for introduction from anyone; she had been standing next to Genevieve who was still very cautious as she held Kendra in her arms. Her own children were standing quietly around her as each introduced themselves. We all had been caught up on how Kendra had been raised, how Langston found out Drezin was still alive. It seemed that Drezin had kept many secrets not just from his family but everyone. As everyone spoke and we had even described what it was like growing up and how we knew Drezin, neither he or Thea had taken their eyes off of us. There were certain characteristics that we noticed were the same as them. Finally, Charley had spoken what we were all wondering, why keep things so private to the point so many thought he was dead and why did he need to hide us? Why do experiments if he thought it would put our lives in danger where he had to hide us in the first place in such an elaborate plan?

"I know I could have had everyone's help except I would have put all of your lives in danger. I never want to risk anyone else's life because of myself. I worry that I put Thea in the danger that I do. Unfortunately, it's not something I've been able to avoid and for the time, it was the best I could come up with." Drezin hesitated to try to think how exactly to word it.

As Drezin started to explain not one person interrupted, the whole reason for going into hiding and faking his death yet again had to do with the council. He started at the beginning to catch all of us up to where we were now. Explaining how he and a group of friends had been changed by a demon that later died leaving them in the care of the council. Drezin had known this could cause stress for his family, especially since he had been kept from them for so long. Later, not wanting to complicate their lives he stayed away until he had lost touch entirely with his family. He had worked for Katherine on the side while still working along with the council. He helped Katherine hoping she would leave the rest of his family alone, realizing what it was that she was after, it had been under her nose, but she didn't realize it. Drezin hoped she would keep focusing on the wrong thing instead of the true object of her obsession.

Working for the council had been rather controversial to begin with, something if you were chosen you did not turn down or you faced death. They hadn't liked being rejected and very few were allowed to leave by their own choice. The council had been governed by the presidium for many centuries after the Augustus family had gone into hiding, not exactly for the reason most thought. They had simply grown bored dealing with fellow vampires and other creatures. Most of the presidium either disappeared or were absorbed by the council. Drezin never liked working as an assassin however he was able to keep his family safe and still work on the projects that he enjoyed. Eventually, one of the jobs he had to complete he had run directly into Lorah and Valafar, not being able to hide the fact he was still alive, they agreed to keep it silent. At the time it would have been too complicated to show up and be seen by the rest of the family if they had known what he was working on. They had also been waging their own war which Lorah never fully went into detail with him about.

Drezin found out the plans Katherine had, of eliminating the McAllister family, taking out the council and any other group who had been fighting for control over vampire and human. She wanted to control everything. If she had, there would be so many needless deaths simply because she felt only vampires should exist and no other creatures should, especially magical creatures, to her it meant possible power over her or something that could defend itself. She felt these powers or gifts should be taken from them before they were put to death. She learned how to extract these gifts from others. The Augustus family placed a curse on her causing her never to be capable of dying, even though other vampires around her for one reason or another could expire, she was to pay for the horrible torture she put others through, the Augustus family planned the most torturous ending for her. She would be tortured for several centuries and not until then would they decide whether or not she would either gain freedom or be put to death, they assumed she would come to them begging for death. As fair as the Augustus family had been, they had not turned down the chance to show their ruthless side. For the most part, creatures learned to stay out of their way, even with fairness, if a trial were held, it did not mean they were not cruel themselves when they felt suited for it.

Katherine could only remain in her own body if it was bound to certain elemental forces — forces the Augustus family controlled because of past guardians of the life stone. Without them, her flesh would wither, rot from the inside, and her soul would be torn loose, hurled into another vessel like a parasite seeking warmth.

The borrowed bodies never endured. They split under the strain of her, collapsed as if her immortality were poison in their veins. No mortal frame was meant to cage something that refused to die.

There had once been others who knew how to restore her. To stitch her soul back into the body she had been born in. The Augustus family made certain those people did not live long. Some were executed as traitors. Some disappeared into the catacombs beneath the city. A few, driven mad by what the rituals required, ended their own lives before the family could reach them.

The curse was never mercy. It was design.

She had been promised eternity, but not sanctuary. Not

ownership of her own skin. The Augustus rulers ensured that whenever her body failed, she would survive to feel it. To remember it. And so, she kept trying.

Because if she could reclaim her original body, bind it to powers they could not sever, she would no longer be their experiment. She would be their reckoning.

She wanted an experiment that Drezin created. This is when he had gone into hiding. After a while he found out Katherine had been destroyed by a special magical force, his own family had been behind it. Except now others from the council learned about it and now wanted power for themselves. They planned on killing off the rest of the council, taking the power from his experiments as well as inherit the curse Katherine had in order to be invisible from all others attacks, never fearing death.

Even now, Katherine continues to exist, only keeping physical form for a short period of time until it could be completed by the right elements that she would gain her physical existence all the time. As far as she understood, Gerard and Lydia would be working as her servants as they had in the past, except this time, they had not planned on keeping her in the form she was expecting. They wanted to permanently destroy her, not allowing her to take full form again, taking her into themselves so that they would then possess the power itself. They needed the help of the elements that Drezin's daughters had. They were willing to kill anyone to get to them which they had. Now that the council knows and are fighting against each other trying to rid the group of the defectors, they are finding there are more of their people in the council than expected. Gerard made many promises that he had no intentions of keeping even though he had many following him and his every word.

Their hope now was to make sure Gerard never got a hold of the girls, to keep Katherine from ever permanently forming. They hoped to hide her where no one would ever find her and where she would never find a way out. Lastly would be the most difficult and hoping they were not too angry from all of this;

would be to convince the Augustus family that the girls were no more a threat to them than any other creature or human that existed. Even with all this answered there was still a question the girls and I had. Taking a look at each other, I decided to step forward and interrupt.

"Why didn't you keep us hidden with you if you were going to make everyone think you were dead, it sounds as if the council thought you passed on, whatever made them think you would still be alive?" I wanted to know so badly it hadn't bothered me for the first time to speak out in front of a group of people I barely knew.

Usually, Rachelle was the brave one speaking for both of us.

"It was far too difficult to hide all of you; with your special gifts that you would inherit. We knew you would all live. When the others found out what we were going to do, we felt it was easier to hide you with other mothers, people would naturally assume you were their children. We hoped no one would question it. I didn't want to risk Thea being pregnant with seven babies, so we found mothers who wanted children but couldn't have them. It worked out for all of us. We always kept in touch and all of you were raised in quite healthy and happy homes. We had to risk relocating so many times, it was safer for all of you not to be with us." Drezin was having a difficult time explaining without getting to emotional or personal.

"Who are Kendra's parents since she's not entirely our sister? Did you manufacture her or is she related to us somehow?" Rachelle asked rather quickly.

"We had been spotted and never had a chance to insert Kendra when the rest of you were, she had been kept frozen for many years later, otherwise, she would have been your same age. We kept her safely stored at a cryobank until we could collect her later when it was safe. We were worried being frozen for so long that there would be problems." Thea had trailed off just a little.

"A special friend of ours was passing away from an assignment she had been sent on; even though she completed it she was badly damaged. Her special gift would be passed on genetically. Except with so many mutations it was no longer passing on naturally, instead of letting it die out, she was able to help us pass it onto Kendra, and it helped her survive." Drezin finished for Thea when she was too emotional to finish.

"So, who are her parents then?" Lorah asked as curious as the rest of us.

"The father doesn't even know who he is. Thea carried Kendra almost full term which is why she was born so small and is still slightly smaller than her age group. Thea is naturally her mother; with the gift it helped reanimate her cells for a short time. However, it did not work with me, so I did a horrible thing, Kendra isn't technically mine, and we were already attached to her." Drezin's voice lightened again as he tried to speak.

Not needing to finish his comment, we all looked directly at Langston, the only one in the room who looked so similar to Kendra. As we did, the moment of realization came to him, it was why he felt so connected. There was still an envelope in his pocket that he never read from a gypsy reader. Being clarified by the envelope, Sophie recognized it as being one of Maddie's letters. All it said inside was, "congratulations on being a father, if you're now reading this you have now earned and are ready for it." Langston hadn't looked horrified, just in shock or rather disbelief.

Chapter Ten

New plans

For now, we were far enough away from the Augustus family, not that it would take them long to come here if they knew we were all here. With the way the McAllister family had grown, they almost rivaled the Augustus family in size and most definitely with family abilities. Several joined them when Katherine made her biggest mistake, instead of making the family more vulnerable, they inherited more strength. There wasn't much time, after a while Gerard would be desperate enough to hire more killers to find us or the Augustus family would and with the threat of Katherine coming back, it made us appear more of a danger then harmless. We already had one portion of Katherine; if she was already forming temporarily, then she had been able to collect most of the other parts. All she needed was the elements and one last key ingredient to permanently solidify herself, making herself even stronger than before. The new search hadn't been for Katherine however to find her location for the ritual. As dangerous as it was Drezin felt if we found it, we could destroy and put an end to it there. Unlike any other area, there had to be a reason for it to be performed there at that certain spot, especially since it was formed before her temporary death. The group searched several of her favorite areas that she used in the past, however many looked untouched or even paved over from mortals moving in.

Originally, I had been having nightmares for a few months before all of this started. After they had lightened quite a bit until we all had similar dreams about seeing Katherine, it almost seemed as if she had already been formed. It was something we continued to see and wasn't exactly sure if it meant it was going to happen, or it was giving us insight into exactly what we should do. The only thing we kept seeing was the image around her, certainly not a place we had ever been to. After the family searched the only places they could come up with, we thought we would suggest our dream, after all it might be a dream, or it might actually mean something. Most of the family had been gone except for Drezin, he was working on his plan of attack with Katherine even though for the most part he already had his plan from the moment he made us. Now he mainly concentrated on trying to find a way to negotiate with the Augustus family. Absorbed in his project I cleared my throat getting his attention.

"Do you need something Willow?" Drezin set his pen down when he asked.

"We think Katherine has a place your family hasn't seen yet, not that we have seen it in person, but we are positive we know what it looks like. The only problem is it seems more like a dream and hard to tell if it's real." I wasn't sure how to bring this up; it was much easier discussing with the rest of the girls.

"Most dreams are nightmares; I've rarely seen them come true." Drezin no doubt was responding to our comment earlier when we tried to bring it up, only Charley seemed interested at the time.

"We were able to describe her perfectly and had it confirmed when Charley and Sophie told us what she looked like. We had never seen her before and the only way we have, has been in our dreams in the exact same setting every time." I was beginning to feel frustrated.

"No one can manipulate your dreams unless you allow

them which means you would have seen her at some point." Drezin seemed more irritated then anything.

"Charley said they've dealt with dreams, especially ones that lead you to the physical." I kept hoping if he thought any-thing of his brother, he might at least try to find the place we described.

"I'm busy trying to figure this out right now and listening to dreams and fantasy is only taking my time away from me, go spend time with your sisters and do something until we can fig-ure this out." Turning not saying another word Drezin seemed to be absorbed into his work again.

Taking a quick glance, I wondered what a few of the sym-bols meant, nothing I had ever seen before, however what would he need those symbols for? Not saying another word to him. I left quietly heading back to my sisters who were all watching waiting for a response. Not saying anything I simply gave them the signal to follow me. Something wasn't right and I didn't want to risk saying a word inside the house or to close by in case he could hear us. The other girls knew from the way I gestured and the expression on my face not to bother trying to speak be-fore we had left. Charley and Lucian noticed when we left the place giving a questionable look on their faces as well when they had first returned watching us leave. At least Drezin would be assuming we had taken his advice to occupy ourselves outside. The others noticed the way we were reacting when we had gone walking and that we were not staying close by this time. We had gone quite a distance from the house. Lucian, Charley, and Rose either followed us to make sure we were safe, or they were wor-ried we would take off. Finding a spot to stop at I turned to face the others.

"Willow, why did we need to come out this far, it might not be safe?" Rachelle was worried in case we were attacked again.

"Don't worry we're not alone, they are still watching us. We needed to get far enough away from the house so I can tell you the news." I hoped they would understand or at least pick up on it the way I had.

"You're acting as if we're not safe at the house?" Piper asked rather quickly picking up on my mood.

"We're not safe. I don't think that's Drezin at all, I think it's Katherine in disguise. I can't prove it and I don't know if it can be done but that's not Drezin. He was always excited and acted differently. He would listen to ideas until each one would be disproven, and we would start thinking of new ones. He never shot us down like that before and the way he talked to me isn't him." I wished they heard the exact way he had spoken to me and then they would understand.

"Maybe it's the stress he's under; this isn't easy for any of us." Dahlia tried to come to a logical reason for his snapping at me.

"Even Thea is different, since we've been here and seeing them again, she hasn't been herself. She's always been like a second mom. Now she won't even hug us. Ever since we found out the truth, she acts like touching us physically hurts." I was still trying to prove a point.

"Maybe she feels guilty for lying to us all these years?" Piper was trying to sound hopeful.

"We let them know we accepted their explanation so why continue to hold back? I can't help it but it's like talking to two completely different people. There has to be some way of proving it." I couldn't help it; this was something I couldn't let go of.

No longer just watching in the distance, the three had come directly over to us with a questioning look on their faces. Charley looked distant for a while until he focused back on us again. We had guessed they overheard our conversation no doubt trying to make sense of it. The few of us that had been questioning what they were thinking and no doubt they were doing the same with each other. The short time we had been standing there with them Lorah had come and joined us.

"Have you noticed anything unusual about Drezin? You know him far better than the rest of us." Charley asked her to find out if there was anything to my questioning him.

"I think he's stressed out since he's under so much pressure, he knows if he messes up there's far too much to lose." Lorah seemed rather optimistic even though her own voice wavered a bit.

"Maybe I should speak with him? At least to see how he's doing, maybe it would give us an idea how he's doing mentally. I know this is all stressful, but we still need to be careful, anything dealing with Katherine has potential for danger." Charley had given a nod of the head then taking off.

Not ready to head back to the house. We stayed on the hill for a while longer. I couldn't shake that feeling if we stayed here any longer, we would be in a waiting trap. Eventually we followed behind Lorah and Lucian back to the house, Rose stayed out a little longer wanting to check on something. Even when we were back in the house nothing seemed to lighten up the feeling I had. All of us were on edge even though we tried to act as if we were alright, trying not to alarm anyone or make Drezin question us. Maybe I was being overly cautious or paranoid since we had been through so much. We had been in the living room watching music videos when Charley came in, shaking his head looking at Lorah I could almost guess how his chat with Drezin had gone. Even Lorah had gone in to speak with him except this time he yelled at her to leave him alone while he worked out his plans. We hadn't waited long when Thea came out into the living room with us sitting down next to us letting us know she wanted to talk.

"Drezin doesn't mean to be so angry, he's very stressed out and can't afford to get this wrong. He takes his work personally and professionally, and this involves more than just himself, which makes it much harder for him to deal with. This is when he prefers to work alone, it keeps his mind clear." Her voice had still been light but there was something missing from it.

"We understand he's stressed except he needs to let us help him; he's not alone in this." Charley made it clear they were here to help out as much as possible.

"We appreciate it. Unfortunately, Drezin is very stubborn

and prefers to work things out in his head before he gets others involved." As Thea said this a strange look crossed Lorah's face.

"I think I'll show the girls where they will be sleeping." Lorah waved to us and turned expecting us to follow her.

"We have their room already for them, we figured after what they've been through, they would prefer being together." Thea had spoken before we left the living room.

Following Lorah to the upstairs there had been several rooms up there. The castle had been large enough we could have gotten lost. We walked past a stretch of silent rooms until the corridor opened into a large sitting area. Without slowing, Lorah led us down another staircase. Two floors deep this time, then along a narrow hallway before stopping at the door to the room she'd chosen. Opening the door Lorah stepped in with us. Facing us she was bracing us for her news.

"Drezin may be under a lot of stress. However, to be careful, I wanted to make sure there is a way out. This isn't the room they were expecting you to be staying in. If anything happens then use the doorway in the closet." Pointing out the door that was covered over we were at least feeling more comfortable in the room, especially with Lorah, at least someone might believe us.

"You believe us?" For a second, I felt a slight bit of hope.

"There is something there. I'm not sure what it is." Lorah gave her best honest answer.

Leaving us alone in our room. I kept waiting for something to happen, a sound or a quake. Maybe everyone was right that I was searching for something? If it had truly been Drezin and Thea, I was very disappointed. Not sure what I was expecting, perhaps the enthusiastic way they would always greet us or the way they would speak to us as if the world could be falling apart and they were still calm enough to handle anything. Laying back on the bed. I had a hard time sleeping. Rachelle had taken the trundle bed that pulled out. Hannah and Dahlia have been inseparable since we got here. Piper and Taylor shared the bed by the window. The only one who was not in the room with us had been Kendra, she insisted on staying with Genevieve. Eventually feeling tired enough, I had fallen asleep. At least I knew I wasn't the only one having a problem sleeping, Piper stayed silent, but I knew she was awake as she stared at the ceiling.

Early in the morning we woke up to see Lorah smiling at us, apparently, she wanted to make sure we made it to the kitchen without getting lost. There were so many rooms and hallways in the castle it could take days if we were to get lost. At least having Lorah around. I felt much safer. Drezin still hadn't emerged from the study. After eating breakfast, we got stuck together this time. All going down to the beach to relax. Sophie felt with all the stress it would help us relax since there wasn't anything we could do yet. Genevieve joined us with Kendra; we almost forgot why we were here when we watched her play in the sand with the other children she had grown up with. It was still hard to believe they would have given all of us up unless there was more to it, unless of course that was more my hope. Sitting down next to the little girl while she built her sandcastle, I helped her collect a little bit of moist sand to strengthen her castle.

Looking around I hadn't seen Genevieve; she must have felt the little girl was safe with the rest of us, even though this would be the first time she was away from her. Her other children started to notice she hadn't come back, leaving to check where she had gone, they had not come back either. Not wanting to scare the little girl. I had the others come closer in case we needed to protect each other. We knew we were being watched by someone at the edge of the woods. The movement was difficult to hide; however, they never once made a move to come into the light where we could see the person. It felt strange for the first time not to see someone watching over us from the McAllister family, they always had a way of letting us know it was them. Knowing the person in the woods was there and not making it clear who they were didn't feel right. Rachelle and I learned whenever we felt that strange intuition feeling, we understood not to fight it, that it had been there for a reason.

"I think it's time to go back to the house." Keeping my voice as calm as I could, I didn't want to scare Kendra.

We started walking back but stopped before the tip of the hill, there had been no one outside of the house, even though the castle was huge, usually we could see someone in the entryway. None of us wanted to go back until we had seen someone. Kendra seemed to be questioning why we were not continuing, whispering lightly she wanted Genevieve. Feeling a cold breeze on our backs as we looked at the castle, a moment of panic kicked in, turning around there were three people standing there. Jacob, Rose, and Lucian. Letting out a temporary sigh. I couldn't help but worry from the expressions on their faces.

"Don't go back to the castle; we're not sure what is safe right now. Drezin isn't himself and Thea was only in disguise. Willow, you were correct that there was something wrong with him, the imposters are waiting until Gerard and Lydia along with their guards arrived." Lucian sounded frustrated, not catching on to this earlier.

"We need to find a place to hide until we can figure out how to free the others, all of you were correct to worry, that wasn't Drezin and Thea, it was Katherine and someone else pretending to be them. They called the family together to fill them in on the plans except instead the form changed and it's how they found out, she can't keep her form long, which might have been why she stayed in the study for so long." Rose obviously kept a lookout as she spoke to us.

"Someone has been watching from the woods no doubt waiting for nightfall or enough shade to come out for all of you, they don't know we have any information as to what's going on. We need to act normal but let's go for a slight walk." As Jacob said this, I couldn't help it that it was already difficult to pretend to be normal, when Lucian was covered from head to toe in clothing that was covering his skin and sunglasses.

The family hadn't told us to much other than some could handle the light, others simply had no troubles with it, and a few could not even be caught out in the sun. We walked on foot acting as if we were taking a relaxing stroll. Dahlia played it up a bit by collecting wildflowers along the way. Keeping Kendra close by me. I had let her walk, occasionally she would lay on the ground rolling having fun. It looked as though we decided to take a walk. Once we had gone up the steep hill away from the meadow, we could see the ocean in the distance. Apparently, the family had a home here before it was destroyed, even the little town not too far away had been rebuilt years later. At least Lucian, Rose and Jacob knew the area well enough. Trying to stay far enough away from the other direction, Lucian was concerned the ritual place might have been in the old city of the Eurubian's. No one had rebuilt the place and neither returned to it, instead they created a new home in an entirely different area hoping to forget their past and the dangers that had gone on there.

We stopped at a large body of water. They would have swam us all across except there were too few of them and more of us. We walked along the edge out of sight not allowing those who had followed us to find us to easily, as Lucian said, we might have to fight if it came to that. Picking a small cave where we could hide during the dark, Lucian kept watch hoping if we slept now during the night then we would have energy if needed if we were attacked. Rose kept reassuring Lucian that Jessica would be alright; she doubted they would do anything until after the ceremony. Knowing what Katherine was like, she no doubt would want to eliminate her own family when she was in full form rather than let someone else do it, especially from all the anger she has held onto over the centuries. She always chose what might emotionally cripple a person the most before finishing them off physically. As she's told others many times, she viewed the killing part as prize for her.

Oddly enough, I slept. The sand held the day's warmth, cradling us in a way stone never could. After nights spent on wooden plank beds and cold stone, this almost felt gentle. Safe, even. For a little while, it was easy to pretend we weren't hiding.

Rose's hand on my shoulder pulled me back.

"I heard something," she murmured.

Her voice wasn't panicked. Just careful. The cave entrance was nearly impossible to reach. When we'd arrived, there had barely been enough ledge to balance on. Jacob and Lucian had lifted each of us inside, steadying themselves by pressing their hands into the cliff wall as if the rock welcomed their grip. No one could simply wander in.

Which meant if there were noises outside…

Lucian was already moving. He stepped toward the narrow opening and disappeared beyond it without a word. The cave fell quiet again. Too quiet. We listened to the wind drag across stone. To our own breathing. Waiting for it to mean nothing.

Or something….

While we waited, Lucian searched the old house looking for any clues that someone might be around. The entire place was empty giving no clue anyone had even been there. Left on the front doorway had been an envelope with several names on it. Picking up the envelope except not reading it, Lucian made his way back to us making sure no one followed him.

"No one is in the castle anymore except someone left this envelope on the front step." Holding the envelope in his hand we all saw it was still closed.

"I don't recognize any of the handwriting; I'm assuming because the names listed on it, this was meant for the girls?" Rose looked the envelope over inspecting it.

None of us made a move to claim or try to read the envelope. Almost too nervous to read the note, Jacob had taken it from Lucian crushing a rock over it, as he had there were a few crunches heard. Not sure what they were at first, his main reason for doing it was to make sure nothing dangerous would come out and harm any of us. Unsealing the envelope, Jacob made a second gesture to us in case one of us had changed our mind wanting to read it for ourselves, not getting anyone to do it Jacob emptied the envelope onto the ground leaving the smashed remnants of bugs known as the African assassin bug or better known as the Platymeris biguttata. Opening the letter and reading it out loud it stated:

"To the seven daughters:
There will be no end to this until you cooperate, unless you wish for those who tried to help you be killed. We suggest you come only with your sisters willingly to our designated area."

The letter had given directions from the castle to the area they wanted us to show up at. Lucian and Jacob knew where the area had been except, they hadn't remembered anything actually being there, it was before the Eurubian city. Rose stayed behind in case anyone else was to show up while Jacob and Lucian made their way to the area to check it out first. The instructions had been for us to stay put while they were gone, or until they could find a way of freeing the rest of the family. We all hated being left behind never knowing what was going on, always waiting and hiding. Instead, we opted to stay in the cave; there was a very long tunnel. At least this way we wouldn't be very far from the last place people knew we were and Rose would not be left alone. We might not have been vampires however we were learning we could take care of ourselves if we had to.

While waiting for Jacob and Lucian to come back, we decided to investigate the rest of the cave, it can't hurt to know where the tunnel goes. From the mouth of the cave, it had been a long drop down below to the ocean, at least it was a deep end if we were to fall in. We hadn't wanted to risk any riptides or simply being crushed against the rock wall. Following the cave inward we were fascinated by the walls, they had shined quite a bit almost looking as if they were covered with a diamond dust, except if you looked closer it more resembled quartz crystal. The tunnel had gone far enough it actually went under the castle and further past. We noticed that one tunnel that had gone off from the main looked different than the rest, no doubt put there intentionally. First checking it out, we had found this is where our escape area had gone that Lorah wanted us to follow in case anything happened. We filled Rose in on what we talked to Lorah and Charley about when we first noticed something was wrong with Drezin.

After a while the tunnel was so dark, we couldn't see a thing, even Rose made sure we held hands so that no one would be left behind or in case one of us fell in a hole we could not see, the rest of us could help them out. Rose had some traits of a vampire however the incredible eyesight with darkness wasn't one of them. Going slightly slower, we could tell the tunnel was curving but then after we had been following it for quite some time, we had no idea if it had curved away from the castle or in what direction, it turned so often. The only thing we were sure of is that it hadn't brought us back to the ocean, we no longer heard the waves crashing against the rock. We were all thankful that Piper was always prepared for anything. She was always worried about being away from home and not having anything to eat. Before we left the castle, she grabbed a couple breakfast bars assuming we would probably eat them later. Even after waiting for Jacob and Lucian for about a day we had not even felt hungry simply from nervousness, except now it was kicking in. Handing out the bars to everyone we continued to walk while we ate them

Looking at Dahlia's watch, we had been walking for at least nine hours; my legs were feeling sore and tired. Sitting down on the ground, we rested a while on the dirt ground until we started moving again. I was beginning to doubt this tunnel was ever going to end but then if we could see we might have been walking much faster than we were. Off in the distance there was a small glint of a light or rather glow. Walking a little faster towards it we hoped it would be a safe place to emerge. We stopped at the end of the tunnel; it had led to the largest underground water well we had ever seen. The water glowed so brightly it lit the entire area. The water felt strange, almost like a jelly, except it hadn't stuck to our hands when we touched it.

"I've seen this before; it might not be the exact same well

except the royal family used one of these in the Lipedian and Eurubian city. My brother used it several times, I don't know if it would end up in the same place except it would take us out somewhere. Make sure you hold hands when we step in. Don't worry, it's not deep at all and don't let go." Rose was so sure of herself; she grabbed Willow's hand as she stepped in.

Not taking too much time. I followed behind holding my sister Rachelle's hand, she in turn held Piper who was holding onto Kendra. Not able to hold onto the next sister's hand, Piper had held onto the corner of her shirt as she was followed by Hannah and Taylor and Dahlia. We were all immersed inside of the well and she was right; it wasn't deep or like stepping down. We were completely surrounded by this thick gel substance. Holding my breath for a while until I couldn't hold it any longer, I took a breath thinking I was going to drown. I wasn't the only one who was shocked by the non-liquid. Looking around. I couldn't see where we had first stepped in at. I hoped Rose knew where she was going. Following along with her in a long chain, we were now stepping out of the substance into a rather unusual place.

We emerged from the strange liquid and found ourselves standing in a city buried deep beneath the earth. Everything around us, the walls, towers, streets, had been carved from gleaming black onyx, as if the entire place had once been a single massive stone.

Silent lampposts stood along the roads, but none were lit. A narrow opening in the ceiling allowed a thin shaft of light to pour in, barely disturbing the darkness that swallowed the rest of the city.

It was such an amazing magical looking place. Apparently, the well was another escape out of the Eurubian city or also known as the dark city.

"I don't know if this place is safe or not, it's fallen apart quite a bit since our family had the fight here and Katherine destroyed it more later on, I'll have to explain it sometime but it's definitely a depressing place." Not wanting to push it we followed Rose along a long corridor that lead to an even larger area.

We stopped rather abruptly when she was pulled into one of the little buildings that had been built into the side of the onyx wall. Racing in to help her, we realized it was Genevieve and Langston. They hadn't been taken by the others. Kendra lit up excitedly when she saw Genevieve that she practically jumped into her arms.

"At least now we know why we hadn't found anything here earlier when we inspected it with Drezin, I wish I knew what they did with the real Drezin and Thea and if they are still alive." Langston was spying out the window as he spoke to us.

"We tried to find all of you when we went back, we were ambushed except we took care of the ones who attacked us, we haven't found or heard from the rest of the family yet." Genevieve had spoken softly as she held a very happy little girl.

"We need you girls to leave here; how did you get here in the first place? It's not safe if they catch you, this place is covered with Katherine's foot soldiers." Genevieve meant well except we were tired of hiding, just like Lucian and Jacob made the point, we can't hide forever.

"Just tired of waiting for what seems like the inevitable, supposedly we have these gifts, and we don't even use them. We can't hide forever and there should be something we can do?" Dahlia had spoken what we were all thinking.

"It's great you want to do something except right now if you try anything, your gifts will be exploited and not helpful. We need you to go back the direction you came as long as it's safe and wait out there, I'm sure Rose can help you hide." Langston made his way to the door with Genevieve following, leaving a reluctant Kendra disappointed that she had been left again.

Watching as they left, we let out a collective sigh that even Rose understood. She let us know what her childhood was like. Unlike other vampires. She had been the klutz, or rather the one everyone had to look after. The only gift she found she inherited from her own family had been immortality. Which explained why they hadn't moved us fast when it was just her.

She moved much slower at our speed than anyone else. She was so much easier to relate to especially always waiting for others and left behind wondering if everyone was going to be alright. Instead of heading back to the long tunnel, we decided to stay in the little building we were in right now. After all, since the tunnel was pitch dark and none of us could see in it, we would never know if there was someone waiting in there for us.

"This place is so amazing I'm surprised no one lives here?" Piper was still checking out the onyx wall.

"It's not exactly a safe place to live, yes its beautiful inside and there's this amazing waterfall outside except this is where Katherine did many of her experiments. It's difficult to say how many might still be alive outside or if they've moved into the city now that the inhabitants are not here, and the gate is not guarded." Rose had given into a chill remembering how dangerous it was to even step beyond the gates.

"You said there was another water well here?" Dahlia was already thinking of another way out if we were too far from the first spot.

"There is, it's at the far end of the city, it was used by the royal family. They mainly resided at the other city except they made frequent trips here and usually used the well since it was faster and safer." Rose was picking up on what we were thinking.

"If they are here, where do you think they would be holding them?" Taylor asked while she stared out the window.

"If they want to stay hidden in case the Augustus family came to check this place out, they will hide in the far back part of the city, it's an exact replica of the royal family's home, not that I want to run into Langston again. Even if he is on our side, it worries me that he's worked for the council for so many years as their assassin." Rose looked worried except apparently not too worried to help us out.

"We'll follow you; we need to find them and maybe we might find a way to help them? It's clear outside we should get going now." Taylor was already getting excited while keeping watch at the door.

Following Rose out, we had all crept along the side of the wall heading down the stairs, staying behind several of the buildings, instead of going through the middle of town, we took the path to the side where the stairs were narrow. We continued to take the steps as they led past several more of the homes that had been built into the side of the wall. The left side of the city had been special shops with a huge center, another row on the right side of shops and then only separated from the housing was the thin walkway with stairs now leading upward away from the town center. There was more housing down on the second level below the main street, except most of it collapsed when the forced workers were collecting certain stones. Katherine's sister Alana had forced them for a while until they had been freed. The city itself was larger than we expected it to be, it was a mile long in four different directions. We were getting closer to the end of the city; except we had to go slower now because it would be much easier to be spotted while some areas we had to step over rubble from areas that had crumbled. It was rather eerie not to see any guards standing watch, at least none that we could see. Staying low on the steps they had gone up quite high; we reached an archway that led into the largest part of the cave so far. It looked as if we stepped into an old English castle with all the marble flooring, black onyx walls and thrones perched just right so they could sit there and look over a large percentage of the city. There were only two other doors leading off from the main room we were in. Rose was hesitant trying to decide which one to take, especially as she voiced to us it was strange, we hadn't run into any of the guards or at least lookouts. It was difficult to believe Katherine would assume she was this safe or invincible here.

"I don't feel safe; this doesn't feel right. She has to know we are here." Rose wasn't the only one questioning it.

"We can't go back or all we do is hide, what if Genevieve and Langston don't come back like Jacob, Lucian or the others, what are we expected to do then? Keep hiding until we get trapped somewhere? I know we need to keep our gifts from them but at some point, we are going to need to face them." Rachelle was right, either way it was going to happen eventually.

We skipped the first door which would have led to personal rooms or living spaces for the royal family when they stayed here; it had also been used for hospital rooms. Instead, we had taken the second door which led straight down to the basement. None of us were looking forward to more steps especially these since they were half steps and steep. We walked by a few rooms that Rose said were small, more like personal offices. We went all the way to the bottom to find three rooms on one side of the hallway. One you could look into and there was nothing in it, the other two were closed off and one door locked. The one room we could look into had a shiny mirror on the one side of the wall which Rose said could be viewed from the second room, she wasn't sure what was in the third room or why they would have locked it. We heard no noises of a footstep, speaking or breathing. It was still silent. Turning around to leave we stopped dead in our tracks; it hadn't been Katherine or her guards; it was three members of the Augustus family.

"What are you doing here?" The rather tall intimidating man who was dressed all in black roughly asked.

"Looking for family." Rachelle blurted out without giving much thought to it.

"You do realize that Katherine is here. She would be rather excited to find all of you; it would be a rather fortunate find for her, sad to say we have to kill all of you." As he spoke it seemed as if Rose was silently pleading with a person standing behind them.

"Whose idea was it to make her so invincible in the first place? We heard your family cursed her except if she can keep coming back, it's still long enough to figure out even more ways to solidify herself permanently, so who is this curse supposed to affect?" Not trying to start an argument, Taylor was hoping to stall for a few minutes.

"You dare question us?" His voice never changing in pitch but remaining calm.

"Yes. I do, supposedly your family is this ruthless group that doesn't let anyone step out of line and we're supposed to accept this when you give such a dangerous power to an evil person who breaks all of your rules and threatens the existence of your own?" Not wanting to cause a problem except making her point rather clear, Taylor wasn't going to back down.

"You think we were cruel?" His gaze did not waver, "death is a mercy, child. Even for Monsters. We denied her that mercy. Execution would have been a kindness, a blade, a flame and instead, we severed her from the natural order itself. We made her die a thousand deaths, in fire, in hunger, in solitude and each time we pulled her back. No release. No fading. No oblivion. Only endurance. Tell me… what is hell if not being forced to survive forever tormented?

She had been under our control until she found someone who supported her goals which resulted in that person releasing her. We have put an end to her supporters, protectors, and anyone else who has covered for her. She always has someone working for her, that way if we show up or something goes wrong, they take the fall." The way the others looked at him as he spoke, we had a feeling there was more to it."

"Why keep someone who wants power around unless you intend on using it for something you don't want others to know about?" Dahlia asked this time while Taylor again asked more.

"Are you actually going to take care of it this time or keep killing everything she starts or gets connected with or had no choice? Sounds like a lot of unnecessary work for you especially if you are trying to prove she has no power over your group." Taylor was getting bolder by the second.

"We should kill you all right now for questioning our power." His voice had risen slightly as though he was about to carry out his comment.

"What else are we to think when you wanted to kill us simply because we have gifts and yet she mocks you every second showing you she can do what she wishes and not get caught, she makes the vampire community wonder if your family is losing their control, you can do something about that, but I guess it's easier to kill us instead of being done with it." Taylor continued to bait him.

We were beginning to wonder what she was trying to accomplish from it, other than stalling.

"I highly doubt she is even here other than the one taking her fall, we have lost control of nothing, and we have cornered her last project. After this she simply exists in pieces, she was never meant to stay whole." Letting out a deep laugh as if he was trying to insult us.

"I doubt we are the only ones she could use to solidify herself; with all the time she has been around. I'm sure she has yet another backup. She doesn't seem to be an ignorant person. She's not even solid and she's still able to accomplish what she wants. If it's true what I heard, is that you can't kill her now if you wanted to." Taylor had been on a roll.

"Where did you hear something like that?" Now she had all three of them glaring down at her except she hadn't budged at all.

"It's not hard to hear it, heard it from several places we've been. Apparently, you no longer have the power to kill her, it's the real reason you don't finish her off the way you would anyone else. We have to face her eventually; we could do it except we need to know how to kill her for compensation." Taylor had worked it in perfectly.

"You wish to get paid?" The man seemed a little surprised.

"Not paid, our lives for hers. Simple as that." Now he seemed to understand what she was getting at.

"We do not strike deals." He stated rather roughly.

"Actually, it's more than a deal for you, no one has to know we did it, they can assume you have some strong power no one knows about, which strikes more fear into people, and it allows us to live. Besides, we could have plenty of witness's who can say they saw her die, they wouldn't tell anyone it was us either, they would let others know it was your group. Not really striking a bargain just a work arrangement. No one ever said you couldn't lose interest in a bunch of kids." Taylor tried to make it sound better for them if they were to go along with it.

"Then we'll figure out something, she has to show up at some point if she wants us. It's one of the few times you know as a definite she's going to be there and not leaving a fall person for her. Just follow us where we go, and you will find her also." As soon as Taylor suggested this the three started speaking to each other in a language we hadn't heard of.

No doubt deciding what they wanted to do. Without saying another word, we could only assume they agreed with us, at least it's what we were hoping for. None of us were sure if we could pull it off except, we had to try. With no idea how to kill her or stop her if she did anything, knowing we were the reason she comes back, and the Augustus family could end up killing us either way, none of us were feeling to good right now. The last thing any of us wanted to do was actually search her out, find her and face her not knowing what was going to happen to us and those who wanted to help us.

We started walking back up to the main room again, this time instead planning on searching the other door hoping to find something there. Looking back briefly we no longer saw the Augustus family, even though there was that strange feeling that they were definitely there following us as they agreed they would.

It didn't take long to find the hallway. It looked narrow at first, almost unremarkable. Then we stepped through the door, and it opened wide, and the world beneath the world revealed itself.

The city rose around us in black onyx, walls gleaming like polished night. Homes and tiny shops were carved straight into the stone, stacked in careful rows that curved with the cavern's spine. Windows glimmered faintly, some draped in tattered fabric, others standing open as if their owners had just stepped away.

Dust hung in the air, soft as mist. Every footstep echoed

too loudly.

We should have been afraid. We were buried deep beneath everything we knew.

But all I felt was awe. I know we were in a rush when we first entered but somehow it looked much more impressive on our way out and it took my breath away.

It was ancient. Beautiful. Untouched by the modern world above. Even in ruin, it felt sacred…. like we had stumbled into something not meant for us, yet waiting all the same.

None of them looked occupied anymore and neither had they looked as if Katherine was using them. We were covering a lot of the area in a short time. Staying close to each other for protection, keeping Kendra as close as possible not to lose her. We kept waiting for something to either jump out at us or unexpected thing to happen, which it never did. We came down to the one building that looked used. Fresh red drapes hanging in the window.

"I think this might be it." Dahlia stated rather lightly.

"The direction here looks off, but it does look like the picture on that paper they left us, maybe they gave us different directions to get here?" Piper seemed unsure as the rest of us were.

After opening the door, we couldn't see anything. There hadn't been any light to see if it had gone straight out or straight down. Feeling along the wall inside the door we hadn't found any outlets either to turn on a light. Feeling along the floor we found there were steps. It felt better having Rose along not that she could see any better than the rest of us, but she could help fight if we needed help. Not that we were hoping for that. The steps were rather small and went down sharply, feeling our way down careful not to fall. When we felt no more steps, we kept walking blindly in the dark hoping not to walk into something dangerous even though that was what we had been looking for. It hit me as strange; usually I would run away from a nightmare, this time I was searching for it. Reaching out touching a wall that had a handle. I could hear Piper take a breath before she opened it, hoping there would be light, there hadn't been. Opening the door walking in, as soon as the rest of us had been in. The door behind had slammed rather loudly, it hadn't been us except we were hoping it was the Augustus family. Listening, we could hear a light sloshing sound; I could feel this wet feeling entering my shoe. We were standing in water, stopping for a second. I reached down to touch the water. It was a cement floor with the slightest bit of standing water. Not sure how much deeper it was going to get since we had only walked a few steps more before it happened.

There was the slightest light at the far end, we were able to follow it to where it was coming from. After coming out of the hallway, the room was rather large and hollowed out from stone, there was a small round rock flattened on top with tables on one side, so many vials and bowls full of ingredients. We hadn't recognized the items other than knowing the beakers were the same as we found the ashes in. The set up was exactly the same, even the hollowed-out walls. Only thing it was missing was a gothic-looking bed and this one was surrounded by water. Walking to the center and out of the water. We looked around, so far, we hadn't seen anyone there.

We couldn't tell where the water was coming from or how it managed to remain, trapped in a room with no doors open to the rain and no cracks in the stone. It spread in a slow, deliberate circle around the center altar, as if it had been poured there on purpose. It gathered in a slow, glassy pool around the center altar, perfectly still, like it was waiting. There was no drip, no draft, no sour rot of stagnant water. No life in it. No decay. Just a cold, mineral sharpness that stung the back of my throat.

And the longer we stared at that perfect ring around the altar, the more it felt less like a leak… and more like a boundary.

"Is there anyone here?" I called out.

"We haven't run into one other person other than Langston and Genevieve; we know they have to be here somewhere. Where is everyone if this is the place, they were supposed to meet us, you would think they would have signs up or something in case we were to get lost?" Rachelle was doubting this had been the place unless they left already, perhaps, maybe they knew the Augustus family was here?

"It seems like this is the place, maybe they are waiting to see if we are alone?" Rose had been paying attention to the surroundings quite a bit.

"Do you think they kept the others here? Maybe they kept them somewhere else?" I hoped they would be safe at least.

"This place looks so familiar; I was young when we were here except, I think this is the exact place Katherine had been when my family first tried to get rid of her. You might be right Willow; they might not want the others here in case things don't work out or if you don't show they could use it to get you somewhere else. I think we took a wrong turn, I don't think this is the right room, but it certainly looks like it." Rose hadn't sounded thrilled when she realized she'd been here before.

Looking around, we started to notice something changing in the room. The rock almost looked as if it was leaking water except it hadn't been. They were incredibly dry to the touch, feeling nervous about it we moved back away from it. The water dripping off from it slowly turned into a smoke swirling outward covering the ground. Standing at the center of the room still, it was too late to make our way to the door since it was no longer visible through the smoke. Staying close, we kept watch on the smoke as it now formed distinct figures, not sure yet if one had been Katherine or how she would show up, eventually we could see the faces of each one as they stood around us in a circle.

The last piece of smoke that formed at first looked like Drezin. For a split second I hoped it was him until I remembered it was Katherine impersonating him. We had all guessed that neither he or Thea was even alive if Katherine kept using their forms. Trying not to appear scared or giving any reaction, we all stood there as still as stone. The closer she came to us the angrier I could feel myself getting. I knew I had to control myself except I wasn't the only one feeling it. She slowly changed herself to the form we had all gotten used to in our dreams when we would see her. Covered in a thick black lace with black leather gloves and boots, her hair was as dark blending in with the smoke that still continued to swirl around her.

"I was beginning to wonder if any of you would show. Nice to see you again Rose, you've grown since the last time I saw you." Pretending to be friendly she attempted a smile that hadn't worked very well.

"Where are the others, we know you have them." Rose asked rather quickly.

"They are silenced for now." Katherine sounded rather proud of herself.

"If any of them have been killed we won't perform anything for you." Taylor made her point rather clear.

"When you get done finishing my orders, I will let them go." Her voice was rather angry sounding not that we trusted her.

"You intended on killing all of us anyway. Why say you will let them go. If we are going to do this for you, I want them to at least know why they are dying, I want them here." Taylor challenged back not changing her own tone and keeping it calm.

"You don't mind watching them die? Little disturbing on your part, you might have been interesting to keep around later if I hadn't already planned on killing you. Can't have someone that can actually tear me apart around." Katherine seemed curious by Taylor.

Signaling to the others lined along the wall, they had separated for a few minutes, wondering if anyone would walk through, we had seen Charley and Sophie from one direction walk in only so far before they were stopped. As soon as Lucian and Jacob came from another direction, Rose let out a sigh of relief. We still hadn't seen Langston or Genevieve, not that the others showing up had come through any doors we had seen, she must have moved them through magic.

"How do we know it's them; there were no doors there for them to come through. How do we know this isn't an illusion the way you pretended to be Drezin and Thea?" Rachelle asked as the last person walked in.

"What? Don't you trust me? You can see them as clearly as I do." Sounding rather sarcastic.

"No, I obviously don't trust you especially since they are not reacting or even standing the way the real ones would." Taylor pointed out not trusting the puffs of smoke.

As soon as she made her point the people had turned into a puff of smoke disappearing in front of us rather quickly. Neither sides trusting the other and not attempting to move as her guards still standing still. We heard the actual door open with a new group of people coming through. This time from the way they walked, the sound of their steps, we knew they were real; the smoke had been unrealistic and very smooth in its movement, not a wrinkle in the clothing as it had moved. This time we were all sure they were the right ones, even the concerned looks on their faces gave them away where the others had been far too emotionless. There had been fourteen standing along the side no doubt feeling nervous knowing we were here exactly where Katherine wanted us. For a split second I swore I could have heard Charley's voice, not that his lips had moved for one second. He was telling the others to simply "trust us."

Chapter Eleven

Final Move

"If you wish for your loved ones to live, do exactly as I instruct you," Katherine paused for a second looking over at Charley before saying, "most of them you won't miss if they die, however my favorite toy Charley, he will be missed but as always, everyone is replaceable."

This was it; everyone was here as we all watched Katherine, not sure what was next. Our new friends who wanted to help keep us safe were now captive standing against the wall worried if we would help her carry out her plan or not. One thing was certain: none of us really believed we'd survive this, especially since we all knew we were bluffing our way through it the best we could.

Already working as a unit, at least we agree whatever happened, we would be together for it. Not that anyone else noticed, Langston was not fully stuck but then I was pretty sure as an assassin he was used to getting away, right now he seemed to be looking for the right moment to strike. I hoped if he had, it wouldn't start a little war in here killing people.

Katherine had us standing around the middle stand, as she explained exactly what she expected us to do, she kept looking us over giving us a rather strange glance. Occasionally she would fade out, she temporarily used the water on the ground instead of taking over yet another body. We waited for her to return as she put on her own original form. The McAllister family and Langston were not the only ones waiting to see how we would react with Katherine's demands. We didn't have to wait for things to begin. Objects began moving around all on their own as either Katherine or her followers were now controlling them.

The water pooling on the ground now slowly crept up until it formed almost a perfect replica of Katherine. One of the canisters on the side that held nothing more than dirt slowly did the same and solidified with the water.

Katherine ordered me to keep the objects connected with strong winds. As she had asked, I made the wind in the room gust as strongly as I could to keep the objects from separating from each other while at times it would lose its shape when Katherine had. She would reform looking more tired each time however she would reform the objects, she added smoke and several other items each time. Keeping the wind going wasn't easy since I felt tired however the others around and nervousness helped keep it going. Then she asked Hannah to create an electrical current to run saturating the items in the wind. While she did that Dahlia added fire strong enough to match that of a burning kiln. To keep all of us from getting badly burned or killing us from the heat, she had Piper add rain to the source to keep it from drying out and Taylor added a light snow to the outer area to keep us cool. As she did, before it even reached us it melted turning into a warm rain, which was better than feeling the full effects of the fire.

We knew she had a reason for all of us except we still were not sure what she intended on using Kendra for? She had been standing next to Taylor in awe over what she was seeing, almost as if it had been a huge magical television show for her. Katherine eventually motioned for Kendra to come to her. Hesitating she had hidden behind Taylor refusing to go to the woman. I heard a gasp from Genevieve knowing it was scaring her to see

Kendra be used. Still continuing to cool the room and us, Taylor picked up Kendra assuring her she would protect her, and she would be fine.

"If you feel any pain or uncomfortable just tell me and I'll stop it." Taylor whispered quietly to Kendra.

"Alright." Kendra barely whispered back.

They walked to the center not far from the very object itself. Hoping they would not burn, Taylor had surrounded both of them in an almost cocoon of ice that rapidly kept melting. This time Katherine had also walked over closer now standing right next to the object we had all been focusing on, she stepped into it rather slowly, now reaching out she wanted to hold onto Kendra's hand. Not liking the idea except hoping to find a way to still protect her, Taylor let Katherine hold her hand temporarily but refused to let go of her.

As Katherine held Kendra's hand there was a white glow that had gone from her arm through her hand and out to Katherine. She was slowly healing Katherine repairing the pieces of her to the formed object making her whole. As the light became brighter, Katherine became more solid no longer losing her form as she stood there. The texture of her skin had even begun to change. During all of this we still had not formed a solid plan, not that anyone was stopping us from doing it so far. Katherine's guards had been ready to handle anyone from stopping the progress so far. Then it had come, Kendra tugged on Taylors shirt with her free hand mouthing a few words to her. As she had, her own skin texture began to change and we all understood what Katherine was doing, she was absorbing Kendra into herself.

"Hurts." Kendra barely squeaked out.

Grabbing her firmly Taylor pulled her as hard as she could away from Katherine breaking the connection of the two. Stepping back quickly holding onto Kendra making sure Katherine couldn't grab her again, she rushed over near the rest of us voicing in her mind what she wanted us to do. As she chilled the sleet making as much ice as she could, we all focused on Katherine. If we were to help her giving her the forces of the elements then we should be able to overload her, even if we were not able to permanently stop her, we could at least stop her and hopefully keep her from regaining enough power to temporarily form. Possibly hiding her ashes again or making them unusable. Taylor was barely able to continue keeping the rest cooled; each of us started to develop a slight burn on the skin even though it could have been much worse if she hadn't been doing her part. Katherine started screaming for Taylor to bring Kendra back to her, trying to lash out at us she was unable to make it past the wind tunnel that kept vacuuming her back into the center that was created. Even the strong swirl of fire aided in keeping her in the center. The stronger we had become the harder it was on those around us.

Katherine's guards tried to prevent us from attacking Katherine, as they came after us. The McAllister family, friends, Langston, and Genevieve did their best to stop Katherines guards from interrupting us. Standing there. I could feel a bead of sweat dripping from my forehead that stung my eye until I realized it wasn't sweat at all; I was bleeding from all the scourging fire. Katherine had no longer kept her original form, she was now nothing more than a swirl of black smoke, even her voice disappeared no longer shouting curses at us from the center. Only one of Katherine's guards made it past the others not that he ever laid a hand on us. Without the protection of the cold keeping the fire from killing us, he had dropped to his knees before he could stop any of us taking his last breath dying next to our feet. We had stopped all at once; I was just as worn out as the rest were barely able to stand on our own feet from ex-haustion. The swirl of smoke simply landed on the table before us not moving or forming into anything. Everyone around us looked thoroughly burnt from the fire. None of us could get over the powerful act we had just performed since it wasn't that long ago, we had no idea we could even do any of this until Gerard and Lydia had Amber teach us. Now the last we thought we had to deal with was the Augustus family, which was now standing in the doorway. There wasn't just the three of them anymore, there were ten of them. Hoping they would allow us all to go free and not simply tempt us to do just a horrible thing we would never forget and yet still kill us all.

"Willow, what are you doing?" Rachelle seemed a bit surprised to see me moving around yet, everyone else was still exhausted.

"We need to be careful since we don't know if she is truly dead or not." Taking out a small plastic container that had held onto our snacks from earlier, I brushed the dusty ashes left from Katherine's body placing them inside and closing the container.

The ten Augustus family members had stood there watching all of us waiting for us to react to them. As I closed the container, I walked directly over to them not needing to say a word handing the ashes to Valafar. The group seemed more interested in the ones behind us. As I had taken a look back, two had emerged from the group. Langston and Valafar, we had known Langston was there except none of us had been introduced to Valafar yet.

"You are a part of this Valafar?" Angelita seemed surprised.

"I had to make sure it was finished. My assassin Langston and I were here all the time to make sure it was finished, or we were to eliminate everyone here who assisted the Madam." Valafar tried to sound as official as he could hoping his own family would not retaliate against us.

"Are we to assume you have cleansed the council of Gerard and Lydia's followers along with Katherine's in the council and the presidium?" Angelita asked sarcastically not believing the situation, no doubt frustrated she was not able to enjoy killing anyone yet.

"We still have to find Gerard and Lydia; once they realized something wasn't the way they planned, they left immediately. We still have to make our way back to the council; we have friends inside helping snuff out the others except I will need the girls to help finish." Valafar never once took his eye contact away from Angelita.

"Fine, then you take the girls, and we will take care of the rest here." With her voice changing to a deeper tone Angelita was staring directly over at Charley and his family.

"I know you want to take out your anger except it won't help any killing this family, we can use them to our advantage, there will be plenty for you to kill later." Valafar was quick to respond before Angelita could pounce on the others.

"We've never needed anyone." Scowling her answer already moving closer to the others.

"We still need to make a mark otherwise we will be busy cleaning up after this for a long time. We need to do what's best for the group as a whole and not just your ego." Valafar stood now between Angelita and the others who were poised to strike.

Now Charley and his family and friends were standing closer to each other ready to defend themselves the best they could against the Augustus family. With the rest of the seven sisters ready to defend those who had done their best to help us, we were ready as much as we could be in case they wanted to kill the others. Eyeing all of us, even Angelita was searching for the weakest area to strike first, which hadn't taken her too long. Even though Kendra was behind all of us we knew she was staring at her.

"That little thing is what we've been looking for this whole time? She's what Gerard was willing to risk his eternal life for?" Kristopher barely spoke even though his deep voice echoed everywhere while he was staring at Kendra.

"Leave her and the others with us, take the six sisters with you to finish, and as soon as you are finished meet us at the "center" to find out the outcome of the others. Dear brother, you may think it's my ego, however it's far more than that. I won't compromise any more than that." Angelita grinned rather evilly making everyone question what she was up to.

"I don't have a choice; I might need Kendra for this." Not wavering his voice at all, Valafar hoped to at least keep the girls together and come up with a plan to get the others hoping she wouldn't kill them for spite.

"I guess you're losing your touch brother, at one time you never needed anyone to finish something. You've gone as soft as this puny little flesh bag." Angelita never once looked away from Kendra.

The room began getting much more crowded as a bright flash of light in a circular sphere appeared in the middle of everyone and Jessica, Aaron, Delaney, Alexandra, Anwen and Lily stepped out from it. We were not expecting to see them at all.

"There's an emergency in the headquarters for the council and the presidium." Jessica quickly informed sounding nervous.

"What is the meaning of this. If there were something going on we would know. You might have gained a larger group of people over the centuries however you do not have the power we possess." Angelita's voice was raising with anger.

"Pollux Moretti, Regulus and Ruby are dead from the presidium. It's difficult to tell who the ones are that died with the council since their bodies are barely recognizable except for three of them which are Gerard, Lydia, and William. We sensed where you all were to protect the remaining members." Jessica never once lost eye contact with Angelita.

"Langston, are you aware of any bids to wipe out the council?" Kristopher asked calmly.

"There are always attempted hires to wipe out the council however no one is stupid enough to accept them. I know that Gerard talked Lydia into assisting him however if they are dead, I have no idea who else it would be unless there is still an inside person doing this. I would recommend we all go to the haven until we figure out who has done this and deal with it accordingly." Langston sounded unnerved by this.

"I second it, not a matter of safety but practicality. Then you won't need to worry about anyone dividing up, Langston can handle this while Valafar takes the girls and Charlies family to the Haven. It's not as though the girls are needed at the center anymore to handle Gerard and Lydia since they are already disposed of." Damar stated in a way that gave us chills.

Langston had been Damar's personal assassin for several centuries and knew how cruel he could be, started wondering if he was willing to take out his own followers. It felt strange that Gerard and Lydia could be thwarted like this. He seemed far to calm and the look in his eyes were a giveaway, something Langston learned when Damar was up to something or had it waiting, he had a certain look to his expression. Angelita insisted on getting herself to the Haven along with Kristopher. The guardians were much better at escorting people out so they took two at a time while Valafar took the remaining ones following him to the Haven simply telling them to trust him, at least he trusted that Langston had a plan, otherwise he wouldn't have been insistent on going to the Haven, hopefully it wouldn't turn out to be a trap.

Chapter Twelve

The end

The Haven wasn't what we were expecting it to look like. For a group who hid in this place for centuries while others could not find them or never came across it, the building stood out from everything around it. Almost looming enough to say notice me. Perhaps people were afraid to find out what was hidden inside. We were still a distance away, but it rose high above the cliffs at the edge, a magnificent castle we would have loved adventuring through if it hadn't been for the current circumstances. It was a dangerous climb and thankfully Valafar made it clear we would not have to wait long. Once the guardians had the others waiting for us at the top, they came back down for us. For what would have taken us a week to get here, it only took a few hours as they swooped in, grabbed us and flashed us to the waiting area. What scared us the most was the silence. Everything echoed around us and not one person spoke. The front door made of mahogany opened slowly with a creek, no one standing there as if expecting us to know where we were going. We let Valafar take the lead as we followed him.

As we followed we could only hear our footsteps, there was a set that hadn't matched ours but no one else was near enough and it hadn't sounded like it was coming from in front but behind. A short glance back only to see nothing was there but the sound. It felt as if something was whispering to us, we each asked if the other heard it without saying a word and the voice answered us all by saying yes. It answered its own voice which gave us chills.

The first room we walked through was a large open room with dark marble flooring and silver highlights glowing in the light. High cathedral ceiling with hand painted artwork. What caught all of our attention was the alter in the center of the next room, it was as impressive as the exterior was standing out amongst the mountains and trees as if again, to say it was the most important thing here.

The altar dominated the room. A large black slab of stone was worn smooth from use. There was a slight shadow below the stone, it was hovering over the floor within inches. It was too large and heavy for anyone to move and magically controlled. Looking closer, it was etched with concentric circles of symbols that overlapped like the phases of the moon. They hadn't looked carved in but jagged from a monsters hand or paw. The same silver flecks in the floor wove through the alter like veins. The closer we would get to it; the silver would turn to a dark red with a smoky ripple look as if blood was running around inside the stone. Blood red candles illuminated the room. A small, tarnished silver bowl sat at the center surrounded by dried herbs ready to be used. Incense was already smoldering as smoke rose up. There were various bones placed around the alter and several scattered along the floor however each looked deliberately placed and not carelessly tossed on the ground.

Willow went to touch the bone handled dagger that was heavily stained except it sounded as though it hissed, how could bone hiss? An ornate mirror with cloves wrapped around the edges and instead of a clear glass, it looked like an oily liquid.

The air shifted, it felt thicker, warmer, threaded with the faint scent of iron and burnt resin. Candles along the circular walls flickered to life one by one, not with flame, but with a low, pulsing glow, as if something beneath the stone had begun to breathe.

A voice layered and fractured, too low to understand but it was said in unison as if many had spoken the same words in the same place, repeatedly, until the sound itself had never left being stuck permanently echoing.

One of the Sisters flinched. Not from the voices we could hear, but at the feeling of fingers brushing past her wrist, cold and insistent, guiding her into place along the altar.

The ritual, it seemed, had already begun. And something in the room was determined to see it finished. If we hadn't put Katherine into the bottle, we would have assumed this to be more of a fitting ritual then where we were previously.

"I feel like we are walking into a trap, are you sure this is a safe place?" Willow asked.

"I think your right, but I would trust Langston with my life, there has to be a reason he still thinks this safe place is right. Just because Katherine is in the bottle doesn't mean she won't be able to come back alive. She will keep coming back until her essence and existence is removed. Her remains are only slowed by being in the bottle. I have a feeling whatever is going to happen will be final. If I give any orders or Langston does. Don't question it, just follow exactly." Valafar sounded nervous.

Part of the wall opened revealing a hidden room. Damar walked in dragging in two body bags behind him. Waving his hand over the alter it split open revealing an incredibly hot fire. Lifting each bag at a time, he threw them in and then the top closed back again while the incense that was burning intensified. Langston joined behind us with a concerned look on his face. He whispered something to Valafar, could only guess our situation wasn't getting any better. More people started coming out from the hidden room. Not everyone from the group before. This time it was much fewer.

Damar said something in an ancient language none of us recognized. As we looked around, dead bodies started to glow around us. Many who we knew over the years that had passed away, family, friends and neighbors with several we didn't know.

Langston had never seen Damar do a ritual like this before but heard rumors of those who used to work for him before they mysteriously passed away. As everyone watched what was transpiring in front of them, they realized he was conjuring up Katherine, was this woman never going to end?

"Damar, what are you doing?" Valafar asked.

"She insisted she didn't need anyone to help her. For centuries I thought she was right, she had so much strength and outsmarted everyone for so long. We've waited far too long just to wait and keep trying to find new ways, eventually we will run out. We need to make sure vampires rule the world, she will be our powerful queen, and all things will be right in the world." Damar's voice sounded deeper than usual, almost as though he was possessed by another.

"You're willing to go against your own family to help her? You do realize once she has power, she won't need you. The others won't allow you to do this?" Valafar tried to reason with him.

"I don't need their permission. Our family would have destroyed me if they knew I supported her all these centuries. The curse placed on her was my idea. She was strong enough to handle it. I won't let anyone stop me, I will miss Angelita, her blood lust was the heart of my soul but even she would have stopped me. You and I are all that is left. I took care of the others. I'm tired of these little rituals being done and messed with. For once this is going to be done right and end. Even if it costs my own life." Damar started laughing uncontrollably as he released his own inner personal demons.

"How could you turn on your own family?" Valafar was in disbelief.

"It's simple brother. Certain priorities come first and I couldn't get them to see things the right way. It had to be done. I left you and Langston because I knew neither of you would stop me." His gin made Valafar sick.

A small hidden entrance on the other side opened slowly with a few people not sure if it was safe to enter. The real Drezin and Thea stood there not exactly surprised by what they walked into. Langston signaled for Valafar to join them.

"He's lost his mind, he killed everyone. What do we do?" Valafar thought as he glanced over at Damar.

"I've seen how crazy he gets. We won't be able to get him at his own game; he's planned this far too long while he's waited for one of Katherine's plans to work. This doesn't look like one of his usual set ups. The feeling is off and if it's what I think it is, this is a spell created by a gypsy called Maddie. You can tell her signature spell, its dripping blood from the page he's holding. He doesn't understand the purpose of the spell himself, which makes this more dangerous." Langston whispered back.

"You can whisper all you want over there, I can still hear you." Damar sounded angry.

"We were not attempting to hide anything. You know me, I never get loud." Langston explained.

An all-too-familiar odor started to take over, the strong stench of iron, whether it was coming from something living or something that used to be. The walls dripped with blood, as it slowly dripped and curved, there were impressions of symbols left behind on the wall that glowed a silvery light.

"I think it's safe to say we might not make it out of here this time. I was hoping it was over at the last one, but I should have assumed it was too easy." Langston sighed with frustration.

"Where's your sense of adventure?" Drezin came up behind Langston setting his hand on his shoulder.

"Not exactly my idea of adventure especially when it deals with dark forces and you know your entire family has been slaughtered." Valafar still tried to sound optimistic.

"I swear, my nightmare of that woman never ends." Thea added in as she joined the others.

Charley and Sophie stood back from the other slightly observing the scene unfold. There were not many there with them. The guardians stood near Drezin and Thea's seven daughters. They had already tried leaving except nothing they tried seemed to work now that there was a grey mist in the room. The center became extremely dark while the air felt more pressurized. Again, there seemed to be a figure transforming in front of their eyes. It was something we all expected but kept wondering how it was going to be possible to stop it. At this point it was starting to feel impossible.

The familiar form started to come to life as Katherine stood at the center of the circle. This time it wasn't the elegant smoke she formed her body from, and she hadn't chosen another host. The elements mixed together creating her new body, at least what was left of her. The jars placed on the ground released what was left of her ashes. She rippled in and fractured several times, whole at one moment, her old terrifying, powerful, untouchable self and next she split apart at the seams, shadows and fog slipping through her as if there was another creature inside of her fighting, clawing to escape. She forced herself back together and each time, with sheer rage stitching herself into something barely holding form.

"You will finish it," she screamed with a thundering book, her voice sounded unnatural, "all of you. You were made for this." As she gestured towards the seven sisters and the guardians, then lastly he pointed at Charley.

The seven sisters trembled within the circle, magic tearing through them like fire under their skin. They weren't casting it.

Sophie went to move forward hoping to shield the others with a spell except she found she couldn't go far, something was blocking her from getting near Charley.

"Charley, I don't think we can protect the others, there's something stopping us from getting through. I can't even reach you. I think it's a magical wall." Sophie panicked trying to think of the best way they could handle this or at least how to escape.

"I don't think we are meant to stop this. Century after the last, it all keeps leading up to this. So maybe, as much as I hate this to happen, this is what is meant to be. Then we'll deal with it once it happens or at least figure out our options then." Charley tried to sound optimistic.

The seven sisters looked distressed, even through the pain, the sisters held each other's hands hoping it would keep them brave and strength to make it through this. The elements were being churned and not by Katherine's power, she was drawing from the guardians and the sisters. All seven felt incredibly strong pressure and exhausted as though their life power was being pulled from them, except Kendra. For some reason she was glowing like a bright white shining light. The girls found they were not casting the power, but they were fueling it.

Katherine always like an audience for displaying her powers. Rose, Jacob, Nichole, Anthony and Lucian now appeared next to Sophie. The family strained against the invisible wall being forced to watch, powerful to help the others or to pull Charley back safely to them. All of this made them feel powerless.

"Don't listen to her!" Sophie shouted, her voice cracking as she fought against the force that was holding her, "she can't keep control if you fight her, the ritual isn't sacred, its from evil origins. It's not what she thinks. He's tricking her." Sophie hoped Katherin might spend her only energy fighting against Damar.

Katherine's head snapped eerily toward her, "wrong," too fast and too sharp, "you don't get to speak," she snarled, "not after everything, I changed you after those imbecilic morons couldn't do it right and left you buried under the dirt. I made you. I made what you turned into. This was the eternal spirit spell of my ancestors that my family kept from me. They wanted me to suffer eternally. I'm the only survivor now and I'll show everyone how powerful I will become."

Her body glitched again as if she was partially here and in another dimension at the same time, her arm and neck distorting, looking loose and broken before snapping back into place. It didn't seem like Katherine could get any angrier except she was, cursing in several ancient languages as she stared at the exhausted guardians as she was consuming their energy. They didn't have to use their powers; she used them as a vessel and steered the power where she wanted as Damar continued to chant ancient words out loud. Even she was coming undone.

"This is it," Drezin said under his breath. "She's not going to stay physically together for too much longer if this isn't completed properly."

"Why would she use a spell that isn't going to accomplish what she wants, especially one that will stop her? I feel like I'm missing something?" Rose said as she worried about the others.

"I tend to keep souvenirs from everywhere I've been or worked, especially if I can either blackmail or at least use somehow in my favor." Langston said softly to Rose.

What did you do?" Smirking at Langston, Valafar wondered what his old friend was up to.

"I let Damar know I confiscated it from Katherine when I worked for her. It was hidden in the council's safe for years. Lydia and Gerard where the only other ones who knew it was there. I checked on it occasionally and noticed it changed out for lesser spells each time someone touched it. I had given the original to Brunswick. I knew no one would ever search him. He kept it safe all these years." Langston sounded rather proud of himself.

"It might not be the right spell Katherine was hoping for but there's something about it I recognize. For some reason I have this mental image of when I was a child, I think part of this was a chant she used to say around the house." Charley concentrated more on the words Katherin was saying.

"Then we don't stop her or do we, right now other than Charley, none of us can get past this invisible barrier." Lucian replied coldly.

Drezin's jaw tightened. "We redirect her. I made a promise to the girls I would keep them safe, even if they didn't realize the connection. I always keep my promise. Right now, Katherin has only tapped into the guardians power of bringing people here, or from Willow and Rachelle, they have the ability to move object and wind. Once she taps into the other powers, its going to get dangerous. Especially if she figures out what Kendra can do."

"We better figure out something quick, I hate seeing my girls in pain, this might kill them and I can't handle it if it does, we owed them a better life." Thea sounded worried as she tried a few removal curses on the invisible wall which hadn't worked.

It hadn't worked, because there was no stopping this. Symbols in the air, walls and on the bones scattered across the floor, all ignited in flames. The ritual had already begun and was getting much stronger as it grew. Magic surged wildly, violent, tearing through the chamber itself. The sisters cried out as it burned through them, unstable and desperate.

Katherine lifted her arms, dragging the power inward, "finally," she breathed, "mine—"

"No." Charley's voice echoed through everything.

Intense silence…And impossibly…the room listened. The force holding him in place shattered. Not because it weakened, but because something inside of him answered the magic. Immediately it Recognized his voice.

It felt like her own throat seized up on her as everyone barely heard Sophie gasp, "Charley…don't…"

He was already moving toward Katherin. Towards everything in the ritual circle of chaos. Toward something Katherin felt in her chest before she understood it. Finality.

"I remember this," he said softly, as if he was reaching through time itself, "the words… how it was meant to flow."

Katherine's expression cracked, "you were nothing more than a mere child."

"And you should've killed me when you had the chance."

Charley stated with no anger, fear or resentment in his voice, just the truth. Charley reached Sophie and took her hands into his, safe and securely. And everything changed. The magic's focus shifted instead of breaking, but turning, pulling away from Katherine like it had been waiting for something else, someone else.

"I have her," Charley said and Sophie felt it.

Their bond with each other surged into the ritual. It wasn't forced, not stolen, but genuine chosen. It steadied the chaos, filled the fractures, rewriting0 something ancient into something new.

"Now!" Drezin shouted.

The guardians moved in unison, pouring controlled power into the circle.

Willow, Rachelle, Hannah, Dahlia, Piper and Taylor struggled to keep up with the shift that was going on around them. And then there was Kendra. Untouched. Unclaimed. She stepped forward with confidence knowing her sisters were there to protect her, and the chamber seemed to bend around her presence. Katherine saw her and for the first time she was afraid.

"It never was yours," Kendra said softly.

Her power didn't clash. It overruled. The ritual surged, no longer chaotic, but absolute. And at the center Charley became the anchor, the bridge between worlds but also the final cost.

Sophie felt it immediately, as she held his hand, she felt the way the magic was taking it from him, his essence, his life.

"Stop!" she cried, panic rippling through her entire body, "we can find another way, please don't do this."

"There isn't another choice, if it's done any other way this will never end and who knows how many more will be harmed or killed by her. It has to be done this way."

Charley turned to look at Katherine, and the look in his eyes shattered something inside her. Not fear, not regret, just... acceptance.

"You were never supposed to survive this world," he said gently. "But you did. If that power had never shifted through to our universe, things would have been different, you would have been different and none of this would be happening right now. So many people would not have died because of your family. Not that they had a chance to control themselves, when it took over, it destroyed everything in its path but somehow you held on, it couldn't fully dominate you. There were times you briefly shined through, there was seconds of compassion. But if it leaves you. Everything is over, even you, and...." Charley stopped speaking.

Katherine's head shook, tears falling freely now. "So will you."

Charley smiled softly with his familiar smile. "I'm trying."

The magic spiked. Katherine screamed as her form finally failed, unraveling piece by piece under Kendra's control. She wasn't destroyed; she was erased until nothing remained.

The ritual thundered a loud book as it filled the air of the room before everything went silent.

The power in the room vanished as the seven sisters collapsed to the ground, Thea and Drezin raced to their side. The guardians staggered, feeling dizzy as it felt like a hole was created inside of them leaving them feeling uneasy, they were human again with no power. Everyone's attention was on them except Sophie, she didn't see any of it because of Charley, he was falling. She caught him, dropping to her knees with him in her arms, heart pounding far to fast and loud to her or notice anything going on around her, other then Charley, as if she were to hope strong enough she could force him to keep going. But Sophie didn't see any of it

"No," she whispered, her voice and heart breaking. "No, no, no... stay with me... please..."

His skin was much colder than a vampire should be, far too cold, his breathing was… shallow. Then much weaker…then…

"Charley!" Her hands shook as she held his face, her tears falling against his skin, "don't do this," she begged, "you don't get to leave me like this… you promised… you said…"

His chest barely moved. A fragile, fading rhythm and then… nothing. The world stopped and Sophie froze. Sophie's breath was caught somewhere between a scream and silence.

"No…"

Sophie was now surrounded the rest of the family as the others looked on not being able to do anything. Rose collapsed next to her parents, her voice unrecognizable, she felt something inside of her collapse as Anthony tried to console her.

"No, you don't get to…" Rose's voice cracked completely, as her grip tightened desperately on her dad, as if she could pull him back through sheer force. "You don't get to be gone… we've all been through so much." Her tears pooled on shirt.

A pulse of energy rippled through the chamber, the same way it had when Kendra first walked toward Katherine but somehow it was different, much softer and no violence, not all-consuming magical with chaos surrounding around it..

Kendra stepped forward slowly away from Drezin and Thea as her expression was unreadable except her eyes were fixed on Charley.

"He's not gone," she said quietly.

Sophie looked up, shattered in denial with the slightest hope. "I can't feel him anymore."

"He's not gone," Kendra repeated, kneeling beside them.

Everyone watched as she placed a hand over Charley's chest. She closed her eyes concentrating on Charley, and for a moment nothing happened. For that brief moment everyone had not moved or dared breath, but nothing happened. No one knew her full power yet but Kendra, the shy little girl was now an incredibly confident powerful being. She hadn't moved from her place next to Charley, then a faint glow came from her hands connecting with Charley.

An ember of a glow emanated from Charley, one that refused to die. They were all watching for Kendra to make any kind of reaction to know if it was working, if he was going to make it.

"There's too much magic in him," Kendra whispered. "It didn't leave—it burned through him; he was the vessel this entire time and he took it all inside of him. If I pull it out wrong… he goes with it."

"Then don't pull it out," Sophie said instantly, her voice was trembling, "do something else… please. Just do something, anything."

Sophie felt horrible putting so much pressure on a child like Kendra, even if she was powerful, she was still a child. Kendra hesitated for the first time since it happened, and she didn't look as confident or certain.

"There's only one option and I can't promise it will work if whatever creature he was isn't compatible. It will definitely change him," Kendra said softly, "whatever he was before, definitely not a vampire… he won't be that again."

Sophie didn't hesitate. The idea of existing without him was too much.

"I don't care," her voice wavered as her hold on Charley tightened, "just let him stay."

Kendra studied Sophie for a moment before nodding in agreement. Without being taught, it came naturally to her as she released her power, softer this time, controlled with impossible accuracy. Everyone standing around watching expected to see the magic to be ripped out of Charley, instead it didn't leave him. It wove through his entire being. She hadn't removed it; she simply redirected the chaotic magic. Her hands hovered over his body before she gave into a smile, 'this would work.' There was a bright glow in the center of him as she anchored it into something that would not destroy him.

Charley's body jolted in an awkward jerking motion. He sharply inhaled as it felt like fire filled his lungs followed by a rush of water as if he had been drowning.

Sophie gasped as she pulled him closer to her. "Charley?"

It took him a few tries before his eyes could stay open but there was something visible about him that changed and was different. Charley looked at Sophie, feeling disoriented for a moment not sure what was going on since this didn't match his last memory, and then he smiled back at her, feeling weak but alive.

"Hey…" he cleared his throat barely getting one work out.

Sophie let out a broken laugh of relief, tears were still falling as she pressed her forehead to his, "you're not allowed to do that to me," she whispered.

"I figured," he whispered faintly.

But his hand, when it found hers was warmer than before. And it didn't quite feel the same.

Kendra stepped back giving them space, "he's alive... but the magic didn't leave him."

Silence settled over the chamber again but this time, it wasn't empty.

"Good," she said quietly, holding his hand tighter.

Because at least he was alive—

And even though he's changed, the world around them would also be different, no constant threat from Katherine or her monsters she created, no more evil magic trying to destroy the family. It was going to be strange for the guardians to get used to regular mortal life, along with six of the sisters. Kendra was the only one who retained her power. Who knows with the change in Charley what the future would hold but either way, he was alive and that would have to be enough.